KU-479-322

The Glasgow Coma Scale

THE GLASGOW COMA SCALE

Neil D. A. Stewart

corsair

Constable & Robinson Ltd
55–56 Russell Square
London WC1B 4HP
www.constablerobinson.com

First published in the UK by Corsair,
an imprint of Constable & Robinson, 2014

Copyright © Neil D. A. Stewart 2014

The right of Neil D. A. Stewart to be identified as the
author of this work has been asserted by him in accordance
with the Copyright, Designs & Patents Act 1988.

This is a work of fiction. Names, characters, places and incidents are either
the product of the author's imagination or are used fictitiously, and any
resemblance to actual persons, living or dead, or to actual events or
locales is entirely coincidental.

All rights reserved. This book is sold subject to the condition
that it shall not, by way of trade or otherwise, be lent, re-sold,
hired out or otherwise circulated in any form of binding or cover
other than that in which it is published and without a similar condition
including this condition being imposed on the subsequent purchaser.

A copy of the British Library Cataloguing in Publication
Data is available from the British Library

ISBN 978-1-47211-268-2 (hardback)
ISBN 978-1-47211-971-1 (trade paperback)
ISBN 978-1-47211-392-4 (ebook)

Typeset by TW Typesetting, Plymouth, Devon

Printed and bound in the UK

1 3 5 7 9 10 8 6 4 2

For Gayla

ONE

Between the shoddy jeweller's at one end of the Sauchiehall Street pedestrian precinct and the low-rise, low-end department stores at the other, Lynne's charity became a compulsion. As her money dwindled, she began to feel a mounting, reckless desire to give away everything to the beggars: her overstuffed weekend bag, her earrings, the fine silver cross around her neck; then still more: her shoes, her jacket. After that, she might twist her fingers and pop off each joint, distribute these too, a controlled disintegration. Surely she would, carrying out this procedure, succeed in locating then eradicating the parts where pain and resentment and dismay resided. For a moment, disposing of herself like this, she felt a flush of liberation. If you could give money to strangers, maybe you could disappear without trace.

The first man she'd given a few coins to had been sheltering in the entrance of a boarded-up sandwich shop outside Queen Street station. After that, some dog-whistle signal must have gone out, because on Sauchiehall Street she encountered more *Big Issue* sellers and more homeless – a vaguely insulting noun, but what else was she to call them? – than she recalled ever seeing there before. They didn't exactly accost her, but each stepped from a doorway in readiness as she approached, and, shifting her bag to her free hand, she gave something to every single one.

Some took from her without meeting her eye, swiping coins from her palm with blackened fingers, their due. Others thanked

1

her, low-voiced, embarrassingly deferential – calling her missus, calling her doll. She made a point of looking them in the eye. They were wounded, wind burned, and a haunted look was common to all. 'God bless,' they said to her, even the most taciturn, and she could imagine Raymond's voice remarking, from lordly height, on the intensity of belief evinced by the luckless. He'd claim it was impressive or even moving, how their misfortunes seemed only to strengthen their faith – he would describe it as a phenomenon. But really he'd be seeking only to mock, his whole speech a trap to be sprung as soon as she agreed with him. What made her think, he'd challenge her, that their godliness was genuine, not simple expediency? He liked to explain the way the world worked, in the process painting her as lamentably naïve.

Better it end today, Lynne thought: the first proper day of autumn, late in coming, inevitable. Overnight, the change in season had put metal in the air, thrawn the year's leaves down off the trees. A time for letting go. Had he woken up and decided, on seeing the frost and the weatherless silver sky, right then, that this was an apt day to make his speech?

Even before she paid proper attention to the man begging outside Menzies, he stood out from the others. For one thing, he did not lift his chin off his folded arms as Lynne approached, but remained motionless, staring into space, cross-legged, back set hard against the newsagent's brick wall. For another thing, Lynne knew his name.

How it happened: she had the last few coins ready in her hand, prepared to withhold them if the man didn't at least acknowledge her presence. How quickly goodwill had turned to entitlement! When at last he lifted his head, she gratefully poured the money into the chewed polystyrene cup between his feet, noticing at first only that his face did not have the same weather-beaten ruddiness as his fellows'. The actual recognition, the actual name, arrived only as a second, delayed reaction.

She hunkered down beside him. 'Angus?'

He didn't speak – wasn't quite making eye contact – but a

vertical furrow appeared between his brows. Up close, she could smell the sharp, soupy aura that surrounded him. His hair, peeping from beneath a grubby black woollen hat, was greasy-sleek and unkempt, his heavy beard riddled with wiry silver hairs, but Lynne knew she wasn't mistaken. 'My God, Angus, it is you.'

'It is?' He seemed no more than moderately interested. He scanned left and right along Sauchiehall Street for the next mark. 'Guid tae know.'

'Don't you recognize . . . ? It's Lynne. Lynne Meacher.'

'Oh, eh, thanks then, Lynne.' She knew that gruff manner, the familiar strong accent she had once, new to Glasgow, struggled to understand. When she didn't move on, he mumbled, reddening, 'Fer the contribution tae funds.' He shoogled the coins in his cup, seeking to ward her off. 'Ah'm, ye know, appreciative.'

She felt she was being watched, from a doorway maybe, but when she glanced around there was no one in sight. 'Sorry,' she said, 'sorry, no. It's just – don't you remember me? From the School of Art?' She gestured towards Garnethill. 'You taught me. Second-year painting and printmaking.'

The line between his brows deepened. 'Lynne . . . Meeker?'

'Meacher.'

'Meacher.' A pause, then: 'Hey,' he said in astonishment, 'you're Lynne Meacher!'

'I am!' Laughing with relief.

'Second-year painting and printmaking, aye!' He jabbed his finger at her. 'Let's see, and weren't ye friendly wi . . .'

'With . . . well, the other English students mostly.' She laughed. 'The other invaders. Oh, and Elena Papantuano. You must remember her – you both came to my house one night back then? We sat up all night drinking.' He shook his head, unconvinced, blistered lips barely smiling. Trying not to let him hear disappointment, she said: 'Well, it's a long time ago now, I suppose. Years and years. But Angus, what are you doing here?'

'Nae ither place tae go,' he said, shrugging. 'None ah'd relish bein, that is.'

3

'You mean you're really . . .'

'Oan the streets? Ah really am, aye. Nae joab, nae hame – scored the double.'

'But how could this have happened to you? You were so . . .' Wonderful, she'd nearly said. Indomitable. 'Well, never mind about that now. Can you stand?'

Angus looked at her with great forbearance. 'Yes thank you, that ah can do. Look, Lynne, no meanin tae be rude, it's kind ay ye to stop and chat, but the thing is, ah willnae make much cash if ah'm jist sat here gassin.'

Lynne, incredulous: 'I'm not leaving you here. How could I? Come on, you're staying at mine.' She stood, her knees aching from so long in the crouch, and felt a momentary dizziness. Sundays usually meant brunch at Raymond's favourite Merchant City café – a place to which, evidently, she now could never return.

Angus had not moved. His eyes were hazy, as if what she was offering was inconsequential. Again it went through her mind: what would Raymond think if he witnessed this exchange? He would have said she was being absurd. 'Come on, then,' she enjoined, more forcefully.

'Aw – Lynne. Ah couldnae.'

How else to speak to him but as to a child? 'Angus, I'm not arguing. I'm telling you.'

She half ran to the end of the precinct, flailed for a taxi, then went back for Angus, who was, despite his protests, clambering to his feet. She tried to take the dusty blue kitbag he'd been sitting on, but he clutched it to him, a wary, shamed scowl on his face. Behind her, the taxi, which had crept on to the pavement, honked its horn warningly. Lynne hesitated, wary too: for a moment it was impossible to see, through the exhaustion and shabbiness, the Angus Rennie she remembered.

He said nothing for the twenty minutes it took the taxi to reach the West End; Lynne, relegated to a flip-down seat so Angus

4

could sit beside his bag, fretted, also silent. Not quite five o'clock but already near dark, all that remained of sunset a swathe of peach sky compressed between black horizon and black cloud, intermittently visible between the buildings they passed. Each time they stopped at a red light, she tensed for Angus to throw open the car door and sprint away into the dusk.

When they reached Glendower Street, she went on ahead up the close's cold stairwell. Angus lagged behind her, pausing on the stair, leaning against the Arts and Crafts tiling. He patted his thigh. 'Busted leg. Sorry. Gie me a second.'

By the time she'd unlocked the front door he had caught up with her, but still hesitated when she indicated he enter before her, as though unable to cross the threshold without an explicit invitation. 'This is really guid of ye, Lynne. Ah've no way tae repay ye.'

'That doesn't matter. It's not . . . I'm just doing what anyone would.'

'Point is, naebdy bothered before you. Ah jist wantit tae thank ye.'

'Well, let's not stand out here discussing it. Go on in. Please. Straight on in and to your right, that's the living room. There's a futon we can roll out for you to sleep on.'

He shook his head. 'That'd be magic.'

With Angus safely inside, Lynne shut and double-bolted the front door, then followed him into the living room. 'You don't mind, do you? Only it's just the one bedroom . . .'

'A sight better than whut ah've put up with lately,' he cut her off genially, looking around. With dismay, Lynne too was seeing the room through his eyes: the dowdy knick-knacks, the framed stock photograph over the mantelpiece, the unburned church candles ranked in the old fireplace to disguise the horrid electric fire she had never got round to replacing.

Rashly, she tried prompting him. 'So, do you remember any of this from when you came before?' She pretended to calculate – 'Five years ago or so?' – not wanting to alarm him with a considerably more precise date.

5

'Nup.' He cleared his throat. 'Sorry.'

'Well, it was just one evening, after all. A long time ago. And it's probably changed a lot since then.' She added this, rather hopefully, despite the evidence of her own eyes. 'Well, anyway, that's by the by. Let me get you some bedding for later.' Even as she said the words, he yawned, hugely as a cat. These curtailed October days did this to a person, daylight barely bothering the visible end of the spectrum; the instinct was to hibernate until spring came. 'Have you eaten? I can throw something together. I'm famished,' she laughed, then worried that she sounded insensitive.

Before fetching the spare sheets from the press, however, she darted into the kitchen and began unpinning certain photographs from the cork board. She had been hoping that being in the flat might remind Angus of his previous visit – what had passed between them then – and was disappointed that he evinced only mild interest in his surroundings. But it's him, she was thinking, even if he barely seems to remember your name; it is still him, and that's the important thing.

She paused over one photograph: Raymond and herself, early on, triumphant at the peak of a Munro. Such good bone struc-ture she'd had, such clearness to the whites of her eyes. She was tired today, and her face had a weary rosaceous shine: these were depredations, she now felt, that Raymond had worked on her. She set the photograph face down into a drawer with the others. She hadn't changed all that much in five years, had she? The younger Lynne from the picture could still come back, just as Angus had.

Angus, as it happened, remembered quite clearly the evening to which Lynne had been alluding, but wasn't yet prepared to admit it. In her absence, he lay back on her couch and busied himself fumbling in his crotch, trying to extricate his right testi-cle, which seemed to have retreated beneath his pelvis.

He had some concerns regarding the reasons for Lynne's

kindness, but a decent sleep in an actual bed, or as good as – rather than passing the night beneath a tree in Kelvingrove Park, in a glassy insomniac trance – was motivation enough not to question too hard. There was food here, light, warmth. You couldn't just turn your nose up at that.

Hearing Lynne scuffling about in the hallway, Angus withdrew his hand from his underwear, sniffed his fingers and, composing himself for her return, arranged his face into what was, under the circumstances, the broadest, most ingratiating smile he could muster.

TWO

Lynne made herself late on Monday morning, dawdling in the flat, hoping her house guest would wake before she had to leave. It was unusual for her not to be first to arrive at the office, but despite what had happened over the weekend, first with Raymond, then Angus, there was no question of taking the day off. In the end she had to run, through the smirr of rain, to the underground station, and arrived into Arundel's offices flustered, her hair damply wadded, an unpleasant trickling sensation under her arms. Late or not, people barely seemed to notice her enter, much less greet her. Only Heather Gillespie, on her final warning for punctuality herself, raised her sleepy face and, to Lynne's horror, winked at her.

She started up her computer, then went to make breakfast – adding milk to the Tupperware box of cereal she'd brought from home. In the kitchenette, Faraz, beard luxuriant but scalp freshly gleaming from its weekly shave, was adding his name to the list for the office Christmas party, due to take place, because of various apparently irreconcilable scheduling clashes, in the middle of November. Beside him, waylaying him, pink in the face, was Struan Peters.

Most of Lynne's colleagues came in on a Monday morning keen to discuss the weekend's football or the new talent contest on TV; Struan arrived vibrating with indignation from a weekend seemingly spent researching ways in which Scotland's failure thus far to secede from the United Kingdom was causing him personal injury.

'What they need to do,' he was telling glazed Faraz, 'is really go after the sixteen- and seventeen-year-aulds. Get them political, get them fighting for their ain country. These guys're our future – they dinnae want Westminster making their decisions for them. They'll vote for independence soon's that pen's in their haund, guaranteed.'

Lynne wanted to speak up – declare that in her experience young people were a lot more conservative than Struan was giving them credit for. But this was hardly true of Raymond's daughter, nor indeed of the young Lynne, who had upped and come to Glasgow alone aged eighteen, on what had amounted to a whim. Even in her silence, however, she was having her customary quantum effect on the debate: observed by Arundel's sole English employee, it began to modulate subtly towards still-deniable jingoism. 'Oor oil goes tae England,' Struan complained. 'Aw they wind farms blighting the hillsides and the moors, the power they generate? Straight down south.'

'Aye, they pay for it, but. And there's, like, tax breaks and that. Och, I don't know, but it's no like we give it away free.'

Struan ignored Faraz's interruption. 'Keep that fer oorsels, we'd be minted, the richest country in Europe. Ye could dismantle hauf they places and still power the whole ay Scotland. What do we need England for anyweiy? No for money. Moral guidance? Aye, right. What they gonnae teach us, how tae pan in windows and steal trainers and TVs?'

Lynne, unable to help herself: 'That's hardly fair.'

Struan's head pivoted jerkily around, putting Lynne in mind of old films with frames missing. 'Whit's fair? Tellin us we'd fail on oor ain? Yis tell us we're stupit even contemplatin it. Way tae win us over, calling us haufwits.'

Barely mid twenties, he acted like someone who'd survived decades of oppression and exploitation. These embittered youths, these independence advocates who behaved like victims of a totalitarian regime: where did all the anger come from?

9

'We're better together,' she told him. 'Co-operation's how things get done, not by antagonism, not by a race to the bottom.' On the TV last night she and Angus had watched a young Tory, who seemed to have emerged from the same dressing-up box as the rest of his ilk, stutteringly make this same point. He had embarked upon a clumsy metaphor about long marriages, at which point Angus, yawning exaggeratedly, had suggested they switch off; and you had to think, if this was the standard of speaker the anti-independence movement were using to put their viewpoint forward, they were either very confident or very complacent. 'Apart, we're less than the sum of our parts.'

'Yous English,' he said, 'want tae keep us in fear. Alwis huv, alwis will.' The kettle popped; with his colleagues distracted, Faraz made his tea and departed the kitchen at speed. 'Ye know full well that without us, England'd fester and shrivel.'

To quell, at least temporarily, the unease rising towards her throat – such was her dread of these daily debates-turned-confrontations – Lynne resorted to exercising her authority, shaky though she felt it to be: 'All right, Robert the Bruce, it's gone nine o'clock. Time to start making calls.' He scowled. 'Try not to proselytize to the customers, will you?' – hoping the word would baffle him.

Suddenly and unexpectedly promoted over Faraz, Struan and the others two months earlier – the interview process had comprised one telephone conversation with someone at head office in Aberdeen whom she hadn't met then or since, followed by an email headed CONGRATULATIONS, which she now viewed ironically – Lynne had received no training in how she should address people transfigured overnight from colleagues to juniors. She understood the pitfalls – too familiar and they wouldn't respect her, too severe and they, longer-serving Arundel employees who already resented her promotion, would turn to openly loathing her – but hadn't yet worked out the right tone to take.

'You'll miss us when ye're gone, boss,' Struan jeered, vying for the last word.

'What makes you think I'll be the one who leaves?'

He smirked over his shoulder. 'Whit makes ye think ye'll huv a choice?'

She watched him saunter back to his desk, insolence radiating off him, even with his back turned. Had the man ever hurried to do anything she'd requested? She tried to console herself, as she returned to her own desk, on its own in the far corner, that his animosity wasn't specific to her. He resented anyone being his superior – would act this way with whoever succeeded Lynne, just as he had with Tony, her predecessor.

One of the cleaners came to tidy around her, pushing aside her keyboard and swiping a bleach-reeking cloth over the desk as though Lynne were not actually sitting there. 'Good morning, Marta,' she said, having made the effort, unlike the other employees, to establish the cleaners' names and that they were Somalian; hoping by example to educate the others into at least acknowledging the pair's presence, a scheme that had not met with marked success. And now, though she tried to make eye contact, Marta's glance slid away from her. For all her efforts to befriend them – to be civil, anyway – the cleaners treated her the same way they treated the people who ignored them entirely. Lynne felt a swell of irritation. Would it crack your face, she wanted to ask, to smile?

She deleted all Raymond's emails, then reinstated them, then deleted them again. Then it was on to work: numbers in columns, spreadsheet cells marked in dayglo. She totted up figures, entered them in the database, plotted the results as graphs. Since her promotion, Lynne was, nominally, department head, although a moderately intelligent child could have completed these tasks – a moderately intelligent chimp. Her real role as manager was to take the calls her subordinates weren't paid enough to deal with: the abusers, the customers who swore they'd come to the office and take revenge. For what? For billing them, albeit belatedly, for gutters cleared, stairwell lighting fixed, drying greens trimmed back from the feral. They had signed a contract, these people, but thought, what, that magic elves carried out the maintenance? It grew wearing being ranted at by strangers day upon day. No one ever seemed to believe that what Lynne said – that she understood their anger, that she empathized – was the truth.

Around her she heard her colleagues making calls – demands delivered with varying degrees of menace. 'I'm sorry,' Faraz was telling a caller, without much sincerity, 'but that's just the way our accounts are made up, six-monthly, in arrears. So you will sometimes see that there aren't that many charges for one period, but those've actually been carried over to the next bill, and that's what seems to have happened here. That's why it's more than normal. So, can I take your credit-card details?' He listened for a moment. 'No, we don't offer a payment plan, sir, I'll be needing the full amount. No. No, sir, sorry, sir, the full eight hundred. There's no mistake.'

Faraz listened for a moment, then set the phone receiver gently down on his desk. When he realized he was observed, he whispered, 'Crier,' and gave Lynne a rueful look. Next time in the kitchen, though, he'd be adding a new mark under his name on the whiteboard. A game Struan had invented: two points for a swearer, three for a crier, the maximum four for any customer who threatened violence or legal reprisals, whereupon they would be put on hold and transferred to Lynne to talk down, this process generally only infuriating the caller further. In the early days they had awarded themselves a point whenever a client hung up midway through a call, but it had started to get away from them. After a pause Faraz lifted the receiver again. 'Sir? Can I take payment now?'

And Faraz was one of the good, the more courteous ones. 'I only hate the Jews,' she'd once heard Struan say, after hanging up on a client, 'because my ex-wife's one.' She watched now as he swaggered out from the gents', a tabloid newspaper under his arm. How long had he stayed at his desk: five minutes? He was sniggering, for reasons Lynne did not wish to contemplate, and on his way past Heather's desk he leaned to whisper something that made the girl recoil, slap at the air, call him minging.

She yearned to fire them all, advertise for a whole replacement staff. Did that fall under her remit? 'Necessary qualifications: you will not make your boss's skin crawl. You will not make her feel sick coming to work each morning.' They were parasites – herself as well – even though being paid to take money away from people represented, she supposed, the ultimate capitalist *reductio ad absurdum*. It did not escape her that the cash she'd distributed among the homeless yesterday, trying to alleviate their suffering a little, she had earned through increasing the unhappiness of a different set of strangers.

So get up, she told herself. Walk out, go back to Glendower Street and Angus. Don't come back. Arundel merely needs a human being, something borderline living, approximately sentient; Angus specifically needs you.

Just to picture Angus in her home provoked a giddy salmon-leap of excitement in her breast. Nobody ever truly grew up: she wanted to call him, but she wanted to be cool too. And when, she derided herself, have you ever been *that*? To distract herself, she imagined dialling Raymond's number instead. Guess what, she'd say cheerfully. Five years ago, when we first met, I wasn't thinking about you, I was still stuck on this other person. I never told you that. And now you've broken up with me, he's come back into my life. What do you think about that? Doesn't that just pull the carpet out from under you? He'd be speechless, she thought proudly – might even, she allowed herself to imagine, break down completely. Him with his 'Can't explain' on Sunday morning, his 'Something just doesn't feel right.' You, she might brag, aren't the only one who can be cruel.

Ordinary human decency prevented her. You couldn't just use one human being as a device for injuring or getting over another. Besides, it was bad faith to assume too much about Angus. He might not, she thought, taking perverse pleasure in pillorying

13

herself, even be there when you get home. The reality is you have no one.

It worked: loneliness caught like a bone in her gullet.

'Sir?' she heard Faraz. 'Sir, please don't raise your voice to me. Sir, you're going to have to speak to my supervisor—'

Lynne snatched up her phone before Faraz could patch through his call, but the phone at home rang out unanswered until the machine picked up. She hung up without leaving a message. Faraz gave her a sullen stare as his caller raged on.

Angus had gone to bed, shivering with fatigue, at eight in the evening. Surely he should be up by now? But then, for him, a full night's rest must be an uncommon luxury. She'd decided against waking him this morning, but had then set about making a noisy fuss of emptying the dishwasher to try and rouse him. She had wanted to explain to him about the rocker switch for the hot water, the boiler's eccentricities, where she kept the washing powder – well, he hadn't been raised in the woods by wolves; he'd have coped with a dicky pilot light before now. She'd settled for leaving him a note on the kitchen table, paperweighting it with the vast bundle of her spare keys, since she could hardly lock him in the flat all day like a pet, nor bring him into the office with her, also like a pet. She tried to scandalize herself, visualizing copies of her keys distributed to every *Big Issue* seller in Glasgow by now, and even that didn't staunch her current feeling of tension – which was not, she realized, the type she was accustomed to feeling in the office, but instead a kind of elation, of anticipation.

'Put it through,' she mouthed to Faraz, who shook his head at her then cut his caller off without another word.

Funny, she thought, taking a deep breath as she lifted the receiver, how a primordial feeling like this could hide out in you until you presumed it extinct, then one day come idling back in, exactly the same as when last you'd seen it. Unchanged, revenant. A coelacanth.

14

THREE

Just as any expert will dream, in addition to the common near-nightmare of the undiallable telephone number or the elevator that cannot be compelled to stop at the desired floor, about the wild failings of his particular specialism, so Angus dreamed about a paint palette grown undisciplined – the colours muddying into one another, the inexplicable vanishment of a burnt sienna he needed to complete some unrevealed canvas – and woke feeling excoriated, the memory of turpentine stink in his nostrils, in a room he did not recognize.

The telephone had woken him, and it continued to ring as, woozy with sleep, he passed it on his way to the bathroom. It did not strike him as worth his while to answer it: hardly likely to be for him, was it? Nor did he pause to read the extremely comprehensive note Lynne had left for him, beneath a Fort Knox-scale wodge of house keys, on the kitchen table.

He peed standing, but washed his hands at least, drying them on one of what seemed to him an excessive number of pastel hand towels. Leave a woman to do up a place and this was the inevitable result: decorative pillows, ornamental throws, so many cushions piled on the folding futon it was near-impossible – certainly not comfortable – to sit on the thing. Soft furnishings gone rampant, pastels, Regency stripes, valances and frills. The lounge walls were shell pink, a wee girl's favourite colour. He prowled the flat in search of the beloved childhood teddy bear, tatterdemalion, frayed with caring, and was not disappointed.

From the lounge's bay window he surveyed Glendower Street, one of a network of well-to-do red sandstone tenement rows packed in dense involutions off the West End's main roads. Across the street, a building site: diggers pulling down remnants under arc lights left burning all through the brief blue October days. It looked like a school they were demolishing, a sixties Scots Brutalist concrete block of the sort in which Angus had been educated, if you could call it that. Nonetheless, he felt sad seeing another eyesore taken down. They had character; more, anyway, than what was shown on the hoardings advertising the new build replacing the school: some artist's rendition of vertiginous glass-fronted towers, happy people ambling the connective walkways under a blue and sunless sky, not a scrap of green space. Luxury apartments, naturally – ONLY TEN REMAINING – at obscene prices. He scoffed. Pruitt–Igoe in Maryhill.

The consequence of all this redevelopment was that well-meaning mid-earners – such as Lynne, he presumed – who'd bought and done up these century-old tenement flats as fancily as their tastes permitted, would find themselves beached at high economic tide. Buyers were ignoring the well-constructed houses across the way, suckered in by duplex penthouses and window walls providing views over – what – the ranks of ex-council low-rises down Partick way; the big crane motionless on Finnieston Quay, workless relic of a bygone age of actual industry. Places like Lynne's were left depreciating, unsaleable. As far as Angus was concerned, the only upside was that the rubble of pulverized buildings got recycled, turned into brand-new pedestrian streets, the pavements you walked or slept out on.

On the kitchen pinboard, among plumbers' cards and a strikingly unflattering photo showing Lynne in full hill-walking ensemble, all sou'wester and crampons, he found a letter from her work: Arundel Property Management. He clucked beneath his breath. So she was the person you called when the lights in the close had gone out and the lock on the close door was busted so any bawbag could come in off the streets and ransack the joint – who you called and called until the company swung into action, weeks later, sending round a crony to botch the repair, followed almost instantly by a vastly inflated bill, and if you didn't pay timeously you'd better believe the next you heard from them would be a letter from the sheriff officers threatening to take you to court. Sometimes – sometimes – Angus felt he was better off out of it.

He was not surprised, having already surmised it from her home, that the letter should confirm that Lynne was not a career artist. The percentage of graduates who made it – who allowed themselves to feel, wonderingly, that they had made it – was vanishingly small. Arts administrators the remainder became, like as not, or went to work for charities – public sector, anyway, which was fine by Angus, who believed that part of an art school's remits was to actuate the lefty tendencies incipient in all who enrolled there.

A career in debt-collecting, though, he took as a personal slight. He parted the photos and Highlands-and-Islands postcards that covered the letter and read, *In line with your promotion, from September 2011 the company will increase your salary to* . . . 'Christ on a bike,' he said aloud, impressed. 'Go Lynne.' Seeing this, he no longer felt he was taking advantage. Although on a budget like that, she might've kitted out her flat with a bit more dash.

The books on Lynne's shelves were best sellers, the CDs greatest hits and soft-core classical: Vivaldi, Handel, Bach, *Dusty in Memphis*, *The Timeless Helen Prine*. And musicals. Some people were beyond help. On the bookshelf he saw and seized up something called *How to Manage*, but found to his disappointment that it was about business.

Further investigation revealed that Lynne was among the few people to own the sole exhibition catalogue ever to have been dedicated to Angus's work, *A Drawer of Knives: Paintings by Angus Rennie, 1991–2005*. He opened it at the end and flicked

17

backwards through the plate section, marvelling that there had once been, for a while anyway, prodigious output.

He encountered first his later paintings, vivid, animated affairs full of colourful lesions, trackmarked arms, arthritically buckled hands grappling empty air. Here was *The Joke*, one he remembered reviewers knocking themselves out over. 'Rennie drags us down into the pit,' his favourite had gone. 'The dead or dying figure lolling on its bier looks back at us – we seem to have dropped to a crouch to stare upwards through the pallbearers' legs, an improbably contorted viewpoint – and its face isn't quite human. This is no Chapman Brothers–Goya détournement, but a creature disfigured, like all Rennie's subjects, by sinister illness. Its caried teeth are bared in a leer, making us complicit in the deception: "They all think I'm dead." And you laugh too, with and at this grotesque, because you get the other, titular joke, the one the monster hasn't understood – because you know that what the pallbearers are going to do next is bury this poor sod alive. At last Rennie has found his place. He's Glasgow's own Caravaggio.' God, how they'd loved that, the drinkers down at McCalls, as though Angus was answerable for the reviewer's hyperbole. 'He is' – because they never could resist the pun, could they, reviewers, resist telling you about their own cleverness as well – 'the Weegie Weegee.'

Strange to see some of these images for what seemed like the first time. Once, he'd been so averse to viewing his own completed paintings that he'd stacked them facing the studio wall, almost afraid he'd catch a stray glimpse – a superstition he had neither fully understood nor tried to. Dust had settled on the canvases' upwards edges. This reluctance to look at his work did not mean he hadn't also resisted selling or exhibiting it; but a man had to eat. Evidently a change had come over him, unnoticed: in those days, he'd have sooner chewed off his own hands than voluntarily inspect those finished paintings.

Colour drained from the paintings as he travelled backwards through the plates, back to when he'd worked in straightforward portraiture – derivative stuff, made before he'd started to feel realism restrictive and stultifying. His old drinking companion Rab had posed on Ashton Lane for *First Pint, Friday Evening*. The page before that was *Girl in a Striped Shirt*: Angus couldn't mind that lassie's name now, though he did recall trying, and failing, to get her to pose without said shirt. Its stripes had been red, he remembered that much, but he'd rendered them in sepia, and his earliest works shared this earthy, grimy colour scheme: browns, greys, blues, storm tones, rutted soil, granite and shit.

When questioned about his restricted palette and the unwell-looking characters he portrayed, Angus referred to these early works as exorcisms. A set-up, plain and simple: 'Exorcisms of what?' his interlocutors would inevitably ask, enabling him to reply, grinning, boasting really, 'All the bad stuff yet to befall me.' Not believing, of course, that it could ever prove more than a glib soundbite.

Each reproduction was a time capsule containing, invisible to all other viewers, his own imago, forever frozen at the age he'd been when he made that painting – the earliest dating to when he was twenty-three, almost unthinkably young. As with any picture album disinterred years after the fact, he had forgotten some of the names and much of the context, yet open this book at random and he could recall, with a clarity that eluded him in many other matters, not just whereabouts he'd made the painting in question – in most cases at his Garnethill studio – but also something about the process, his mental state at the time; even, in one or two cases, what he'd been wearing as he painted.

He remembered working day and night, feverish, not pausing to wash or sleep or change his minky clothing for fear he'd lose whatever fire-thread he was pursuing, and he felt an intellectual interest in the fact he'd once been able to work so fervidly, but the pictures as he revisited them possessed no greater emotional charge than a stranger's might. He didn't mind them, exactly – was not disgusted by the failings he saw in them – but there was nothing left dangling, nothing he could take up now for a new work. Part of him, though he didn't like to call it *inspiration*, a word with unpleasant New Age overtones, had been quietly cauterized. Every artist – so Angus told his students and his interviewers alike – paints himself by painting others, makes himself as he makes his works. So who are you when you stop?

Not the telephone's repeated ringing so much as his reluctance to answer it brought to mind other ways in which he'd rather not be contacted. He upended his blue kitbag on the futon and guddled through the sad jumble of his earthly belongings for his mobile phone: a cheap model intended for scadges, schoolkids and the like, not that the manufacturers tended to emphasize this. Pay as you go, made to last six months at a time on a tenner top-up.

He deleted a text he'd received the day before from Cobbsy, a not-quite-pal from the streets. It was a tip-off, and it contained four vital pieces of information: 'F35, green, W Sauc, 5' – meaning that Cobbsy had sent it out after receiving five pounds off a woman in her mid thirties, dressed primarily in green, last seen heading west along Sauchiehall Street: be vigilant, you derelicts. A fiver was remarkable – unheard of. A few minutes later, right enough, Lynne's green windcheater had swum into his peripheral vision and Angus, as was his wont, didn't acknowledge the do-gooder, only geared himself up to mutter something abusive if she gave him nothing. Then she'd said his name: he'd looked up in proper surprise – confusion – and over her shoulder had seen Cobbsy himself, his texting system made redundant as he jumped up and down in the entrance to the Savoy Centre, pointing and giving Angus the big thumbs-up.

The letter box clattered, startling him. Naturally enough, he went to fetch the post in, first inspecting it – he laughed at himself – for further clues. Two items for Lynne, bills most likely, and a letter addressed to a certain Miss S. McKenzie at this address – given, he was amused to note, as North Kelvinside, though the area was most definitely markedly less glam

Maryhill. He imagined Lynne dissembling as she gave out her address, and liked her more for it.

This letter for Miss S. was the first hint that Lynne might not be the only resident here. He resurveyed the flat and was bamboozled. Two folk sharing a place this size, at any given moment you'd have one person's clean clothes drying on the pulley over the bathtub, for instance. It was a one-bedroom place, and evidently nobody normally slept in the room where Lynne had installed him. This left the possibility that she'd turned lesbian, but despite all the fleeces and leggings in her wardrobe, Angus wasn't convinced.

It didn't take much more searching to find, on the bedroom window ledge, the wood-framed photo of a blonde teenager, sharp-featured, sixteen or seventeen by Angus's estimate: old enough to have left home, but young enough still to receive bank statements with a cartoon character franked on the envelope. Not a daughter, for sure. Lynne Meacher, teenage mother? No way. He examined the girl's picture for some time without discerning any resemblance to Lynne.

He was propping the letters up beside the telephone when it began once more to ring. Angus again made no effort to answer it, counting off the rings. On the wall over the bookcase with the phone on it hung a watercolour in sage greens, foggy blues, regularly sized lozenges of colour that had bled faintly into one another – semi-abstract, though the colours suggested a deciduous forestscape somewhere ascetic and Mitteleuropean. He squinted at the lower right corner: LM pencilled in. He recalled her work now, all a little faltering and delicate. He was amused by the slight conceitedness of her hanging something of her own, though this was no less deserving of wall space than the picture-postcard stuff and stock photos in cheap frames he'd seen in other rooms.

At the eighth ring, an antiquated answer machine clunked into life. 'You've reached Lynne's number,' he heard the recording say, harried-sounding. 'Leave me a message and I'll get back to you as soon as I can.' Another thing this lovingly curated flat was not: a place whose owner's hectic social schedule meant she was seldom home. He listened on, amused, and after the bleep Lynne's less assertive live voice came through. 'Oh, hi, Angus, it's me – just phoning to make sure everything's okay, you're finding everything all right . . .'

Angus stood in the hallway listening to her blether to nobody. Next time. He'd answer the next time she called – he gave it half an hour. You had to save some things to treat yourself. And he didn't want her to worry – did not, above all, want her to come home and fuss over him.

Someone threw you a lifeline, you'd have to be stupid or a saint not to grab it. What worried Angus was what might be expected of him in return. More of the same as last time she'd wanted to snare him: a game of footsie beneath the kitchen table, a buss on the cheek before bedtime? He feared not. He feared Lynne had *designs*.

Well, he'd simply have to take his lead from the not inconsiderable number of women from whom he had, in his time, heard variations on the artful brush-off. 'Let's see how we feel when I get back from my holiday.' 'I'd never go out with anyone I didn't consider a friend, so why don't we try being friends first?' By careful manipulation you might postpone a difficult showdown indefinitely, never quite crushing the other person: unbearable cruelty dressed up as humaneness. In the interests of self-preservation, Angus was not averse to being cruel.

FOUR

'The first thing to say – and this is crucial, Lynne, absolutely crucial – is that despite whut embdy else might say, any ay ma former employers or ma students, ah wis absolutely not guilty ay harassing *any*one.'

'Oh, Angus.'

Affronted, he set his cutlery down on his dinner plate. 'Now that's telling. See whut ye jist did? That conclusion ye leapt tae? You heard a word ah nivver said. Soon's folk hear the word "harassment", they think the "sexual" is a formality, silent there at the front ay it. Don't feel bad,' he fired at her. 'Ye're no the first person tae make that mistake and doubtless ye willnae be the last.'

'I'm sorry,' she said, dropping her gaze.

He waited a good while, apparently expecting her to elaborate, before telling her not to apologize. He collected poached salmon on his knife and drew the blade between his teeth, making Lynne wince. 'It's a bit hurtful for me tae hear, is all, if ye can understand that.'

'Of course I do.' She strained to show empathy. 'I didn't mean . . . But, look, if it wasn't . . . that, then what did happen?'

'Year upon year,' he said, commencing a lecture, 'ye see the same thing. These kids do not appreciate how insanely difficult it's gonnae be for them tae get anywhere wi their art. Almost everywan walks in that door in September's gonnae be disappointit come May. Ah know it and you know it' – an ironic

23

sidelong glance at Lynne's drab office clothes already hung out on the bedroom door for Monday morning – 'but did ye know it back then?'

Yes, Lynne thought: due in no small part to Angus's critiques, she'd known it almost from the start. 'Do something with your talent,' people had kept telling her at high school. 'It's a gift, don't let it go to waste.' She'd heard it put that way so often – the talent was the important thing, Lynne herself merely its vector – that when ultimately she'd elected to move far from home to *do something*, it had felt to her like rebellion, rather than simply capitulating to what she'd been urged. In time, it had come to seem an act of feckless impetuosity, one more misjudgement to rue.

'Ah shouldnae even call them kids. If they're mature enough tae be daein whut they think their future career'll consist ay, they should be mature enough to take honest criticism from folk that know. Whut's mair irresponsible anyway, mollycoddling yir students, assuring them they've got skills they huvnae, or don't huv *yet*, or setting them straight: "Look, pal, ye're a competent draughtsman, but nothing mair. Huv ye considered transferrin tae Illustration?" '

'That doesn't sound,' Lynne conceded, 'like harassment, exactly.'

Angus struck the table with his palm. 'Thank you, Lynne! If ye want to succeed – even if ye want tae fail nobly – then ye huv tae dae the hard yards, and ah see nae point pretendin otherwise. Naebody benefits fae bein lied to, even tae spare their ego.'

'No, but there are ways, don't you think? Ways to make your opinion known without being deliberately hurtful. You were quite harsh with me, I remember.'

He blinked. 'Well, aye. Daresay ah wis.'

' "There's a big chunk gone from the Amazon rainforest where they've cut down trees to make the paper you draw on." Remember that? "Why're you so determined to ensure they died in vain?" '

24

'The thing is, but—'

'You used to say I was too posh for art school.' Somewhere along the way, this maddening condescension had become fondly recollected. 'And I had to explain a few things about Eastbourne to you.'

'Suicide Land, aye, ah mind.'

'And remember that time you made me leave the studio because I'd been drawing with a propelling pencil?'

He laughed. 'Hey, Lynne? It's been, whut, five year? Let it go.'

'It became a sort of contest – who would get the most hurtful crit each week. Who'd be honoured.'

'But it wis well meant, Lynne, ye see? Ah'm no a total monster. Besides,' he said slyly, 'if that wis the worst ah ivver said . . .'

'Anyway, I'm a case in point, aren't I?' No, he had said worse, but Lynne felt it better not to remind him of his crueller remarks. He was right: they had stung, but they had rarely, she could see now, been unwarranted. 'You told me I wasn't cut out to be an artist, and I wasn't. It didn't deter me. If anything, it freed me. All I pick up a pen for nowadays is to sign off time sheets or authorize letters threatening legal proceedings.'

Angus's mouth was working, twisting. Some difficult declaration must be on the way. She waited, intrigued, until he inserted his little finger into the side of his mouth and levered free a shred of gristle; he inspected his fingertip before wiping it, with great delicacy, on the edge of his plate.

'Well, the boot's on the ither foot now, right enough. All ah wis offerin wis guidance. You understood that – but not everywan did. Sumdy developed a persecution complex.' He put on a feeble, griping voice: ' "Mr Rennie disnae take ma work seriously." "I suffered psychological damage because Mr Rennie nivver gave me a pass on my final exam." Wan person complains, then the floodgates open and aw the attacks start in. Before ah know it, ah'm up in front ay the board tae give ma response, and funnily enough, ma honest response disnae go doon so well. Ah shouldnae've . . . och, but ah was angry. Ah knew what wis comin, but couldnae move out the road. Ye mind if ah smoke?' She shook her head, could see he didn't know whether that meant yes or no, but could not bring herself to refuse him outright.

They'd all gone, one after the other: the income from his job, then his severance, then the pittance he could make selling off his possessions. The paintings were long gone; no way, in his anxious state, he could produce anything new. He told her, as he smoked his cigarette down, as Lynne blocked her nose against the smell and looked with yearning at the shut window, that after a while he'd been able to step outside the process of losing everything – developed the traumatized organism's coping mechanism, dissociation – and see it as resembling the way a space shuttle increases velocity by jettisoning the stages that have helped it get airborne to start with – only it was aimed downwards, this rocket, piling ever faster, ever deeper into the lightless earth.

'Of course you tried to find other work.'

An icy pause. 'Ah don't know if ye've noticed, Lynne, but this isnae a brilliant time tae be buildin a new career. What hingmies, transferable skills, huv ah got anyway?' Uncertain, she made no reply. 'Precisely.' He stubbed out his cigarette on his plate, then seemed to realize what he'd done. He looked apologetically at the scrunched dowt, the ash amid the food scrapings.

She went to top up his glass, though he'd barely touched his wine, and his hand shot out to cover it. 'No thanks, doll. White gies me horrific hangovers.'

Oh, right, she thought, feeling stupid. Right. What had her research taught her about the homeless and their dependencies? She withdrew the bottle and replaced the cap without serving herself. She had, now, a sense of what Angus had been describing: a great black chasm yawning beneath the feet, into which only the thinnest, most fragile crust prevented anyone, at any time, plunging. 'So what do you do next, when all that's happened?'

'Sleep in parks.' He lounged back in his chair, pretending to be at ease, a raconteur. He turned the cigarette packet in his hand like a toy. 'On the flatted-out cardboard box ye've took fae roond the back ay the supermarket. Ye head doon Kelvingrove Park, clamber over the railings, locate a tree naebody else has claimed, and bed doon. Take yir chances among the freaks.

'There's three types ay folk frequent parks after hours. Ye've the wans wantin a fight, the wans wantin a shag, and the rough sleepers. The shirtlifters ah dinnae mind, they're jist after company, a wee bit human contact, ye cannae begrudge them that, though you do feel like reminding them it's the twenty-first century, they dinnae need tae make it sae hard on thirsels. Well, mibbe that's aw part ay the fun. Anyway, it's no them ye need tae be watching out fer.'

On his third night out, he told her as he lit another cigarette, he'd risked shutting his eyes. Despite what he'd said, it wasn't the best idea to actually try and sleep in the park, but he'd been so exhausted that, after a few false starts jerking awake whenever his chin drooped, he'd finally fallen into a restive sleep under his tree.

Goblin voices woke him – a stifled chuckling – and when he opened his eyes he found himself facing something pale, vast, alien. Whatever it was, it was too close to him, and he struck at it, his fist meeting clammy, yielding flesh: this minging bastard, goaded on by his pals, crouching over him, trousers down, trying to shit on the homeless guy, while all around, hands clamped over mouths and noses, the others were bursting out with stray noises of fascination or disgust – 'Haw, naw way man, check it' – which were, Angus concluded, in some ways facets of the same thing, didn't she think?

'Hey, hey – don't *cry*, Lynne, Jesus.'

'I'm sorry. It's just . . .' She fell silent, the corners of her mouth tugging down in misery. She wasn't stupid. She understood his subtext: this is what you'd be abandoning me to if you change

27

your mind – the mawkit sewer that courses, invisible to you, just beneath your frankly cushy life. Why didn't he believe she was genuine when she said he could stay as long as he wanted?

'Ignore me,' she said, and tried to smile, to force the unease down like vomit. But when she stood up, Angus lurched from his chair too, his plate in his hand, and on impulse she went to him and he suffered her to put her arms around him. They stood together, quite still, while Angus's breath rolled, warm then cooling, against the top of her skull.

Just tell him. She sat at work on Monday dazed with love, sizzling with it, drumming her heels against the floor until Faraz, sitting nearby, prevailed upon her to desist. The worse Angus's stories got, the greater her urge to fling herself at him. The next time he made the tiniest allusion to five years ago – even referenced the art school – she would just say it. I love you. Sorry, but I do. All this time I've loved you. How hard could it be? It was already taking all her power not to blurt the words any time he entered the room.

Or slip them in unnoticed! Did you hear that Elena Papantuano was nominated for the Turner Prize last year? And by the way, talking of that night, you do know I love you?

But Angus, seeming to intuit her scheming, denied her any such opportunity. 'What ye have tae be,' he resumed over dinner that night, 'is visible. The charities send out these sortay scouts at night, roond parks and that, and if they spot ye three or four times in the same week, ye qualify for help – that's whut they tell ye, ye huv tae be *seen tae be* sleeping rough, so's they know you're genuine, no jist too blootered to walk hame that wan time. That's why ye sit under the same tree each time, lookin out for the scouts, accruing yir points. Same's ony ither application process,' he explained, flippant because he'd come through it. He was meting out his disgrace in instalments, making sure she absorbed each fresh indignity before he moved on to the next. 'After that ye can get a bed at a shelter, a toty bit scran each evening. A wash. And then back oot on the street again during the day, earning yir rent. It gives ye structure—'

'They *charge* you?'

'It disnae grow on trees, Lynne.' A big superior smirk on his face at her naïvety, but how was she to know? 'Three quid fer a night's bed and breakfast, anither couple quid for dinner – bargainous. Some days ye kin make that by lunchtime, just sittin wi yir back against a cashpoint. Then ye can take the afternoon aff, treat yirsel – go hing oot in the Wetherspoons, or huv a kip in the bookshop wi all the sofas. Keep a magazine close by ye, say ye're browsin, they cannae dae nuhin.'

Maybe he honestly didn't remember sitting at this very table five years ago – not just the last night of term, but her last night as a student. Just like now, he'd automatically sat at the head of the table, taken charge. That night, though, there'd been Elena too – Lynne's humourless Greek-Australian classmate, to whom she had, with bad grace, extended the invitation to come back to Glendower Street after last orders and share a bottle of vodka. Angus had been deep into one of his monologues, Elena paying intent, unsmiling attention, while Lynne, having surreptitiously checked under the table the position of Angus's feet, had found herself fighting an almost overwhelming impulse to run her stockinged foot up his leg. And if she did, say she did, and he permitted that much – his eyes flickering momentarily to hers all the permission needed – she might go on to press her foot into his crotch, first gently, feeling against her toes the warmth she fancied she could already sense radiating from him, then more firmly, as he set his own pressure against hers . . .

She'd blushed then and she blushed to recall it. What had possessed her? He was her teacher, and moreover it felt like she'd never given him a second look before, barely even considered him a person; yet earlier that evening in the student union, she'd noticed his shirt collar skew-whiff, adjusted it for him and, at his grateful smile, been seized by sudden, sourceless, inexplicable lust. It was to do with the wild disjuncture between his professional meanness in the studio and his surprising affability outside it – or between the long and fine-boned hands in which he held his drink and the thickly furred forearms his rolled sleeves revealed. The reality of quitting art school seemed suddenly bound up in the idea that she'd never see him again. She had astonished herself by inviting him home, she the shy one or, as Elena had casually called her later on, the sensible one: 'You don't rent? You're twenty-four, with a *mortgage*? Creature, you're so sensible. I wish I had half your sense.' Deadpan: you'd swear she genuinely believed she was paying Lynne a compliment.

By now, Angus had moved on to describing the converted hotel out Dennistoun way where he'd been assigned a bed. 'And when ah say a bed, that wis about the extent ay it. Walk in the room, bam, there's yir bed. Barely open the door. Well, it made sense, the kinds ay people coming in there didnae huv that much tae store. What were we gonnae dae, decorate? Arrange wee ornaments on the mantelpiece?' She opened her mouth and he bellowed, 'We didnae *huv* mantelpieces, Lynne.'

Tonight, at least, she was able to smile. 'But at least then you were . . . off the streets,' she suggested, dabbling in the unfamiliar vernacular.

'For a while, aye. Three weeks oan the street, three nights aff, then back oot again. An endurance test – two endurance tests.'

'That was all? Just three nights?'

He laughed. 'That wis *enough*, ye mean. Worst three nights ay ma life, and that's saying sumhin. You ivver tried sleepin while folk literally scream the place down around ye? Screaming fer drugs, or families who've abandoned them? Brawlin in the corridors ootside? Ye get some right bampots in they places, Lynne. Ah wis so tired ah wis hallucinatin, and still ah couldnae sleep, couldnae relax, too feart some basketcase'd barge in ma door and assault me. People get savaged in they places. This.' He rapped his knuckles on his hurt leg. 'How did ye think this came aboot?'

'I hadn't . . .' She didn't want to admit that the injury had seemed intrinsic to his homelessness, his general ill-fortune. Street people often had these wounds, and she supposed she had concluded that they occurred as part of the same process by which they lost their homes: things that happened all at once, by mysterious means, to people she didn't know.

'Funny thing is, ah'd always taken pride in callin masel a loner. It's romantic tae be self-sufficient, isolatit by choice. Not so much when the description's foistit on you by ither people. Then ye jist feel a reject.'

She could do it now, touch his leg, re-enact that old evening, do it right this time. Back then she had not dared, and so the evening had ground on into morning, the old, fierce, confident Angus holding court and the two girls enraptured in their different ways: brash Elena finding points to argue in his every proclamation, Lynne oddly boosted by his unfailing derogation of any artist mentioned – that one's a failure, she's a bore, he's just an arse – as these remarks put her, who he had derided in similar, albeit milder, terms, in the same general category as these *proper* artists.

'Of course the gender thing makes a difference,' Elena had berated Angus, while Lynne was interrogating her desire to touch him. 'I mean, if you're calling people like Smithson or fucking *Ruscha* conceptualists, you are going to have to make room for Eleanor Antin, Susan Hiller, a whole load of other people.'

'Bull*shit*.'

'It is not bullshit whatsoever.' Elena, standing, levelled two fingers weapon-like at Angus. 'And I am going to tell you exactly why, in exactly four minutes, when I come back.'

Lynne and Angus had sat frozen until they heard the bathroom lock go. Then they sagged, smiled at each other. Angus blew air out of his mouth. 'Talks a guid fight, that one, eh? Ah mean. Who the hell's Eleanor Antin?'

The booze was finished, and Lynne had got up to start clearing

31

things away. Angus had followed her to the sink, still holding his glass with the last inch of neat vodka warming in it. Behind the tenements opposite, light was starting to rise. 'God, wid ye look at it.' He put an arm round her shoulder. 'Ah'm sorry tae've took up so much ay yir time, Lynne. Kept ye up all night.'

'No, no, it's fine, it's good. I've enjoyed having you here.' A current was going through her, bright as dawn. It was the simplest thing to pivot beneath his arm and lift her face to his, already downward-angled; to press her lips to his mouth and feel it yield. Not a good kiss, mouth botching on mouth, but a kiss. What she remembered best was his stubble swiping and scraping over her mouth, and wondering whether she could ever come to like it.

'Oh, right,' he'd said when she stepped back. There was a great grin broadening across his face, but he hadn't even taken his free hand out his pocket during the kiss. '*Right.*'

'Now ah,' he was saying of his brief stay at the hostel, 'hud royally ballsed up, ah don't mind admitting, but at least ah wisnae in denial regardin ma situation. Wisnae castin aboot, unlike some ah could name, for weiys tae blame society rather'n take a bit ay personal responsibility. And what that amounted to, so ah wis told, was that ah didnae huv the right *attitude*, wid ye believe. So that wis me, "Fuck yis aw", and back oot under ma faithful beech tree. Lynne, doll,' as she opened her mouth, 'say "Oh Angus" like that one more time, so help me ah'll skelp ye wan.'

The funny thing was how nostalgic she felt being told off by him. Back in college days, whole lessons had vanished into Angus's famous, feared rants – starting out as regular crits, these had veered swiftly off into invective against, it had sometimes seemed, the first things that came into his head: from the works of Barbara Kruger to the sinisterly bourgeoisifying influence of a TV schedule filled with home-improvement shows. Lynne didn't like to think what it said about her that she had rather missed being so hectored. Even when arguing with her,

Raymond's tone by contrast, had been so unfailingly reasonable that she had sometimes come away uncertain she actually *had* been chastised.

Angus noticed her smiling – not at what he'd said. 'Oh, hilarious story, aye. Ah've spent the last few nights clutchin ma sides, trying tae get ma breath back.'

'No, it was that thing about your attitude. It's exactly what Ray– Raymond said to me last time I saw him.' Lynne, seeking an opportunity to mention him, had focused so hard on sounding offhand that she tripped herself up, gulped his name. There followed a brief interrogation:

'Yir boyfriend?'

'Ex.'

'Recently?'

'Fairly.'

'Long term?'

'Four years, nearly. Long enough.'

'Ye break up by mutual agreement?'

'Not especially, no.'

'How no?'

'I didn't bring – let me see – the right openness, the right flexibility to our relationship. I lacked spontaneity.' She did not add how fresh this itemizing of her faults had been the morning she'd found Angus. 'I'd been under appraisal for three years and this was the firing meeting.'

'A gent ay the auld schuil, eh. Ah wonder – hus there, in the history ay the human race, ever existed a person ay any merit or distinction by the name ay Raymond?'

'Oh, no, he's not as bad as I'm making him sound.' To her irritation, her voice started to skew upwards in pitch, betraying her. 'He's got his quirks, that's all.'

Angus regarded her pensively. 'Christ, we're a couple ay wee saouls, urn't we?' Then a sly look entered his eyes. 'Ah remember, one time in the studio, ah came over tae see whut ye were working oan, and as soon as ah came near, ye threw a sheet over yir easel, stuck oot yir chin and went, whit wis it, "Children and fools—" '

'Shouldn't see unfinished work.' She beamed. Here was a breakthrough, acknowledgement that the Lynne he was talking to now was the same person he'd once taught. 'Something my mother used to say when I'd come into the kitchen and see her cooking. Handling the raw meat, rubbing the lard and flour for pastry. I thought all that stuff was disgusting.'

'Couldnae believe ma ears. Children and fools! Talk aboot the mouse that fuckin roared.' He shook his head in admiration. 'Ma point is, that didnae sound like sumdy lackin spontaneity – who didn't ken her ain mind.'

They *had* kissed. It had happened, even if Angus had forgotten the fact; even if for the scant seconds it'd lasted Lynne herself had not been fully able to enjoy it because of the immediate low-level fretting it had sparked in her. They'd kissed and, because of the person Lynne was then and continued to be, her first thought had been to worry whether the futon she slept on then would comfortably accommodate two.

Nonetheless, 'You could stay, you know,' she'd blurted. 'Stay the night – what's left of it.' She had addressed this invitation first to the tumblers she was rinsing of suds, then, having run out of props, and remembering that barbed word *sensible*, she had turned to look Angus unflinchingly in the eye. 'If you'd like that.'

'Oh,' he'd said, surprised, stepping back, and she'd seen instantly she'd got everything wrong. 'Oh, well. Lynne.'

'It's fine,' she'd interrupted, desperate not to hear what he'd come out with next. 'You don't have to—'

'The thing is, Lynne . . .' He butted his shoulder against the kitchen wall. A faint quavering in his tone, the big man; she'd found him so sweet then, until he brought his eyes to her, brows raised, caricaturing sincerity. 'Ah like ye, but ah don't fancy ye – ah mean, ah do, but ah don't. So as long as that's . . . understood?'

'No.' It was not. She did not. Effortfully, she reformulated what she'd been about to say. 'No, you're quite right. It's the student and the teacher, isn't it? I have this rule, you see, about who I let myself get involved with.' A lie, invented on the spot, that must have made her sound conceited, forever fending off the attentions of unsuitable men.

'Ah'm no yir teacher any mair,' Angus had pointed out equably. It wasn't meant to persuade her: it was a way to withdraw his almost offer without offending. In the next room, she heard Elena crossly addressing the lavatory as she tried to get it to flush. They had seconds, and all she'd done was stare at Angus wide-eyed, trying to transmit wordlessly what she wanted – barely knowing that herself.

Then Elena had come striding back in: 'Fucking Christ, Creature, that toilet of yours, I'm telling you. Look, it's five in the morning and I'm due in work at eleven, so I'm calling a cab. Angus? Go halves?' And it had all been over: Angus shrugging, daring to shrug, at Lynne before he followed Elena out into the hallway, where she was already on the phone haranguing a taxi company. Lynne could invent no pretext for making him stay behind. In any case, she wouldn't have dared suggest it a second time. Her nerve had failed her; seemed for a while, as it always did on those infrequent, uncharacteristic occasions when she screwed up her courage and did something reckless – like applying to art school in the first instance – to have failed her in perpetuity, at least until it happened again.

Lynne had sought Elena out in the week that followed, shown far more interest in deepening their friendship than she ever had when they were classmates. All a ruse. Feigning prurient interest, she'd tried to find out what had happened after they left Glendower Street, but Elena's only responses had been tirades about patriarchy and power imbalances, in which Angus was heavily implicated, but which could have meant anything. Lynne imagined their bodies colliding as the cab turned a sharp corner, Angus's hand on Elena's leg, crawling up beneath the wool skirt. She imagined their constant bullying one-upmanship as flirtation, the only way to halt hostilities being to fuck, and

35

this she visualized in every foul permutation her imagination could conjure. The ways they'd stop each other's mouths. Going over and over it, she made herself literally ill – sluggish, inattentive, heavy-limbed. Her eyes streamed: summer flu, though she recalled dire convent-school warnings about the dangers of self-pleasure. Self-pleasure! It should have been her, Lynne, arguing through the night with Angus. After Elena returned to Athens – something to do with the economic crisis and a poorly father – Lynne had found reasons to walk through Garnethill, hoping she might spot Angus on the art-school steps, smoking, so she could – what – proposition him again?

Into this, months later, had come Raymond, sidling in beside her at the church on the Trongate one Sunday when she'd felt especially abject. Sick of her own company, her contorted fantasizing, she had accepted his amateurish advances with relief – too readily, it seemed to her now. It was rare to encounter anyone made more nervous than herself by the cat's cradle of early romance. And here was a man who seemed gentle, who seemed earnest, whose job as building-society branch manager seemed appealingly uncomplicated; who, without acknowledging how much turmoil she must have seemed to be in, had taken it upon himself to try and make her feel better.

'I do, but I don't.' Well, here was proof that *l'esprit de l'escalier* didn't stop generating smart-alec suggestions, even half a decade on. 'You,' she might have told Angus, unflappable, 'need to work a bit more on your chat-up technique.' She could have alluded to that retort now, reminding him; and lightly, without animosity, mention her regrets. What a laugh they'd have then about their younger selves, those two freaks.

It was all good and well, Angus thought, this blether, but you couldn't help feeling that the chat was yawing constantly towards one inescapable nexus, a rowboat dragged towards a whirlpool at sea . . .

He'd missed the opportunity to claim total amnesia and he

was running out of ways to forestall a conversation he sensed could only end badly. No remark was innocent here, no enquiry unfreighted with unspoken baggage. Nothing had changed; back then, Lynne's 'Stay the night' had been code for a much deeper involvement, whereas for Angus, sex after a night's pleasurable drinking and bantering was like a digestif: hardly essential, but a nice way to round off the evening. Nothing lost. That the memory still seemed to possess Lynne was sad – was too much. She had imprinted on him like a duckling.

His best tactic was to distract her. 'Who's the girl in the picture?' he sprang on her as she served up store-bought cake for pudding.

'Oh – you mean Siri?'

Miss S. McKenzie, thought Angus, immoderately pleased with his earlier feat of deduction. 'You tell me.'

'Raymond's daughter – from a previous marriage. She was thirteen when I first met Raymond, so I've seen her grow up. She wasn't very nice to me at first, but we've been close these last couple of years, really close, more than her father and me, maybe. Well, that's probably definite now,' she laughed uncomfortably. She went to refill her glass at the tap. She had not, to his relief, tried to serve wine with dinner tonight, though he sensed she'd taken his line about white-wine hangovers as covering up some more significant difficulties he had with alcohol. 'We were friends, more than anything. She confided in me. But lately she's been . . . well, I don't know. Maybe she sensed things were changing with me and Raymond. But it's like I can feel her pulling away. She keeps secrets from me now, which she never used to. She doesn't come round so often, and when she does, it's – different. I've started to dread her visits. I had to email Raymond this week, to tell him she was coming this weekend, and I . . .' She laughed curtly, unhappily. 'I felt so ashamed, like he might think I was trying to steal her away from him. Or poison her against him.'

'Ach, stuff whut he thinks. Correct me if ah'm wrang, but

he didnae exactly treat ye like a princess, so how come you're makin allowances for his hurt feelings?'

'But he's her father' – frowning, as though Angus was a half-wit. 'I'm just the outsider. She might take his side, and I have to prepare myself for that. Only, I'm afraid that when I see her at the weekend, I'll overcompensate, scare her off by saying how much I've done for them both over the years.'

She was breathless, and that was her own fault for draining all the oxygen from the room. It occurred to Angus that she'd throw anything at him, any drama, to try and hold his interest, or solicit from him some reciprocal disclosure. Instead, serenely, he continued to explain her own life to her. 'Things're bound tae be weird after a break-up. But it's a big gap between thirteen and, whit, sixteen, seventeen? Auld enough tae make up her ain mind. Hang in, doll, she'll come round.'

It was bog-standard psychology of the what's-fur-ye-willnae-go-by-ye variety, but Lynne seemed to swallow it. Then, rattling like a tin full of wasps, she burst out: 'Did you – do you have children?'

'Me! Christ, no. At least ah hope not. Jesus, ah've *been* a kid – ah cannae imagine anyhin worse than huvin one ay ma ain. Ye hud the best ay it, bein sortay step-godmother. Bit like me wi ma students, the ultimate father figure.' He had meant it as a joke, but Lynne sprang up from the table without a word. 'Whit ye daein? Ye awright?'

'Going to my room. If that's okay.'

'Why wouldn't it be?' And off she flounced, leaving Angus bemused. He'd thought it might break the ice, a light allusion to what had failed to occur between them all those years ago. Why was she carrying this torch? He wanted to call after her: 'Ah didnae winch that girl Elena either, if that's whit's upsettin ye. Could've, but didnae. That make ye feel better?'

Lynne drew the curtains and knelt by the bed. One thing she could not allow herself to do was believe that Angus's reappear-ance in her life was part of some divine plan. Profane thinking.

What would he constitute, anyway, the test or the reward? It was hopeless: love had come up around her again, a nimbus, and Angus insisted on speaking to her lightly, ironically, with no sense of any emotion invested in her, as someone who meant nothing to him, someone he barely knew. Okay, that was true, but did he have to make it so obvious?

She was nothing to him: when he talked to her, he was talking to himself. He was smug and implacable: he knew full well what she was desperate to hear, and wouldn't say it. This situation, or so she repeated to herself, hoping she might start to believe it, would not, could not, work out the way she had hoped, because what she was hoping for was a paradox. For anything to happen between them, both she and Angus would have had to be quite different people. Logically, it followed. So why couldn't she listen to herself?

She was asking guidance on this and other matters when Angus himself came crashing into her room. 'Lynne, doll—' She rose in haste. 'Oh. Sorry.' His face blazed: what did he imagine she'd been doing? No, she could tell by his look of impish delight exactly what he thought she'd been up to, crouched half out of sight behind the bed there.

Shame – and she hadn't even been doing anything! – made her speak harshly. 'Yes? What is it?'

'Whut ye up tae, hen?'

'I'm . . . tidying. Tidying stuff up.'

'No ye're no. Are you prayin? Is that what ye're daein? Disnae bother me.'

Lynne, realizing that her hands were still clasped demurely before her, separated them, then didn't know what to do with them so put them on her hips, hardly less silly. 'Was there something you wanted?'

Grinning, he lounged in the doorway. 'Oh, nothin, nothin. Ah was jist gonnae go doon the shop, get milk for ma tea. Wondered if ye wanted anyhin was all.'

'No, that's all right, you go ahead.'

Still he didn't move. 'Ye dae this often?'

'Once in a while I find it useful, yes. It's not . . . I'm sorry, but it really isn't any of your business.' His tone wasn't mocking, exactly, but curious, which she thought worse. Abruptly, wonderfully, he infuriated her. 'God, Angus, can't you just go for a nice walk or something?'

The smile vanished. 'You're the boss.'

'Get some fresh air,' she added, trying to moderate her tone. 'It'll do you good.'

'Aye. Fine. See ye after.'

She knew she'd been condescending, and she knew she'd offended him. Good. But come eight o'clock the next evening, Angus rubbed his hands and announced that he was off out for *a nice walk* – parroting her words, though his tone was neutral – and the next, again at eight. Evidently he believed he was making a point. The third time it happened, after he'd let himself out quietly with a sad wave goodbye, she ran to the living room's bay window and watched his rangy figure limp off along Glendower Street beneath the patchy street light. She felt a clutch of guilt, cold blue beneath her tailbone, at joining those people who'd banished him – given up on him.

Certain streets, Angus knew, he'd have to dingy. He could go no further down Byres Road, for instance, than the Ashton Lane turn-off, because his old regular, McCalls, was on the next corner. Nor could he dodge left on to Ashton Lane itself, since that was just pub after pub: student hang-outs serving from midday until two in the morning, an all-day challenge he had met numerous times in the past.

Great Western Road was a safer choice, though even then he had to stick to the terraced crescents on the north side, because over the road were its Belle, its Coopers, its Captain's Rest. There was Walker Fontaine's, from which he'd been barred for surreptitiously draining the dregs from other people's abandoned glasses after kicking-out time one night. He was bounded

40

on all sides, he realized as he explored, by establishments that might appear innocuous to the uninitiated, but were in reality packed with compressed memories ready to expand at frightening speed, like those dried flowers that bloomed when steeped in water or some other liquid. Worse, these were not at all unpleasant memories – the opposite, in fact, altogether too tantalizing. A worry: alcoholism might be inscribed in his genes, a hand-me-down. Just because he'd never gone too far didn't mean it couldn't still happen.

Treating the West End like a maze, each familiar pub a dead end, he walked the quiet moonlit streets night after night. Kicked out that first time, he'd stayed cross with sanctimonious Lynne until it occurred to him that it wasn't the worst idea for him to be out that flat a bit more. That sad house of memory, whose every tiny gewgaw came accompanied with a backstory she felt compelled to relate to him – what did he care who'd given her it and when, how could that possibly matter – these wee ditties cladding Angus like paste-sodden paper, trapping him just as they had Lynne.

Though the town centre had been gutted by recession, these nightly expeditions yielded evidence that the West End was undergoing a counterbalancing, equally unchecked process of gentrification. Money had spread outwards from the city centre over the decades, and middle-class wealth now surrounded the fallen centre in a palisade. Even the most affluent graduates could no longer afford to move to the South Side as previous generations had; instead, they stayed close to the university, and their demands were changing this area instead. Everywhere shops were selling organic this, hand-foraged that. The sign in the old ice-cream parlour opposite Hillhead Underground now advertised gelato and semifreddos; the fishmonger used bunches of samphire, rather than the old fake-plastic grass, to partition trays marked RED MULLET and TUNA (SASHIMI GRADE). Could you pick up a good old-fashioned fish tea on Byres Road these days? Like fun you could.

Wednesday night he took a right off Byres Road after the big supermarket – newly done out in a style they were calling Mediterranean, meaning, as far as Angus could tell, that they'd laid down lumpy terracotta tiles your conspicuously non-upgraded trolley could no more navigate than it could the Gobi bloody Desert – and up into Dowanhill, where he noticed a sweet smell, like almonds. He laughed to himself; even the air round here was posher. He wandered the rabbit-warren back streets behind student halls and student houses, a bit lost, but in a way that felt safe, and emerged eventually on Great Western Road, where a private school's playing fields faced rather cruelly on to a private hospital, so any players puffed out could stand by the subs' bench, bent at the waist, hands braced on their knees, and gaze over the road at their inescapable destiny. Back along towards Queen Margaret Drive, past the black trees and ghostly domes of the Botanics. He strode with purpose, hoping the exercise was helping his duff leg. Forty minutes' brisk walk and a good few smokes, in the mist, in the silence, alone; that was what he needed, heartening solitude.

He stopped to inspect the noticeboard outside the deconsecrated church on the corner of Byres Road – now an arts centre rather than, as per every other conversion in the city, jerry-built luxury apartments. Here were signs for theatre productions and meditation courses; appeals for missing pets. A solitary VOTE YES sticker: aye, good luck with that. Then, on one A4 sheet he read: DRAWING CLASSES AT GLASGOW MUSEUMS AND GALLERIES. THURSDAYS, 6–9 P.M. NO EXPERIENCE NECESSARY. It tickled him to think there might be people to whom this description literally applied: hairless nude six-foot foetuses who'd never learned to so much as focus their eyes. Still, he didn't walk on. He missed working, that was the truth of it; moreover, flicking through his old catalogue the other day had given him a pang of quitter's remorse – the feeling that, because he'd given it up, drawing was the only thing he'd ever truly loved. He lit a cigarette and reread the ad, and scoffed, and did not outright dismiss the idea.

After all, he couldn't picture himself working in Lynne's flat, great light though there was through the big kitchen window – not because of the demolition across the way, which seemed to be on hiatus, but because the place was saturated with sorry self-deceptions that would creep inevitably, inexorably into any work he attempted there, tainting it.

On his return to Glendower Street, he made the mistake of mentioning the classes to Lynne, who, predictably, lit up like a Belisha beacon. 'Oh, but Angus, that's a terrific idea. When do you start?'

'Ah only said—'

'It'd be so good for you. Exactly the thing you need to get yourself, well, you know, back into the swing of things.' He eyed her in astonishment: the *what*? 'It might even be good for you,' she suggested, oblivious, 'to be a pupil again, to remind yourself what it is to be a teacher.'

'Hold up a minute there, Advice Shop – ah nivver said ah wis definitely gaun.' He wondered, given the way she'd wired straight into the psychobabble, what qualified her to know what was or wasn't good for him. 'All it's gonnae be's ould wifies widowed twenty year, bored ay the bridge club, the community tea mornins. "How's about we gie these wee classes a go, Senga?" These places are a, a vortex ay talentlessness, Lynne, and whut's more,' he warmed, 'it's infectious. Ye might turn up knowing how to draw fuckin . . . stick figures, but ah guarantee by the end of the night they'll have managed tae bore even that skill out of ye.'

She held up her hands. 'All right, all right! Sorry I spoke.'

'Ah'm no gonnae humiliate masel,' he insisted, 'in front ay some Cambuslang graduate hauf ma age who wants tae teach me the proper way tae hold a pencil. Ah've mair dignity than that, believe it or not.'

'Angus. It's fine. You don't want to do the classes. Now, can I go to bed?'

'Yes,' he shouted. 'Fine. Night.'

43

He'd barely raised his voice, yet Lynne had a face like fizz as she ran a glass of water and swallowed her nightly valerian tablet. It wasn't fair, her simply shutting down discussion like that, just because she didn't relish confrontation. In Angus's opinion, a frank airing of views would do them nothing but good.

Perhaps that was why, come morning, he found his indignation had turned to firm resolve. 'Ah'm gonnae try they classes,' he informed Lynne as she was heading out the door. It was as much apology as she was getting.

'Sorry if I snapped,' she muttered back, collecting her raincoat and her brolly. He had to admire how she gave no hint how much his decision must have pleased her. Hell's teeth, he was thinking, you had to keep an eye on Lynne. Underneath it all, she was a sly wee operator.

FIVE

In recent times he'd been more familiar with Kelvingrove Park itself than with the art gallery at its centre. On Thursday night, after ten days under Lynne's roof, he entered the park with his stare fixed dead ahead, feart – he'd freely admit it – that lurking in the gardens' shelters and dead ends and traps were creatures who knew him, watching him approach, readying themselves to pounce. But the reason he'd originally selected this particular park to sleep in was precisely because of the gallery, a place he knew of old as a sanctuary.

In Angus's day the gallery's turrets and crenellations had been black with the decades' shipbuilding smog rolling up off the Clyde. Recently, though, money had been found from who knew where to do the old place up. There was scaffolding over the main entranceway; to its right the untouched wall was still discoloured, but to its left the sandstone had been restored to its former fierce ruddled fox-red. The effect was startling, and the intention behind it not necessarily dishonourable, but Angus, whose da had been laid off from the docks in the 1980s, could not help but feel this was the last stage in a revisionist Thatcher-era project to efface any sign that there had ever been such a thing as industry on the river.

Oh, but there were ramifications time didn't erase: there were those men, Angus's da among them, beached redundant, skilled for nothing but the ships, and needing something, anything to fill the hole.

As a child, he'd been brought here after mornings spent across the way at the Yorkhill – the sick kids' hospital, still standing, its salmon-pink mirrored windows reflecting the sour Glasgow light. Inside, you'd sit silent on the brown pleather sofas, awed by the waiting room's centrepiece: a nicotine-coloured rocking horse you were first too small to go on, then, seemingly without an interval, too big – or all along too afraid. It had wild rolling enamelled eyes and bared ivory teeth, and there were sooty dowel holes on its glazed neck where an overenthusiastic rider had wrenched out plugs of its black nylon mane. This maiming horrified you, and you half wanted to show your da, your then-immaculate da, what you'd noticed. Yet there was something unspeakable about the holes – they were rude, somehow. Sooner or later you'd be called by nurses you recognized from last time but who didn't recognize you, and who got your name wrong the same way each time – 'Rennie? Rennie Angus?' – making you wonder, even that young, what the hell sort of name that was, your earliest notion of identity and disguise provoked, you believe, by their recurrent error: your vague sense that the person being summoned both was and was not yourself, and there was a minuscule gap in there that you might one day squeeze into, exploit. It also gifted you a treasured memory, the old man pissing himself laughing: months after it first happened, he still, to your bafflement, sang 'Walk Away Renée' any time you exited a room, for which recollection you remain grateful.

Angus loitered outside by the scaffolding tower, smoking a steadying cigarette, until some folk he felt certain were drawing-class attendees had entered. Matching jackets, matching portfolios; he knew the sort. After a brief wrangle with the revolving door, he followed them in.

A group had gathered at the far end of the main hall, beneath the vast church organ that dominated the whole wall, and beside the entrance to a temporary exhibition of Egyptian artefacts pilfered, he supposed, from the tombs of kings. No surprise, the blue-rinse brigade were present in droves, all fawn anoraks and fingerless gloves, more females than males. Angus approached, his rubber soles making a mortifyingly loud squealing on the marble floor. Orange plastic chairs had been set out in a semicircle, and the students were clustered, nattering, around a small guy with a shaved head who was doling out stationery and platitudes. 'Who needs supplies? Alice? That's a pretty dress, dear.' He wore a sticker: HI! MY NAME IS DEAN. 'Oh, and Campbell, I should have known – needing pencils again, right? Right.' Didn't the old dears realize they were being treated like bairns? Maybe that was how they liked it.

Of course Angus had no equipment either, and had to queue up with all the other losers for paper, pencil, eraser, talking-to. 'You're new!' Dean greeted him when he reached the head of the line. 'Did we speak on the phone this morning? Angus?' Angus gruffly admitted it. 'Well, welcome to our little gang. Here' – applying to Angus's jumper a sticker like his own, with Angus's name felt-tipped on. 'Now, you said you'd done some drawing before? Excellent. How it'll work tonight is we'll start out with some group work here first, and then after an hour or so people peel off and do some solo investigations, picking an object that interests them and drawing it. Then about nine o'clock I round everyone up, like a big old sheepdog, and we let the good people keeping the gallery open late for us go home. How does that sound?'

How it sounded was like death on toast, but Angus capitulated, choosing the last chair in the line, away from the others, where he sat silently, radiating, he hoped, a dinnae-speak-tae-me vibe. Everyone around him was gabbing away like ninnies. His chair was warped and he took pleasure in rocking back and forth on its misaligned feet. What had Lynne meant about it doing him good to imagine himself a student again? A bullshit thought experiment she'd lifted from her *How to Manage* book. All it made him feel, to be back in a classroom but not in charge, was as sullen as a teenager.

Dean clapped his hands. 'Are we all ready? Campbell? Well,

47

tonight I'd like to talk to you a bit about shading. *Shading.*' As he spoke, Dean began sketching a portrait of the replica statue advertising the Egyptian exhibition: a serene androgynous face on a long, slender neck, bargain-basement Modigliani. 'Now, that's a start, but she's a bit flat, isn't she? So what I'll do now is . . .' He held his pencil on the angle and started to fill in a triangular area to one side of the nose. 'And what else am I going to tell you? What is it I'm always saying is your most important skill?'

He mouthed the word, and 'Ob-ser-*va*-tion,' the old dears chorused back, kindling in Angus a crushing sense of purgatorial damnation, week in, week out the same call-and-response, a geriatric circle-jerk of mutual congratulation.

'Right! So I want you to *observe*' – Dean left his easel and began walking around the group, several already having embarked on their own drawings – 'where light is coming from, and where it falls. What shadow is cast, heavy or faint. What shape it makes. Don't just guess – *look*, properly look. You're working from . . .' Ruefully he waved a hand at the statue. 'Well, from life.'

Although inclined to sneer at Dean's manner, Angus found that both the tutor and the environment were actually helping him to relax, though the fact remained that a statue was a bloody silly subject for sketching. Picking up his pencil and beginning to make lines, he found himself navigating his way back into a mnemonic space he'd thought no longer accessible. An old desire reasserted itself: the wish to excel, to show how much better he was than the others. It did help, although he was not old – grizzled, that was how he liked to imagine himself, there being some wiggle-room for romance in that word – to be bossed around by someone so young. Antipathy was crucial, something specific to rail against. Maybe in Dean's imagination his shaved head gave him more authority, but all the onlooker saw was a big-eyed neonate whose bare scalp gave the impression that he'd had problems with late-onset head lice.

48

Angus finished a preliminary outline of the statue, but its features were too inhuman to be satisfying. Bored already, he fell to wondering how Lynne was coping without him for a whole evening. Writing sonnets dedicated to him? Ha, no, probably glad to be rid of him – probably up to her tits in an orgy right this minute. He sniggered. Poor Lynne was so uptight she probably didn't even like to *think* the word.

Footsteps approached from the entranceway, clopping like hooves on the marble. A chair scraped back and he heard Dean's voice squeak out, 'Come on in, China, we're just starting.'

It was nearer seven than six. Are we fuck just starting, Angus thought, but when he saw China, he understood why Dean was cutting her this slack.

'Sorry. Hi. Sorry.' She came sidling into the group, long black coat and a nest of slate-coloured hair seamed silver, though she was maybe mid twenties at most. Angus wasn't left open-mouthed by her beauty or anything, but then again, here was that Nordic colouring he liked, indigo eyes, skin so pale it neared blue . . .

'We thought maybe you weren't coming. Don't worry, don't worry, let's just quickly get you set up. Wherever you can find a space.' Angus, acutely aware of the spare seat beside him that no one had risked taking, dropped his head. 'How about over beside, er, Angus there?'

Ha, that's the ticket. He smiled sidelong at the newcomer, who looked back at him without expression. Then, as she manoeuvred her way into the circle, her bag struck the easel set up by one of the more enthusiastic students and brought it crashing to the ground. Equipment spilled and clattered – the old dears responding with wordless, vaguely censorious clucks and coos – and as China knelt to gather her pencil tin to her, ignoring the pensioner she'd jostled, Dean scurried to assist her with a solicitousness Angus recognized, understood, filed away.

Ruckus over, the older students returned to their work, showing one another their experiments in shading with as

49

much delight as if Dean had demonstrated how to transmute base metal into gold. By contrast, the concentration on China's face as she set to work was ferocious, though her line was light and fleet on the page. Seemingly she carried no more than three pencils, and to Angus's mind this meant that she, alone among the amateurs overloaded with every coloured felt tip and set square you could buy, had come prepared to do some actual work.

Dean had been moving around the group, offering comments and correctives, unfailingly positive. He was soft, but the last thing a group like this needed was someone mean in charge – an Angus. When he came to the end of the line of chairs, he inspected Angus's sketch in silence. Unnerved, Angus picked up his pencil again, pretending to have paused rather than given up; but without a word to him, Dean clapped twice. 'All right, everyone, time to split up. Find something that inspires you, pick a good spot, and get to work. I'll be around in an hour to see what you've come up with. Remember, it's not a contest, so try to choose something nobody else is drawing. China, a word before you head off?'

'Just one?'

Angus lingered too, unexpectedly wounded by Dean's failure to praise him.

'You were a bit late. I just wanted to check everything was okay.'

'To be honest, I was swithering. I wasn't all that sure I was going to bother.'

Dean, with what seemed to Angus misplaced gallantry: 'It would have been our loss.'

'Yes.' The colouring, the petulant set to her mouth as her smirk developed – blue eyes, black temper, the right side of insolent to interest Angus, just as she herself surely knew that her cheeking Dean only boosted her allure.

He was all set to pursue the girl into the galleries when Dean stepped into his path. 'And how's Angus doing?' Angus, who detested the con man's trick of addressing you in the third person, rose on his toes over the wee guy and didn't respond. 'That was really rather good, what you drew. I didn't want to say in front of the others, but it beats them into a cocked hat, if I'm honest. I'd make just one adjustment . . .'

Eraser in hand, he dived for the picture, but Angus snatched his sketch pad away. 'Ah actually prefer it the way it is, if ye dinnae mind?'

'Oh, of course. Of course. Now, did you need any help finding your way around?'

'This place?' he said with scorn, mimicking the high-handed tone China had taken with the guy. 'Don't you worry aboot me. This is familiar territory.'

Sketch pad under his oxter, pencil box rattling in his free hand, Angus stotted the Kelvingrove's dim-lit halls and chambers in search of China. Compelled almost to mutter under his breath *jist looking fer ma friend*, in case anyone asked why he hadn't begun working yet. When he did encounter other students – several had ganged together, in contravention of Dean's instructions, and were accomplishing precious little work in between their yak-king – he smiled, inspected their efforts and with great difficulty resisted pointing out their various shortcomings.

In a front gallery he encountered the slate-grey dinosaurs he knew from his childhood visits. Still impressive, too: none of this modern-day animatronics shite you found elsewhere. These vast immobile sentinels had never changed – well, they wouldn't, dinosaurs, nature's losers – and still gave off their familiar freshly sculpted, coal-dust smell. One whiff of that, any time, anywhere, and Angus could've hand-drawn the creatures from memory.

He shook his head, moved on, remembering the routine of thirty-plus years back. After the appointment at Yorkhill, the treat: over the road to the Kelvingrove to see the monsters, the samurai, the knights in armour – the same exhibits each time, in the same sequence – and was it coincidence, it occurred to

Angus tonight as he wandered from one gallery to the next, that these had all been fighters, figures of strength: had he been receiving tacit life lessons? The tour completed, he'd be allowed a jam doughnut or square of fly cemetery in the canteen, to boost blood sugar brought low by the morning's tests and injections at the hospital. The canteen was fitted with fluorescent tube lights and a squeaky black vulcanized-rubber floor, and this made it, to Angus aged nine, the acme of sci-fi sophistication. The old man had had to tell him several times each visit to stand up off the clarty ground, since – though this had been as inexpressible as his troubling feelings on noticing the puncture marks in the rocking horse's neck – to trace his finger around the embossed circles on the floor, sixteen per tile, was a highlight of Angus's day, the hospital appointment for which this was compensation by now all but forgotten.

He passed spearheads and sidearms; Mackintosh chairs, ormolu clocks, stuffed reptiles; Beryl Cooks and the Dalí Christ. Artefacts from unrelated epochs, forced to mingle in the vast cold rooms like guests at a wake. A funny feeling stole over him in places like this: he heard footsteps in distant rooms, the metronomic plod of adult feet set against a child's adagio, and felt just for a moment that he might round a corner and see, through an architraved doorway, his father and himself as a boy, the sickly child.

Someone blabbed, of course, the instant he'd achieved any measure of success. 'Oh, you didn't know? Yeah, *seriously* ill as a kid. They say he was lucky to survive.' And oh, the critics' relief, now that they no longer had to pretend to be divining hidden meanings, but could give anything they liked or disliked in his work the most banal, reductive biographical gloss. After that revelation all they saw in the underlit rooms and looming gronk faces he painted was the lingering psychological drip-down of childhood malady. At first, he'd been amused by the naïvety: he'd laughed at a review of the 1998 CCA exhibition in which he'd shown *The Losers*, not knowing that all subsequent reviews would resemble it: 'Rennie contributes a vast and cine-matically melancholic canvas, all austere deep Victorian browns and blacks, and, in faltering chalk marks, two huge malevolently grinning faces, personifications of disease bearing down on the feeble patient . . .' Cheek, spouting all that claptrap then only awarding the show three stars. When reviews praised the work, the artist could take no credit; when they were harsh, he was the one felt the blame. Worse still, once the story had got around, Angus could no longer deliver his stock line about tragedies yet to befall him, all his interviewers now supposing they knew him better than he did himself – hence no bugger making the effort to find out whose double portrait *The Losers* actually was. One early death, one disappearance. Aye, well, maybe better that remain Angus's secret.

He finally found China in one of the taxidermy rooms. She was sitting cross-legged with her back to the wall, before a vitrine in which various Arctic animals stood in unnatural prox-imity on jablite tundra. A sketchbook was open on her lap, and he keeked down to see what she was drawing: the Arctic fox, which, going by its dead dumb eyes, its snaggle teeth and bald muzzle, dated back to the flood. She had lightly pencilled in guidelines for herself: cylinders for its body and legs, a tangram of differently sized wedges for its head. He almost laughed. This was what Dean was teaching the poor fuckers?

'That's – interestin,' he opined, nonetheless. She glanced up, unsurprised at his seeking her out, or feigning it. 'Good, is what I mean.' Her expression didn't change. 'Ah've been tourin aboot, ye see, and the other folk . . .' He trailed off, and, either self-conscious or uninterested, China went back to her drawing, starting on the scraggy ruff of fur round the fox's throat. 'Even the ones drawin properly, like you – well, it's still comin oot two-dimensional.' A dim sense of propriety kept him from a more candid appraisal. 'Nae understandin there's anyhin beneath the skin.'

'Uh-huh?' China replied, on a rising note, as though intrigued by this information. She threw aside the pencil she'd been using, took up another, and started shading, just as Dean had taught them.

'Aye.' He cleared his throat and then sat beside her on the polished floor, which was a more complicated and painful process than he had anticipated, involving dropping into a crouch then arranging his sore legs like a puppet's beneath him. 'That there's bones, and muscles and tendons, and . . . other stuff. Ye know, the same workings that're inside us aw.' His bad knee, folded back on itself like a flick-knife, chose this moment to click into place, emitting a crack that seemed to echo in the hush. Embarrassed, he fell silent, opened up his pad and began to sketch – without the aid of any geometric shapes, mark you – the same Arctic fox, from a different angle. After observing without overt interest what he was doing, China returned to her own work. Frowning, she drew the line of the fox's back, glancing up at the vitrine every few seconds, wary, birdlike, in case the creature might have moved in the meantime – taken a hesitant step forward, ruined her composition.

In a sense, by watching China work, he was obeying Dean's first principle: observe. She was using soft pencils, 2B, 3B, and she was leaning rather heavily on them, with the result that the picture emerging was too dark to capture the scrappy fox's spoiled-milk pelt. Rather than mention this, Angus said:

'Interesting, but, comin here, seein aw the different stuff folk're daein.' Ah, *interesting*, the weasel word that could mean anything you wanted it to. 'Ma first class, ye see, although ye probably knew that. Ah wis reassured tae see sumdy more in ma ain age bracket.' This was deliberate provocation – China couldn't fail to be outraged by the insinuation that she was anything near as ancient as him – yet she didn't respond to this either. Tough audience. 'Ah'm glad it's no jist auld biddies here shelterin from the cauld.'

Beside him, China was using a pocket Stanley knife to whittle her pencils sharp, holding up each in turn to inspect its squared-off nib. Under her hand, the scene that was forming was livelier than the stilted set-up in the vitrine. She'd lent the static beasts some dynamism. Painted up, her drawing could've been used on a jigsaw puzzle or a calendar for a child's bedroom wall; that was the standard he was seeing.

With his own fox nearly completed – though he had misjudged the starting point, so the animal seemed to cower at the foot of the page – Angus had a go at adding a fulmar, which hung by nylon threads from the vitrine's gridded ceiling. He wanted to show it swooping low and majestic over the animals' gathering, but instead he inadvertently made the bird look like it was plummeting, petrified, from the air. Flummoxed, he turned the page and debated whether he was better starting over or giving up. Some days you just didn't have it. It was his first time drawing in God knew how long, yet that made him even less inclined than usual to go easy on himself. He tried again, and this time got a couple of the seabirds down reasonably well. What must China think of him, seeing these half-arsed efforts? He found himself wishing he could show her the paintings he'd done in his old life. *The Losers* – he didn't even know who owned that any more. He'd held off selling it as long as he could, then let it go hastily, reluctantly, for an insulting sum, to keep body and soul together that bit longer. Whose wall did it hang on now? Whose attic was it shoved in, waiting to appreciate in value? It was not about who owned it, he corrected himself; it'd always be Angus's, no matter if he never saw it again.

He felt the long point of dejection pressing into his throat, and had to switch his attention back to China swiftly. 'How long've ye been comin to these classes?'

'Oh . . . a few weeks now, I guess. Yeah, a month or two maybe.'

She didn't give you much to work with, this one, and he said in desperation, 'Grand place tae come and work, eh?' This time she didn't even open her mouth to reply, but gave a non-committal hum. Peculiar to think that China, though not exactly loquacious, and Dean, whom he found ridiculous, were the only folk besides Lynne he'd spoken to in a fortnight. And how quickly he had come to take Lynne's company, her hospitality, for granted! Sure it was a privilege to use a bathroom you didn't have to share with a dozen other soap-dodgers, yet somehow that made it especially bowfing to find one of Lynne's unconscionably long, wiry, kinky hairs in the sink some mornings. And as much as he tried to remain grateful to her for never pressuring him to go on the broo, or find a wee temp job seeing as he was not actually disabled, even this had started to rankle. Did she not believe he *could* hold down a job? This thinking was no good, he understood, this was not grateful or noble or whatever he'd have liked to be. He couldn't help himself.

'Well *there* you are,' came Dean's voice, preceding the man himself, who arrived via a marine gallery adjacent, aqueous light bouncing off his peanut head. 'We were starting to think you two had run out on us.' He seemed to be under the impression that referring to himself in the plural might bolster his skimpy authority. 'We're finishing up now, unless you fancy spending the night here?'

'Widnae be the worst place ah'd steiyed in ma time,' Angus said, sniffing. Dean laughed like it was a joke. 'Albie Day,' he went on, taking the opportunity to showboat to China, though she wasn't, ostensibly, paying him any heed. 'Ye heard ay him? Used tae sneak intae places like this just before closin time and hide, so he'd get locked in after hours. He'd wait there the night then reveal himself next mornin to whoever opened up. Ta-dah! Performance art, he called it – ah'm no so sure masel.'

'Day,' mused Dean. Angus noticed that the tutor had positioned himself closer to him than to China, body-blocking him. 'No, never heard of him, I'm afraid.'

'No, well, that's no more than the guy deserves. Horrible artist. A horrible human being full stop, come tae that.' Dean blinked in surprise, but that was how you separated the wheat from the chaff: no artist worth his salt hesitated to slag off his peers and precursors. You had to think about the alternative: lavish praise on someone as uncontroversial as Picasso, say, and you were what, a follower, a slave. Artist, let not the word *influence* slip from your lips. As for more obscure figures, why give them the free publicity?

China, ignored, was packing away her equipment. Angus sensed disaster a moment before it occurred: she fumbled her tin and pencils spilled across the marble floor, delicate leads shattering. He and Dean both dived to be first to help, China scrabbling up the pencils but the sketchbook slithering out then from under her arm. Trying to catch it, she seemed to lose her balance, staggered like a drunk, and Angus suffered a momentary hallucination: China toppling headlong into the display case, shattering it, letting air into the vacuum inside – struggling to her feet while the threadbare specimens in the scene, unbound from their long paralysis, stared around in astonishment . . .

Jesus! He fought Dean off, scooped up the sketchbook and returned it to China, and she regarded him with eyes as blank as those of the creatures in the vitrine.

'Well,' Dean nearly shouted, his friendliness seemingly exhausted, 'I've just got to make sure nobody's done an Albie Day, and then we're finished. Maybe after that—'

Angus, who could see where this was going – we three are the real talent here, why don't we find somewhere to hang out together – talked over him at China. 'Want me tae walk ye out, doll?' She didn't reply in words but favoured him with what you could almost, at a stretch, describe as a smile. You could project almost anything on someone so silent: already old Angus was making plans for her to find him charming – shifting things around in his head, wishing he had more than just pennies in his pocket so he could suggest they stop for a drink on the way home. Maybe not a *drink* drink at this stage – though now that the thought was planted . . .

Leaving disconsolate Dean behind in the fake Arctic, they

57

passed into the fake Atlantic from which the tutor had come. The room was lined with tanks of lifeless fish, static-swimming in one direction around the walls. At the centre stood a peculiar diorama: several small tropical sorts arranged in an otherwise vacant aquarium tank maybe fifteen foot across and eight high. China strode right past, but Angus, curious, stopped to read the signage. A curator's note explained that this display illustrated symbiosis, the mutually beneficial arrangement in which these butterfly fish cleaved close to a hammerhead shark to feed on the parasites that troubled it, nuzzling its cartilaginous hide, liberated in their proximity to the super-predator from their normal position in the food chain. Well, that was how you survived, turning your disadvantages around until they started to look less like problems and more like things you could exploit.

But the shark was absent from the display – removed, according to a supplementary note, for maintenance. Angus barked when he read that: wasn't that just like a god? So now these fish hung baffled in blue formaldehyde, kissing up to empty space, experiencing, he imagined, the very mildest existential crisis, their scant few seconds of memory never permitting them to fathom what it was that had disappeared so abruptly from their lives.

SIX

She liked to stand alone in the living room – his room. Open the door, pause, then just a few steps inside, so she was still more or less on the threshold – hardly *in* his room at all. It had become a habit since he'd started going on his nightly walks. Where was the harm? The harm was in telling herself it was a harmless thing to do.

From loitering it wasn't a huge leap, knowing he'd be out at his class all Thursday evening, to searching. She pretended not to know it was wrong, narrating to herself a justificatory monologue: just seeing what he's done to the place, making sure he's settled in okay. She did not succeed, by these means, in hushing the other internal voice, which chided her with the real reason for this snooping. She'd revealed so much to Angus these last ten nights – confessions he absorbed as a black hole absorbs light, disinterested, pitiless – and had obtained almost nothing in return. What more did she know about him now than she had five years ago? Horror stories about sleeping rough, a cast of grotesques. She felt he offered these scraps only to obfuscate. Who was he to let her run her mouth off and give nothing back? With Angus volunteering no meaningful revelations, she had, at some point she couldn't identify, concluded that it was her right to seek them out herself.

And if she was caught? She free-associated her rationales. For one, she might claim she wanted to check he wasn't concealing anything illegal. Homeless people were often substance

59

abusers – half the reports she'd scanned blamed drugs for the individual's homelessness; the other half claimed that homelessness led to drug use – so you couldn't condemn her. But what if she found something, as she almost wanted to, some leverage? Would she even know drug paraphernalia if she saw it? In her heart she didn't believe he'd be capable of hiding an addiction from her, any more than she'd be capable of throwing him out – which, she imagined, he would immediately challenge her to do. How, anyway, was she to claim, if she did find syringes beneath the mattress, for instance, that she'd just happened upon them?

It brought her up short when she opened the chest of drawers and saw the two checked shirts, the dun chinos, the five days' change of underwear neatly folded. He'd barely worn half the clothes she'd chosen for him. Long having viewed with suspicion those who treated shopping as a leisure activity, Lynne had nevertheless relished picking out these clothes, carefully choosing colours, shirts whose labels promised they'd never need to be ironed, smiling as she identified foibles she'd imagined for him – disinclination to iron his clothes, a general aversion to any housework – which were in truth characteristics of Raymond's she had imputed to Angus with no idea whether they were true.

Every other lunchtime, she struggled back to the office with fresh carrier bags from Buchanan Street. Safety razors and aftershave balm, a toothbrush and dental floss, unscented deodorant, nail clippers, coal-tar soap, anti-dandruff shampoo. He liked tea; she bought him four different varieties. She left her parcels in a prominent position beside her desk, waiting for her colleagues to remark them – willing even to be mocked for them, the important thing being to make it known that she was able to have secrets, another life that people would realize, even as they jibed at her, they knew nothing about. But her colleagues, if they even noticed, didn't say a word.

She ran her hand over the shirts, feeling sadness: why? It was herself – the lonely woman shopping on her lodger's behalf

– she felt heart-sorry for. Angus had his walks, his classes, was growing back into himself despite all his difficulties, while she was doing . . . what exactly? Mooning. Mourning.

And intruding. Here was a better excuse: she was tidying up, ready for Siri's visit at the weekend. This was still her living room, after all. But to her surprise, Angus, who piled used plates and glasses in the kitchen sink as if having ideological objections to carrying the washing-up process any further, had kept his room almost preternaturally tidy. He'd not just made the bed, but folded the futon away and replaced the plumped cushions so that it looked unused. It struck her that if for some reason he did not come back tonight, she'd be unable to convince anybody he'd ever been there.

The only evidence was the books he'd stacked on the little cabinet by the sofa, a sort of bedside table. She picked these up one by one – two of the pop-science books Siri persisted in giving her for birthdays and Christmases, and, to her amusement, Angus's own catalogue – then panicked that she'd betray her presence by failing to replace them in the correct order.

The little cabinet, brick-red ersatz chinoiserie from the furniture shop on Kelvin Bridge, was locked. A cheap padlock had been fastened to its dulled brass latch – the cheap padlock, Lynne realized as she rattled the door, she had bought to secure her seldom-used suitcase. She must have inadvertently included it with the keys she'd given Angus. She wondered what treasures he could want to lock away.

Without interrogating what she was doing, she hastened to the kitchen for her own key ring. A digital camera, she reflected, as she searched for the tiny padlock key. You could bring a camera in with you to photograph things as they stood, and that way be sure you'd put everything back properly afterwards. Undetectable. But that would be a tiny bit excessive, would it not?

The cabinet was stuffed full of fabric. A smell she identified as Angus's, a faint sour gaminess, not unpleasant, came strongly off this bundle, and she realized, as she removed it and it fell apart into a shirt, jeans, that these were the clothes he'd been wearing when she had found him begging. She found nothing in the jeans pockets, no stash rolled up in the disintegratingly soft shirt. Why hadn't he laundered these clothes? Why had he hidden them?

She pressed them to her face. That smell, redolent of life persisting in lightless places – its *himness*, the same scent discernible through his deodorant and the fresh and staling sweat when he came home at night – made her lift up on her toes, made her feel like she was about to lose hold of herself: not necessarily a bad thing. It frustrated her, though, that she could not turn this inchoate feeling into any fantasy life. She could imagine an embrace – they already hugged each other anyway; sometimes he let her kiss his cheek good night – but when her imagination tried to elaborate on these chaste moments, even just turn his mouth to hers, it felt like trying to recall a dream, the attempt to marshal the details chasing the whole away. Some nights she lay awake for hours, readying herself for something that never happened – fantasizing about having fantasies about him.

Out in the hall the telephone began to ring. Lynne sprang up, face burning. She stuffed Angus's unwashed clothes back into the cabinet, and it only struck her as she clicked shut the padlock that the clothes themselves must be the secret – that what he had sought to conceal was his fear that he'd have to wear them again.

'What's the matter?' came Raymond's voice as soon as Lynne picked up.

'Nothing,' she stammered. She was so relieved it wasn't Angus, or someone calling about Angus, she was almost pleased to hear from him. 'Why?'

'You usually answer on the second ring. It's one of your "things" ' – suggesting by his tone a whole portfolio of tics he'd once found charming but come gradually to despise.

'No, no, I'm fine.' She had a bad liar's voice, bright, high and brittle. 'I was just finishing up dinner. A lasagne. I was putting it in the oven.' She fell silent, wary of somehow incriminating herself.

'I thought . . . Well, I was rather expecting we'd have spoken to one another before now.'

'I've been busy,' she said, hating the defensive creep in her voice.

'Evidently. Making lasagnes at nine at night.'

'You know I like to cook for the week ahead.' They weren't strangers, so why did this exchange have the same tenor as their earliest, most faltering conversations? Those first awkward dates at the Russian tea rooms, Sunday afternoons after church. Five years swiftly extirpated, two intimates turned back into strangers. Don't panic, she told herself: you spend all day at work saying things you'd rather not to people you have nothing in common with; you know how to speed a conversation along. 'Raymond, why are you calling?'

'Do I need a reason?' She could see him passing a hand over his brow in consternation. 'Yes, I suppose so.' He laughed, contrite, and that made her more nervous. 'I wanted to see you. That was the reason. That's a good enough reason, isn't it? I was hoping you'd be able to come round this weekend. Are you free on Saturday?'

Luckily, she was able to answer honestly that she was not. 'Siri's coming for lunch.'

'Is that so?'

'Yes.' Lynne had to fight hard not to apologize. 'It's been arranged for weeks. I did email you.'

'That's too bad,' Raymond said, after a pause. 'Sometime next week, then, Lynnie, is that better? I do need to see you. You left so abruptly last time.'

As if he'd had nothing to do with that! She was about to give an angry retort, but the words jammed in her throat as she heard footsteps on the stairs of the close. An arrhythmic tread, one step emphatic, the next slurred: Angus, favouring his good leg, trudging his way home from class.

Raymond, oblivious: 'Well, maybe Thursday, then, if . . . Lynnie? Are you still there?'

She was barely listening. 'Next Thursday, yes. That's fine.' Even uncoiled to its fullest length, the telephone cable didn't stretch far enough for her to look round the door frame into Angus's room and ensure she'd put everything back as she'd found it. 'Look, Raymond' – Angus's silhouette looming in the glassed front door – 'I have to go.'

'There *is* something the matter—'

'I'll call you back.' As the key scraped in the lock, Lynne slammed down the receiver. With no time to go elsewhere, she remained beside the phone, one hand resting awkwardly on the bookcase, for all the world like she'd stood there for hours awaiting Angus's return.

He came in, yanked the black hat off his head and blinked gummily at her. 'Creepin' Jesus, Lynne, whut happened to you? Sumdy run over yir cat?' The heat of her guilt she assumed Angus would immediately detect what she had done, and when he simply strolled past her, whistling, patting at his hair, she detached herself from the bookcase and followed him into the kitchen.

'How was class?' To her, her voice still sounded unnaturally high.

'Who wis that ye were on the phone wi?'

'Oh, nobody. You seem awfully sparky all of a sudden. You enjoyed yourself, then?'

'Funny business,' he chaffed her, 'getting a call aff ay naebody. Nae wonder ye look spooked.' He put the kettle on, then hung his jacket – another thing she'd bought him – over a chair. Underneath he was wearing the black jumper and blue checked shirt she'd chosen, the jeans still with the crease in them. He didn't put those other things on during the day when she was out, did he? Didn't still go begging with a cup? The dirty clothes she had—

'It was braw, aye. Interesting. The class?' he clarified, rolling his eyes, mistaking Lynne's panic for incomprehension. In fact she was trying desperately to remember what she had done with her keys when the phone had rung.

She patted her pockets: nothing. 'And it was . . . the Kelving-rove you went to?' Surely she'd set her keys down beside the telephone? She couldn't see the bookcase from here.

' 'Sright, aye. Don't let me keep you,' he said snidely, as she inched towards the door.

She halted. 'No, I'm not going anywhere. But, so, tell me. What did you have to do? What were the other students like?' If she couldn't escape the room, perhaps she could waylay him here indefinitely instead. It wasn't much of a ploy, but nor, as her foray into espionage had shown, was Lynne much of a plotter.

'Actually, ye know whut, hen? Ah'm bushed.' He lifted the bag from his tea with his fingertips, tossed it dripping into the sink, and turned to her, opening his mouth in a theatrically vast yawn. 'Amnae used tae these late nights. Think ah'll jist head straight to ma bed. Ma . . . fut*on*,' putting strange emphasis on the second syllable.

Defeated, Lynne took a seat at the table. Angus paused in the doorway and scowled at her. 'Sure ye're awright?'

Lynne nodded. 'Never better.' When he withdrew, mouth pursed, she groaned quietly and rested her forehead on her arms. Well, so what: either the keys were in his room or they weren't, which meant it was fifty-fifty whether she'd been discovered. She readied futile excuses. It's my house. I had every right. Then, when Angus didn't come charging back through to bawl her out, she raised her head. The living-room door was shut and no sound came from within. Cautiously, Lynne allowed herself to consider the possibility that she had got away with it after all.

SEVEN

They called it the clockwork orange: a tiny subway chasing its tail in a perpetual loop beneath some rum parts of the city. Train carriages scaled down, suited to troglodytes. Time was, Angus would have joined his students on a Friday night for the traditional crawl – sinking a pint at the pub nearest each station, then back underground and onwards to the next stop, fifteen in all. The high point came with his charges' trepidation on alighting at Cessnock, a place whose name threatened to oversell its charms, comprising as it did one massive flyover and a maze of pebble-dashed back alleys, walls topped with scribbled battlements of barbed wire – defence against what, who knew; what could there be in these sagging houses and junk-filled back yards worth thieving? Angus riffing on this theme as he led the way to their destination, an auld-man pub whose Friday-night air of barely suppressed violence – Friday night, hell, any night – thrilled the youngsters. With Angus there to protect them, they were free to feel dangerous. He knew the regulars. They'd never lay a finger.

None of that today, more's the pity, the cramped wee train with its distinctive staticky, fusty smell rattling through a mere three stops, Angus emerging into the city-centre fug: stale smoke, vinegar, the ozone of recent rain.

When Lynne's call had come, he'd made sympathetic noises and promised to search the flat top to bottom for her lost keys – all the while withholding the information that they weren't lost at all, he could see them right now, exactly where she'd left them beside the books on the red cabinet. Either that or the paint-chipped Snoopy fob, which got him feeling sympathy for the daft mare despite himself, had come to life and walked itself into his room. Snoopy was right – creeping round, checking up on him. Were her daily phone calls home to ensure he hadn't topped himself or burnt the flat down not enough? He'd called back after a decent interval to say he'd found the keys, and agreed to come and drop them off at her work.

The city centre had a special air of desolation about it this lunchtime. With the bone-white daylight already fading, Angus hurried through dreich streets, spooked by the atmosphere, as well as by the prospect of encountering one of his erstwhile peers: Cobbsy; needy wee Bobby Imison, always on the lookout for the rich older guy who'd help him off the streets; the mental bam girl who sold drugs out the baby carriage she wheeled about the place. On the streets, you quickly learned a whole lot about what had happened to whom, and one constant was that you weren't given fair go if it got out you'd found accommodation. Just look at these whole office blocks lying empty, but: their blank or broken windows, the TO LET signs drooping, efflorescent with scum, from their walls. Here was the solution to your *homeless problem*, as the politicians called it, like an abstract conundrum: the old Odeon on West Regent Street, boarded up and years obsolete, but in decent condition nonetheless. You could accommodate everyone in there no bother, put a roof over the heads of everyone needing it.

He was eyeing the restaurants he passed, too, though the only things that seemed to be prospering were shoddy Italians, all-you-can-eat buffets. He was getting ahead of himself, not least in the small matter of his lack of disposable income, but you had to have plans in mind for all eventualities. Next time he'd disarm China with his old-world charm: flatter her with questions – make her feel she was fascinating – then suggest, as if the thought had just occurred, this Italian place he knew . . . Think positive and you're halfway to success. He scoffed

67

at himself. Says the guy hasn't two brass farthings to his name. Who could resist? Leaving the gallery in her company the night before, or walking beside her anyway, he'd asked if she had to dash off, or . . . Stupid way to phrase it: just meant she could agree she did and swan off with a peremptory 'See you next time.' Then Dean had emerged, head turning like a surveillance camera, and Angus, in the tutor's full view, had loped off without a word in the opposite direction.

It wasn't altogether surprising to discover that Lynne worked in a basement, given the perpetually sun-starved look she had to her. Not even a decent basement, either, not even a renovated one from which the faint reek of its nearby neighbour the sewerage system had been entirely expunged. The only natural light seeped in from scuzzy light wells set high in the walls, tiny panes yielding an ant's-eye view of pedestrian feet tramping down St Vincent Street. Packs of sweeties lay open on every desk, the employees seeking to comfort-eat their way out of the oppressed feeling the place gave them – the consequent bad skin jaded further by the harsh overhead tube lights. Loaners', lawyers', benefits offices: they all had this same despondent sweaty air. He bet people cracked wise here and called the office the orifice. He bet there was a lottery syndicate. Five minutes waiting for Lynne, on a purple sofa set oddly close to the cludgies, and he was contemplating taking his own life.

In the middle of the open-plan office, in plain view of colleagues and underlings, Lynne took back her keys without, somehow, acknowledging how they'd come to be in his possession. Almost admirable, the scale and extent of her denial. Angus was keen to get back to the West End and safety, but Lynne, to his dismay, chose this occasion for one of her daily pep talks.

'We didn't have much time, did we, to chat last night' – colouring on this last phrase as she realized she was making oblique allusion to her wee slip-up. 'I wanted to make sure it had gone all right, the class?'

68

'Oh, aye, uh-huh. It was grand.' He glanced upward, feeling like the polystyrene ceiling tiles had descended an inch or two since he'd arrived. 'Useful an aw.'

'Well, I think it's great you're going out there and doing it. Brave, too.'

Oh, this was low, keeping him talking like this. She must've been hoping to set her subordinates gesturing to one another behind their cubicle partitions – here, see that, ould Lynne knows people, ould Lynne has friends after all. From what he could tell, though, no one seemed that fussed. Few seemed to be at their desks, even: the slaphead with the mad beard who'd let Angus in was collecting empty cups from the unoccupied desks; a fattish bird was hunched over the photocopier, unaware that her shirt had ridden up at the back and she was showing off her G-string, the sight of the black fabric taut across mottled white back-flab obliging Angus to visualize, unhappily, the gusset sunk deep in her flesh like cheese wire.

Lynne, not realizing that his attention had wandered, was in full flow now, havering on – with, apparently, no irony whatsoever for somebody who spent her days in an airless subterrarium, overseeing folk any disinterested onlooker could tell didn't respect her one jot – about how these classes were the first step in enabling him to resume what she called normal life, as if that was a thing anybody in their right mind should aspire to.

'Oh aye,' he interrupted her, 'about that, ah've actually a wee favour tae ask.' He jiggled from foot to foot, acting bashful. Ladle it on, son, ladle it on – though in truth he did feel just a smidge of guilt about the coming deception. 'The thing is, there's some, like, equipment ah'm needin fer next week. Pens and that. Ah mean, there's no rush, but ah wis wondering . . .' A phone was ringing, ringing. He had planned to trail off at this stage anyway, but was as astounded as any petty larcenist seeing a far-fetched scheme come off that Lynne was already pulling ten-pound notes from her purse. 'Hud tae ask to borrow a sharpener aff ay sumdy last night,' he continued, startled by how much cash she seemed to be carrying. He began to wonder who was playing who here. 'Pretty embarrassin . . .'

'Is fifty enough? It can be expensive, that stuff, as I remember. It's a shame you didn't drop in before lunch, I could have come with you to the art store then, in case you needed more.' She frowned at her watch. 'You know, I could probably—'

'No, no,' he cut across her in panic, 'that'll be plenty, ah'm sure.'

'Well, here' – eagerly pulling out still more notes – 'take sixty anyway.' She believed, no doubt, she was buying his silence about the spying thing. 'But you will let me know if you need more?'

'Oh, definitely. Defin-*et*ly.' How far would sixty quid stretch? Enough for a meal for two, surely, without wine or dessert? Angus hadn't eaten out, not counting the hostel's dismal canteen, since the SNP came to power, not that he suspected any causal link.

'Excuse me,' Lynne suddenly bellowed over his shoulder, making him start. 'Is anyone going to answer that phone? Struan!' A blond youth nearby turned round, none too urgently. 'How about taking your finger out your backside and doing some work for once? – So sorry.' She dropped her voice, laughing uneasily when she saw Angus's startled expression. 'They're driving me nuts today.'

'Well, eh, ah might go aff doon the art store, anyway. Thanks, Lynne, it's really – really guid of ye. Again. Eh . . . do ye mind, before ah go, if I use the, eh . . . ?'

Lynne giggled, which was, if anything, more discomfiting than her shouting. 'Of course you can use the eh.'

A sanctuary in a place like this, the bogs – more dimly lit and not air-conditioned to buggery like the office outside. He retreated to a cubicle and settled in for the customary extended stay on the throne. Spending your days camping out on damp pavements wrought havoc on that side of things. He had a haemorrhoid back there that big he could draw a face on it and give it a name. He often wished the human race would hurry up and evolve into sentient light waves or something.

Such was his distraction that it did not immediately strike him as odd that a collage of women in the scud should be stuck to the back of the insultingly brief stall door. Angus, who was as interested in the female form as the next guy, inspected the nudes with middling interest while he waited for nature to take its course. They were pages from newspapers – page three of your Scottish *Sun*, to be precise, the sheer volume of T&A mildly diverting, and that was why it took him a moment to notice how the images had been doctored.

Every office had its colour photocopier, and somebody had gone to quite the effort to run off pictures of Lynne – her rastered likeness scaled up from an ID badge or the like – to stick over these girls' faces. He blinked. Well, it was a tiny bit funny, her eighties hairdo and faintly glaikit gaze atop these young bodies, and the thought bubbles apparently emanating from the clone-Lynnes' brains: 'Curvaceous Kelly, 19, thinks bankers need to get real. "These huge bonuses they're paying themselves aren't fair when the rest of us are struggling to make ends meet." We know whose end,' the bubble concluded, '*we'd* like—'

Obviously someone didn't think much of Lynne. But if you hated her, Angus wondered, studying these topless chimeras, why paste her image over these superficially alluring bodies? A man who sought to undermine a female in authority either feared her outright, or subconsciously fancied slipping her a length and couldn't cope with the Oedipal implications. This was the work, he concluded as he emerged from the bogs, of one fuck of a sorry and conflicted individual.

Well, there might as well have been a neon arrow indicating the culprit: strawy-haired, his podgy puce face low over his keyboard, defiance in the set of his shoulders – the young guy Lynne'd bawled out earlier for failing to answer the phone. An open-and-shut case of workplace foes. What gave him away was the way he was studiously ignoring Angus, while every other employee bar none was openly gawping at him, not in a friendly way.

He stood there until he unnerved the cunt into looking up, whereupon Angus poured into his glare all the warning he could. Don't mess with ma Lynne, you little wank stain. You do not know what ah am capable of. The wee guy feigned bovine indifference, but Angus could tell he was rattled.

Then the victim herself materialized at Angus's side. 'You've not a class tonight, though, do you?'

'Oh – no.' He broke away from the staring match. 'Jist wan a week. More'n enough.'

'Then I'll see you at home later? Thanks for . . . you know.'

'The keys,' he reminded her, not to spare her. 'Aye, nae bother.' That Struan guy still had an eye on him, waiting to be exposed. Belatedly it occurred to Angus that he should have torn down the display in the bogs. Why hadn't he? Maybe because it was, in some sense, despite its meanness and crudity, still a kind of artwork.

When he looked at Lynne he saw a wee soul, high-strung but harmless. Likely she was a terrible boss, but still Angus found it extraordinary that anyone could take such exception to her. Nothing. Do nothing. No need to be cruel, taking her in there to confirm what she either suspected or knew full well already – that she was despised.

Leaving Arundel's offices, Angus did indeed set off, as though Lynne might be monitoring him, towards the art store: not the one in town where the wannabes shopped for their handicrafts crap, but the serious one up by the School of Art. Be as well, he figured, to buy a few bits and pieces, give the impression he was putting Lynne's loan to good use, and better yet not to have to use the cheap stuff Dean had given him. Plenty money left for his other purposes. The apprehension he'd felt earlier at the thought of running into Cobbsy and that lot had dissipated. And if he met someone he knew at the art store, so what? He was a man with money, a man with secrets, and until such time as one or both ran out, he walked with purpose, he owned the streets once again.

He cut through Blythswood Square – a lot less prostitute-rich by night than by day, it turned out – then broke into the first tenner Lynne had given him to buy himself twenty cigarettes. The headline on the hoarding outside the newsagent:

CITY POOR

SMOKE LESS

DRINK LESS

FEEL SAFER

– reportage or edict, he couldn't tell.

He lit a smoke to help him up Dalhousie Street's killer hill. There was a bad ache in his shins, in addition to the usual pain in his gammy leg. Bone scraping on bone. The gash pavements didn't help – here were potholes, fissures, unbedded flagstones that recoiled when stepped on and made his leg shriek; one deep rift between patchworked zones of friable tarmac had been filled in with just random chunks of rock, courtesy the Department of Roads, Lighting and Fuck It, That'll Do. Cold air, smoke and exertion made his lungs feel wire-woolly. How weak he was, how lacking practice. Worse, one consequence of visiting Lynne's office underworld was to have lit in him that rare, fierce desire for a drink, a feeling that only intensified when he turned the corner and came in sight of the School of Art.

Here, in a cold room under the eaves, Mackintosh leadwork on the tiny windows, Angus had taught his first-years, through torturous repetition, the rudiments of drawing. They had only one subject the whole year: an old high-backed dining chair with a busted seat he'd found on Woodlands Road one morning. The rubric was simple: in week one, he'd ask them to call out adjectives; thereafter, week in, week out, he quoted from the list they themselves had put together. 'Draw the chair as if it's curious.

73

Draw it lonely. Draw an embarrassed chair.' If they coped with the banality without cavilling too much – though he did welcome signs of resistance once they grasped that this was going to be the extent of things, a certain spirit – it showed they were ready to progress. In their second year he might even get around to inspecting the portfolios rammed with the life drawings, sensitive charcoal portraits, pastel fantasia, *unicorns*, that'd got them on his course to begin with.

He did not tarry at the art-school gates – too cold to drop pace, for one thing – nor enter the art store after all, but carried determinedly on down the hill to where the street became a cul-de-sac abutting the motorway. His desire to drink didn't vanish when the school was behind him; the pride he felt in bypassing the locus of his cravings soon began to pall: like betraying no recognition when you passed an ex-lover in the street, afterwards all you felt was nigglingly, unquantifiably depleted.

To his left stood a row of disused warehouses, a wide ramp leading down to former loading bays, and as Angus was passing these, he saw movement – the cessation of movement – out the corner of his eye. He turned, squinted. A figure, silhouetted on the dimming sky, had paused on the ramp: someone who'd been caught short and nipped down between the overflowing dumpsters for a cheeky pish, no doubt. Angus started to move away – then heard a high, nervous voice call his name: 'Angus?' He faltered, kept walking. 'It is Angus, isn't it?'

His shoulders dropped. Recognized twice in a fortnight – getting on for celebrity. 'Who's that?'

'Ah'm no wrang, am ah? It is you.'

Over his head the red street lamps warmed to amber, and Angus, taking two steps towards the warehouses, made out round glasses, a cadaveric face. 'It's nivver Rab,' he called back, trying not to let dismay into his voice.

'As I live and breathe.' His grin twitching, Rab came forward into the lights' shallow cone to confirm it, though as far as living and breathing went, the old man had only ever seemed barely to do either.

'What in God's name you daein here?' By *here*, Angus meant more than the merely geographical. He was trying to remember if he had ever before seen Rab in daylight. Pubs at night, that was where you found him, and once he'd hitched on to you it was impossible to dislodge the bastard. He'd cling to you all night, encouraging you into bad habits, cajoling you, 'Jist wan mair scoop,' expertly managing to ensure he was served at the same time – and Angus had never been much averse to being led astray. The merest thought of a drink and who should materialize? It was as if the wish, misdirected, had brought his old acquaintance into being.

'Ma neck of the woods,' Rab said, sounding astounded that Angus didn't already know this. 'Ah'm alwis somewhere hereaboot.' He came forward and, fist balled, slung his arm around Angus's neck. How much weight had he lost? The clothes were hanging off him. 'You, but. Huvnae seen you oot an aboot in' – he calculated – 'pure ages.'

'Takin a bit ay a break fae aw that,' Angus said, shrugging. 'Nae big deal.'

'Angus Rennie, taking a break fae the bevvies?' Rab scoffed. With great scorn: 'Ye're no in recovery or sumhin?'

'Aye, right.' How could he explain? Quite simply in one way: when I reached the age my father was when he died . . . Rab wouldn't get it, or, worse, he would understand completely, evince sympathy. 'Naw,' he settled for saying, 'jist keepin a low profile a while.'

Rab released his grip, tapped a finger to his nose. 'Say nae mair.' Angus wondered what he'd managed to imply. 'Which way ye headed anyway? Chum ye along fer a bit.'

You had to give the guy credit: he'd found a formula that worked and stuck to it. 'Just bein friendly,' he could claim if anyone resisted; and what was Angus going to do, tell him he didn't want to walk beside him?

They crossed the bridge over the motorway, cars bustling beneath them – halfway across, Rab leaned over the edge, sniffed clotted matter into his throat and hawked a mouthful down on some unsuspecting driver below. With Rab at his side, Woodlands Road became for Angus a magic-eye painting in which every other doorway was a boozer: the heraldic gold motifs painted over the doors of the Uisge Beatha; vile Sam's Bar; Russell's, where for a bet he'd once shaved the eyebrows off a comatose drinker, sustaining severe bruising after Angus's so-called pals woke the victim up; the Cellar Door, Bar Bola, Barracuda, Harvey's, the Hamlet . . . Not helped by the chuntering monologue Rab maintained the whole time, a factoid for every establishment they passed: which bartenders had moved where, which regulars had disgraced themselves and how – none of it of interest to Angus but its ceaselessness good reason for him to keep silent.

Soon enough, though, Rab switched his attention back to Angus. 'So whit's gaun oan wi you yirsel, big man? They've bin askin after ye down at McCalls.'

'That'll be right. "When's that tight basturt comin back tae settle his tab?" '

'Noh, man. No like that.' Rab, grinning slimily: 'Nae fun without you there – place is deid these days. Big Shelagh's never done askin if ah've seen ye.' If you were unversed in it, you could mistake Rab's obsequiousness for genuine warmth – could start to believe you really had been missed.

On their right: the Ravenscroft, the Dolphin Bar, O'Ceallaigh's – daft Davy Breen once paid a dealer there fifty pounds for what proved to be a gram of salt, then spent the evening smearing the stuff on his gums, swearing he could feel it starting to kick in. These memories! He had to get off Woodlands Road. To the left, after the cash and carry – SPICES AND PULSES AT WHOLESALE PRICES – a relief: the park. He managed to steer Rab through the gates and they went crunching up the hill through the blue grass and frost-stiffened leaves, Rab at last leaving off talking.

Twilight was coming in and the cold starting to bite, but it made the place beautiful. When a breeze flurried up the fragments of leaves, Angus found himself moving quicker, chasing them, stamping them down to powder, Rab joining in: a pair of auld jakeys japing about like kids.

You couldn't do it for long – breath catching thick in their throats – and they collapsed, laughing a fog around their faces, on a softly rotting bench.

'Come wi me down McCalls for a bit,' Rab suggested, trying, as Angus had expected, to sound nonchalant, like the idea had just that moment come to him.

'Come aff it. Loon.' In a way, he was relieved: now the inevitable proposal had been made, he could get on with rejecting it.

'Jist the wan, that's aw. Be like auld times. Big Shelagh'd be over the moon tae see ye.'

'That'd be right. Prolly keeps a shotgun loaded neath the bar in case ah ivver show ma face again.'

'Well, we've got tae go somewhere,' Rab said peevishly. 'Ah'm startin tae no be able tae feel ma toes.'

'Shoe shop's whut you need, no a pub.'

'That reminds me, ye know who's still aboot? Remember Wullie? Still sittin there all day, every day, hauf a pint shandy in his haun, watchin the telly. Nae place else tae go, ah shouldnae wonder.'

'Wullie wi nae shoes, wis that whut we used tae call him?'

Rab cackled. 'Aye, well, that's a story. Wait'll ah tell ye.' He settled his jacket around him and rubbed veinous hands together, swelling with raconteur's pride. 'No joke, right, this guy comes intae McCalls one eftirnoon – bout a month ago, this was – no a regular, but Big Shelagh reckoned she'd seen him a couple times before. Anyway, in he comes, big box unner the arm, marches straight over to where Wullie's sitting gazing intae space, tuned tae the fuckin moon as ivver. Plonks the box down in front ay him. "Here ye go, big man," he goes. "Winter's comin." And whut d'ye think's in the box? Brand-new pair ay shoes, expensive an aw, hard-wearing, guid grip on the soles. Guy comes up tae the bar, passes Big Shelagh an envelope and says, "Here's the receipt. Gonnae gie him a haund if they're no the right size?" She's giein the guy wan ay they looks ay hers could melt a hole in steel plate, but she says yes anywise, and that's it, aff this cunt goes again wiout anither word. All the while Wullie's kept starin up at the idiot box, eyes like marbles – but right enough he makes sure and takes that shoebox with him when he leaves that night.'

'So he's Wullie wi shoes these days,' Angus ventured.

'Well, that's the thing, isn't it? So next day Wullie's back sittin in, hauf pint shandy, starin up at the racing oan the telly, same auld same auld. Oot comes Shelagh fae behind the bar tae see how they're fittin him, but there're his wee white toes keekin oot the ends ay his troosers same's ever. "What the hell," she goes, "did you dae wi that nice man's shoes, ye ungrateful so-and-so?" But Wullie just plays dumb, acts the daft laddie, like, whut's that, ah nivver heard anyhin about any shoes.'

Lines of students, the autumn term's new influx, straggled past in the gloaming, heading back to halls, uncertain-looking, soft as newborns. The dry leaves drove up in the wind, eddied, fell back, made no sound.

'Ye've missed yirsel,' Rab offered after a while.

'Sounds it, aye.'

'Why don't ye come for a bit at least.' A querulous tone had entered Rab's voice. His teeth were worn to nubs, a dismal colour nearly green. 'A wee swalley.'

'You'll get my dander up,' Angus warned, trying to sound good-humoured.

'A wee hauf jist.'

It touched Angus, the effort it must have taken to get that out. When someone was prepared to make that kind of sacrifice, you did have to compromise, you had to meet them halfway. Besides, sixty quid in his pocket, and where else to go but home to Lynne? 'Fuck yir hauf,' he scoffed, howking back his shoulders. 'Whut are we, wimmin?'

They wound their way up Gibson Street, heading for Byres Road. Five o'clock, and dusk coming in: by now, in another life, Angus would've been scouting out a place to stay the night. The warehouses where he'd met Rab? No, he'd scoped those out with a practised eye. Rainwater, bin juice and worse would stream down the entrance ramps and in beneath the doors. Roof was in all right nick, but the buildings stood on an exposed corner, and wind'd cut right through the wooden doors and askew windows. Weather this cold, someone might drop off as a man and be discovered the next morning just a body. It didn't happen often, but often enough. There but for the grace of Lynne Meacher. He did not intend to tell Rab about his experiences. He didn't want the facts to turn into anecdote, the horror to be diluted.

He patted his hands together and blew into them. A weird smell like acetone in the air here. 'So tell me,' he said to Rab as they reached the top of University Avenue. On their left rose the uni's jagged towers, speckles of blackening sky visible through the golden-lit, stencil-cut main spire. 'Catch me up. Ye still see whut's-his-chops proppin up the bar? Alwis used tae try and sell ye pills?'

'Oh, Barney, aye. Nup. Got put away, didn't he?'

'Barney did?'

'Tellin ye. Last year this wis, mibbe? Year before? Possession wi intent tae supply.'

'Fuck's sake. Whit he get?'

'Three year, sumhin like that? Judge wantit to make an example ay him – nae matter the useless cunt couldnae've selt ye a bucket watter if yir face wis oan fire.'

'Nae luck, eh.' But what interested and saddened Angus was not John Barney's shame – even taking into account the forced camaraderie of barflies, they'd never been pals – but the notion, since he was sure he'd seen Barney last time he was down at McCalls, that it might have been years since he'd set foot in his regular.

The pub was visible now, down the bottom of the hill. The

paintwork had been done up, red now rather than the black finish he remembered, and with the brass-covered lights coming on over the frosted windows for night-time, the place looked braw. Angus swallowed. So welcoming, so inviting, you could say that objectively, and now it wasn't just the gradient of the hill making his pace pick up. These lights on Byres Road went in a long sequence: you didn't get to them at just the right time, you could wait an eternity to cross the road.

McCalls: less a pub and more an entertainment complex for the alcoholically inclined. There was a dive bar in the basement – walls painted black, snakebite on permanent special offer – for students, who might find the street-level lounge bar that bit too auld-mannish for their liking, but also to benefit the auld men in question, who did not like to be reminded about such things as youth, as potential. A gaggle of youngsters was heading in now, each essaying a pimp's loose-kneed gait, glancing around before descending the stairs, pretending they were up to something illicit. Oh, and they were, they would be.

Next to that entranceway, the off-licence open till midnight for takeaways – Angus peered over, and there he was right enough, Cairry-Oot Aidan, a sweet guy with a fierce expression, who'd been working there since he was a student himself: more heavily bearded than Angus recalled, but otherwise essentially unchanged for a decade or more now, an elemental. Each time you saw him he was wearing the T-shirt of a different death-metal band. A man of few words, he just glowered out from behind his counter, where he guarded the bottles, the quivering fridges of Tennent's cans, with the air of someone dealing in arms, which – well, you only had to walk down Sauchiehall Street on a Sunday morning, glass from Buckfast bottles crunching underfoot, to see that that was actually perfectly true.

At last the lights changed. Gammy leg nothing: Angus was across that road like a greyhound out a trap.

Into the lounge bar, the familiar smell hitting him as he

entered: hops, spilled spirits, peppery underarms, with a nicotine top note still lingering, ineradicable, long after smoking had been banned. The bell-shaped wall lamps, the framed Tennent's ads going back decades. And there behind the horseshoe bar, Big Shelagh herself – six foot nothing in her stocking soles, the black polo shirt he remembered from years back, hair dyed the yellow of a smoker's fingers – performing the old ballet, stepping *en pointe* from the lagers to the stouts and back, then a wee pirouette and lunge, one hand aloft pressing tumblers to the optics, the other down at the fridge picking out a miniature of mixer. See nothing else of her, you'd still know her by her arms, the way the tendons stood up as she worked the taps.

'Well, well,' she went, clapping eyes on him, though she didn't so much as pause in her routine. Rab hung back, looking sheepishly between Shelagh and Angus, trying to decide which one he had betrayed. 'Look whit the cat dragged in. Cara-fuckin-vaggio.'

'Christ, Shelagh, ye no self-respect? Barely one step in the door and you're already off tryin tae entice me wi yir vaggio.'

'Finally happened, did it? Ye finally got barred fae every single other pub in toon.'

'Hie, hie,' he protested, waving his arms. '*Wan* time ye telt me ah'd overdid it. Can a guy no live down his mistakes?'

She never even needed to ask him what it'd be. Dodd and Wilson's, pint, just the colour of the stuff as it filled the glass – a deep maplewood red, head the colour and consistency of buttermilk – switching something back on in Angus's head, dabbing some dormant taste centre in the midbrain. 'Saved ma life,' he told Shelagh, taking back the handful of shrapnel from his second tenner, but all she did was curl her lip.

Rab took a seat beside him at the bar and contemplated his still-settling pint of Guinness. It seemed that simply manoeuvring Angus into McCalls represented the limit of his ambition, which made Angus feel slightly like he'd let himself down by yielding even reluctantly to the pressure. But he wouldn't have believed anyone who described to him the comfort this drink would provide – slipping down good and easy now, his thoughts already turning pleasurably to a second. This, now, this was what it was all about. He forgot everything else, or everything else came back to him – like hearing a song on the radio you haven't heard in yonks yet whose lyrics, you discover, you still know off by heart. For instance: half an hour ago, Angus could barely have told you Rab's full name, but now he recalled, without consciously retrieving the information, that Rab Hanna only ever ordered Guinness, out of pride for his Irish heritage – pride undented by the revelation one uproarious St Patrick's Day that he'd never once crossed the sea to what he invariably called, making sure you heard the reverential capital letters, the Old Country. Angus, awed by this sudden capacity for recollection, watched Rab raise his pint to his lips and slowly shook his head, wondering what he'd plugged himself back into here. He held up his finger and indicated the half-sunk glass to Big Shelagh. 'When ye've a minute?'

He had been scanning the lounge for familiar faces, still skeery in case the person he did recognize proved to be the enemy he didn't remember making back in the day. It was dispiriting, nonetheless, to look around more openly as he grew braver, and see next to no one he knew. Round the far side of the bar, a choochy wee face – the face less familiar to Angus, in all honesty, than the faded corduroy bunnet atop it – clocked him, craned round the draught taps, confirmed his identity, nodded, withdrew.

'Here,' Angus apostrophized gloomy Rab, 'ivver see anyhin that guy Dooley these days?'

At the mention of the name, Big Shelagh, down the far end of the bar but equipped with superhuman powers of hearing, emitted a cackle like a hyena.

'Got married, if ye please.' Rab gave the word hoity Kelvinside pronunciation, *married*.

'Fuck's sake.' Part of the deal in a place like McCalls was that you understood your social circle to be stable in that regard, its comprising fundamentally unlovable people. 'Bluddy traitor.'

'New burd keeps him on a tight leash. Got him goin to AA an aw. When'd ye ever see him stotious? Wife comes storming in here wan night, bawls him oot right in front everydy, drags him aff haim by the lug. See him mibbe wance a fortnight now? Aw cowardly he creeps in – ye dinnae hardly even notice him at first. Then ye're like, "What's it ye'll huv?" and he's all, "Oh, eh, a ginger beer please." ' Rab's voice dropped. 'Big Shelagh near enough glessed him first time she heard that. "Sure ye widnae prefer a pint ay milk, Dooley?" Ye ken how she can be icy polite when she hates sumdy. "A *coffee* mibbe?" '

Telling this story had perked Rab right up, and Angus tried to bring other names to mind. Even a conversation this straitened had its uses – slowing down your drinking, for one, which must be a what-did-you-call-it, an evolutionary strategy.

'Big Gary Sykes, seen him?'

Rab paused for maximum effect. 'Found God.'

'Christ Almighty.'

'Did we not alwis say there'd be wan?'

Angus shook his head. 'That's depressin.'

What he was pushing for, he realized, even hoping for, was appalling news – for Rab's face to split open in a big sick help-less grin, the sort you can't suppress even when reporting a death. Just as there'd always be one guy in a group like the McCalls lot who got religion, another who got clean, so too there was one they'd afterwards agree had been doomed all along. What Angus wanted was reassurance that somebody else had got there first – that it wouldn't be him they'd be saying it about.

The door opened, admitting sharp cold and a shock of stu-dents, bright eyes peeping out from the gap between muffling scarves and woollen hats tugged down low. A few each year picked McCalls as their favourite, its cheapness and proximity to the uni making it a popular place to recuperate after a gru-elling two-lecture day. They started out in packs like this in the autumn, numbers winnowing down across the year till only the dedicated remained, the next generation of regulars. There'd be one who ended up working here; another – because there was always one of these too, getting carried away – who'd take to walking the West End supping from a Bell's bottle ineptly disguised in a brown paper bag, thinking himself the new Bukowski.

'Here, Angus,' Big Shelagh bellowed along the bar, 'you still a teacher?' – making it sound like she considered this an affectation Angus should have outgrown by now.

'Ah dinnae teach any mair,' he called back, more cheerful than he felt, 'so ah'm guessing ah'd huv tae say no.'

'Still an artist, but,' Rab put in, worried.

'Well, see, that's the question, isn't it? If ye dinnae draw every day, if ye dinnae paint, whatever, can ye still call yirsel an artist? What about twice a week, once a week? Whaur's the cut-off? Ah've been asking masel that a lot lately.' He tanned the last of scoop two, watched the rime of foam slither down inside the glass. The first couple of drinks barely touched the sides going down; you certainly didn't savour them. 'Ye've heard ay the phenomenon,' he said carefully, 'ay the phantom limb? Sumdy loses a body part, in an accident or whatever, but to them it's like they can still feel it. Ah knew a guy' – at the hostel, he didn't add – 'hud his legs amputated, but even years later swore blind he could wriggle his toes, still got cramp in his foot same's he alwis hud.' Nixon, the guy called himself: went round in a wheelchair with a sign proclaiming himself to be a war veteran, serge folded and pinned ostentatiously at the knee, when he'd actually had to have them off because of alcoholic's gangrene. 'Ma point being, if ye renounce yir occupation, then how long've ye got before ye huv to say, "That's no whit ah do. That's no who ah am ony mair"?'

Everyone in the lounge seemed to have stopped talking. Angus, a little mortified, sank his face to his empty glass and fixed his teeth around the rim as though to take a bite out.

'You!' Shelagh addressed stupefied Rab. 'Whaur's yir man-
ners? Get the philosopher here another drink. In fact fuck it.
This wan's on the hoose.'

'Shelagh, such generosity.' Shown compassion by Big
Shelagh, the Arbroath Colossus. May wonders never cease.

She sneered. 'Don't go relyin oan it – ah'm in a good fuckin
mood tonight is all. Ah love it,' and you could tell she was a
professional from the way she could slam a full pint down on the
bar with no spillage whatsoever, 'when one ay ma lambs comes
back tae the fold.'

Angus took up the drink, touched two fingers to his brow in
salute. 'If ye renounce yir occupation', fuck's sake. How many
times would he phrase it like that, imply that it'd been a selfless,
voluntary act, before he'd start to believe the lie?

Rab had evidently decided that this was the moment to
embark on another well-worn scheme. 'Whaur ye steiyin at the
minute, Angus?' Here, the plan was attrition: he'd start with the
innocuous enquiry and slowly, slowly work it round until you
found yourself offering the guy your sofa, zed-bed or, if his luck
was really in, your whole spare room for the night. Maybe even
longer: Angus'd heard stories about Rab inveigling his way into
staying with some poor cunt on the Friday night and still being
there to wave them off to work come Monday morning.

'Oh, eh, ah'm up Maryhill weiy these days.' Smiling to
imagine Lynne's umbrage: North Kelvinside, damn it! 'Just
temporarily, y'know – wi a friend.'

He'd hesitated for maybe half a second, but Rab, busy with
pint two, was straight in there. 'A friend is it, aye?'

'An old pal. Sumdy ah hudnae seen in years. We bump into
each ither randomly wan day, transpires there's a vacancy for a
flatmate, and boom, ah'm in. Pretty peachy.'

'A good Samaritan.'

'Ye could say so.'

Rab, grinning broadly: 'Ay the female variety?'

'Och, it's no like *that*.'

'How won't you tell me yes or no, then?'

Well, Rab had him there. 'A she, then, aye.'

He'd dropped his voice, yet way down at the other side of the bar Big Shelagh's head swivelled around like an owl's. 'Who in her right mind,' she demanded, advancing towards them with a swiftness that suggested she wasn't walking so much as swelling up like a wave, 'takes a runt like you in as a lodger?'

'A guid wan,' he snapped back. Shelagh raised her eyebrows at Rab, but kept on dichting down the bar taps, unimpressed. 'Wan that disnae judge, Shelagh. Wan that keeps me right. A generous woman – see these claithes?' He plucked at his sweater. He was at that stage where he was in danger of being moved by his own bullshit. 'No that ah'd expect the likes ay yous two tae understand.'

'Caravaggio in love,' Shelagh crowed.

'Aw no. Nothin like that. Defin-*etly* no. Anyhow, Shelagh, ye know fine well ah'm savin masel fer you, doll.'

'Away tae fuck,' she scolded, Rab guffawing into his pint, and it was situation normal once again. Pals like these weren't really your pals at all; betray the least hint of finer feelings, they were on you like jackals. It was exhausting, but you had to keep the sparring going. That was the only way Weegies ever complimented one another, via these what you might call backhanded insults.

'Oh, Shelagh? Getting a bitty parched down here by the way.' Angus peeled off another note, careful to conceal from Rab how much cash he was carrying. Fifty-odd remained of what Lynne had given him: more than adequate, he imagined, for his purposes – and if not, he was sure Lynne'd be good for the extra.

An image popped up in his mind then – his rescuer, mouth tucked in at the corners in that despondent way as she told him he should consider the money a gift, not a loan: she'd never ask for it back. Sure it was just a coincidence she should have spotted him in Sauchiehall Street that day, but one whose timeliness could be considered, were you so minded – as Lynne surely was – miraculous.

He clambered down off his stool to pay a visit to McCalls' primevally familiar lavvies. The wee white sugar lumps marinating in the urinal, cloy of lemon freshener failing to mask the baked-on shit smell, Jeyes fluid on dried boak: all of it Angus's madeleine. He glimpsed himself, his hackit auld coupon, when he passed the mirror on entering, then conducted a more detailed inspection while rubbing his hands together beneath the hot tap's incontinent trickle, trying to avoid touching the bullet-mark hole its drip had eroded in the white enamel. He fingered whitish matter from the corner of his eye, rolled it into a tiny lump between finger and thumb and flicked it away who knows where. Well, he looked better than he had done while he was sleeping rough or getting stamped on by strangers in the hostel, but that was about all you could say. So much grey in his stubble, glinting like iron filings, and in his hair too, which stood up either side of his crown in what his poor dead da used to call koala ears.

He'd been alive forty-three years, eight months and a handful of days. Angus Rennie, the pathology artist: criticized by one reviewer as the disease-obsessive turning all his subjects into sufferers, breaking them down, posing them at death's door; praised by another for his unflinching depictions of human misery. Ironic that what pulled him up now was seeing what indignities simple day-on-day ageing, same as everyone else, had wrought on him – as if, a reverse Dorian Gray, he had hoped to prevent his own decay by projecting it on to the figures in his portraits. So ravaged, in the mirror's untarnished central oval – like the frame tabloids put round a school photo when someone died young. Well, how about a promising youngster whose life had tragically gone on, and gone on unravelling?

When he returned to the lounge, he challenged Rab to a round of darts, and his game seemed to improve with each fresh gulp of his pint. 'Painter's Zen,' he told Rab in his triumph, plucking his darts from the board's centre and chalking a line under the game. 'It nivver deserts ye.' Rab clucked his tongue, wiped his specs on his sweater and paid the forfeit: one more round.

Some time later, Angus found himself in someone's living room, surrounded by the students who'd come into McCalls earlier. The room was high-walled, dense with sweet smoke, and lit by a lone red bulb hanging nude from the ceiling rose. He was holding a can of Tennent's in one hand and an unlit cigarette in the other, and he was mid tirade, addressing a crew-cut twenty-something training on him a ferocious frown, borderline psychotic, which would, sustained much longer, come to worry Angus. He hadn't a scooby how he'd got here, nor how long ago, nor where here *was* exactly. Neither was there any sign of Rab. He could tell, however, from certain signs discernible only to the expert, that he was on maybe his tenth or eleventh drink by now: not steaming by any stretch, but on his way. A certain density to his body, sunk low in a spongy black chair whose pleather cover was clammy on his exposed skin. Angus was by some distance the oldest person present, but he did not feel especially out of place, mainly because every other person had a drink in their hand too. Music, obliteratingly distorted, came from speakers in another room, and also – standard issue for these situations – from a twat with a guitar who strummed a continuous chord that occasionally coincided with the key the record was in. Between Angus's feet lay oily papers, the remnants of a fish tea he could not remember consuming: a real waste.

'The poem, y'see,' he was declaring, 'gets it wrang. What ye'd actually like is fer other people *not* tae be able tae see ye exactly as ye see yirsel.' He was emphasizing his rhetorical points with wild gestures, making it impossible for his cigarette to be lit, though the youth continued to hold his lighter steady in his hand, its flame shivering, burning lower. 'Ah mean . . . Galleries. Art galleries, ken? Museums. They've an effect on me. See last year, ah took masel off tae Amsterdam for a week. Two days in the Rijksmuseum, two mair in the St-st . . . the Stedelijk. The Van Gogh. Moochin aboot among the Auld fuckin Masters, yir van Eycks and Vermeers and Rembrandts, then aw the contemporary stuff – yir Beckmanns and Schades. The more ah saw, the more ah startit feelin, like, fingers dandlin over the back ay ma skull. A lover's touch. The first inklings ay orgasm coming doon the line. Surrounded by these giants and ah'd a chub on like ye widnae believe. The light in they Caravaggios. No jist the portraits either. There wis wan wee Mondrian – white, blue, yellow, black, jist squares, barely there at all – and there was ah, creepin aboot in a state a semi-permanent priapism, like a fuckin . . . sex offender.' As light at last met cigarette, he brought it to his mouth, drew deeply. 'Aye, cheers.'

His voice must have been increasing in volume. Other conversations had paused, and people were watching him in silence, some exchanging nodding glances: listen to this, this guy knows what he's on about, by the way. He had them in his thrall, same as ever. He couldn't quite work out what point he'd wanted to make, but it'd probably come to mind if he just kept talking.

'Anyway, later oan ah head doon the red-light zone, as ye dae. And these girls are posing in their garters and their corsets and whatnot, less even, in these windaes dressed as hotel rooms or suburban bedrooms. And in theory' – he drained the can – 'in theory, these should be provoking the same response, the same staundin tae attention down below. And they titillate ye, course they dae, ah'm no made ay stone. But there's something missin too. I was aroused, but ah didnae huv that feeling like static over the surface ay the skin. Which is odd, eh, since on the surface a Hopper painting ay a burd in her medical-sortay underwear sittin oan her bed readin a letter ay abandonment – well, that isnae much different fae these girls staundin in their windae beneath the auld tasselled red lampshade, bestowin thir blank come-hither eyes on the world at large. It's the difference between a really luxurious wank versus sumdy crankin yir erection like changing gear in a racing car, just tae get oan wi it.

They tableaux, they girls, they lack . . . they lack . . .' He click-clicked his fingers, the word's shape eluding him.

'Self-awareness?' suggested a tiny girl sitting on the empty fireplace hearth. Angus, frowning, tilted his head. 'It's commoner than you might think.'

'Naw, they've nae' – pouncing on the word in triumph – '*backstory*. Whut ye see's whut ye get. Punters dinnae want a story, dinnae want potential. They want, not tae be indelicate, a shag and that's it. It's the difference between lust and love, the physical and the brain.' Found himself tapping his skull, for the avoidance of doubt. 'Commerce too, but that's anither story. They ones ostensibly inviting ye in are the ones whose stories there's no way ay sharin. The pictures dinnae ask anything of ye. That's why they get your blood surgin and the hookers dinnae.'

'Fascinating theory,' someone said drily.

Wide bastards. 'Naw, naw. Doan gies that. Listen, let me pit it anither weiy. This wummin ah'm friendly with – Lynne. She's been really good tae me, totally brand new. Anyweiy, she's got this, like, stepdaughter – well, no really stepdaughter. It's her ex's girl. See whut she says to me the ither night? "The moment I felt proudest of her," she tells me, "the moment I felt most like this was my own daughter, was when she was slamming the door in my face – yelling at me how glad she was I wasn't her real mother." ' Angus sat back and was nearly swallowed in the chair. 'The simulacrum ay child meets the simulacrum ay mither, they stage a fake fight, suddenly everyin's happy. That's what weans dae to ye, mind. Doesnae even need tae be yir ain offspring tae fuck ye up. But it's why folk go on havin kids, eh, generation upon generation – because it's their wan and only stab at a medium- tae long-term relationship, dependin on how wily the kid is, wi sumdy entirely blind tae their faults.' He took a deep breath, hoping for a contact high from the druggy smoke in the room. 'Me,' he confided, leaning closer to the student, 'ah got away wi bluddy murder when ah wis a bairn, all because ah wis sick. Know whut they telt ma da? That ah widnae live. What

90

seems at first tae take kin still end up being rejectit. Ten year ah'd live – twelve mibbe if ah wis lucky. "Don't go getting too attached", that wis the subtext. What a thing tae tell a parent! But here ah am, forty-three year auld. And whaur d'ye think he is?' He raised his index finger slowly ceilingward.

'Now you' – he prodded the student nearly in his impassive puss – 'you're too young tae huv children ay yir ain.' He meant it to caution rather than to elicit confirmation. 'Nivver dae it. Stay true to yirsel, big man.'

In the ensuing silence, someone chuckled. It was not a kind sound, and Angus, who had been impressed by the trenchancy of his argument, began to feel perturbed. Maybe these looks going back and forth had not been expressing awe and admiration after all.

'Anyway,' he got out, with the drunk's gruff misplaced politeness, 'time ah should be headin up the road.'

'Yes,' said his pal with the lighter, 'I think that might be best.'

'Only, before ah go' – setting down his spent can and slapping his hands on his knees – 'if it's no too much bother, ah wonder if wan ay yous might furnish me with a pen and a chitty paper? Or a pencil. Ah willnae steal it. Jesus,' he laughed, 'that no wan ay the sorriest promises ye've ivver heard?'

The tiny girl brought him an envelope and a biro. 'You can keep it. It was free anyway.'

'Oh aye, just hurry up and scram, is that it?'

She did not reply, nor meet Angus's eye. Under normal circumstances he would have protested, or tried to charm her – what was he, a gorgon? – but her unfeasible minuteness unnerved him. The frame of, what, a nine-year-old, surely too young to be at the uni – or maybe a superbrain, a prodigy he oughtn't cross. Stuck-up twats, the lot of them, but it wasn't easy to lambast a group whose hospitality you'd enjoyed, very possibly uninvited, for what might have been several hours. He fought his way out the chair, which clung to him, it alone unhappy for him to go.

No way he could compose his note in the threadbare-carpeted

stairwell illuminated by a single yellow wall roundel – he could barely see his hand before his face. Out on the street, in the sharp cold, he slumped against the portico entrance. A clapper-less bell hung on one square column; beneath that, relic of the property's grand former life as a hotel or such, was a printed arrow and a painted note reading RING FOR SERVICE, into which notice some wag with a marker pen and copperplate handwriting had inserted the word ANAL.

Flattening his envelope against the pilaster, Angus carefully wrote: THIS IS A HANDWRITING TEST. Fairly steady hand, all things considered; the letters well formed, the words more or less following a straight line. A sober fellow's writing, this, he'd go so far as to say. He was relieved: if he rocked up obviously gished at Lynne's, he'd never hear the end of it.

The pen he'd been given was one of the efforts charities sent you through the post, cast in a white plastic so soft, so cheap, you could bend it into a figure of eight – and right enough, here it was, the RNLI flag stamped on its barrel, a pathetic attempt to sway you to contribute to the cause, but one that drew honest tears to Angus's eyes: set off not so much by the idea of the lifeboat crews or the drowners being collected for, but the thought of the widows this mean gift would convince to send in their contributions, fifty-pence pieces sellotaped to a bit of card. Drops in the ocean, the little acts of purposeless charity.

He shoved the envelope in his pocket and dunted his forehead against the column. Da, ah outlived ye, and for whit? To be homeless, jobless, aimless, helped oot ma fix by a wummin thinks ah hung the moon but who ah dinnae even – ken why.

The first stage on his journey home – he was back down near where Rab had ambushed him earlier, making Glendower Street an almost unthinkable half-hour's walk away – involved passing the St Georges Cross subway. In the gloom down there Angus could discern two, three bodies sleeping, or trying to: newspaper packed into their clothes as insulation, damp cardboard for a mattress. While over their heads at street level, the warm all-night glow from interior-design showrooms: gold mixer taps and slate flooring, granite worktops, drop ceilings, induction hobs, lifestyle upgrades glinting beneath halogen lights, but tasteful: coldly, spendily tasteful. Throat stinging from a sudden acidic upswell, Angus looked back to the figures huddled in the underpass. He could climb down there with the others, make a pit for himself beside them: no problem, a doddle. He could describe how easy it'd be to anyone who'd listen. What people couldn't grasp was how tempting it was – how sometimes it was your dire circumstances, your abjection, that set you free.

He came clattering in, kicked off his shoes, and was so irate to find Lynne sitting at the kitchen table waiting up for him, exactly as he'd pictured, a caricature of herself, that he started to yell before she had the chance. Could she not have come to open the door for him? Had she not heard him scrabbling around out there for ages, vying with a lock that seemed too small for the key he'd been given? Fair enough, he'd taken longer than expected to get home, what with the brief heated exchange he'd had with the students spilling out Clatty Pats at closing time; then his urgent need for a pish and frenzied search for a spot to do it – ending up behind BBC Scotland, aiming his stream between the wrought-iron railings, melting the frost on the undergrowth. He'd put himself away and turned around, and what a fright: this wee fox was standing in the road watching him, bright orange in the street light, and when Angus had taken a charmed step towards it, the bold thing hadn't fled but only trotted a few steps then looked back at him, like Lassie wanting him to follow . . .

Lynne was talking, but Angus was too busy laboriously checking his pockets to pay her heed. To his dismay he seemed to have misplaced his handwriting test; now she'd never believe he was sober. It tickled him to imagine the fox wandering the West End with Angus's envelope crumpled in its jaws – though smiling proved not that politic a response to Lynne's diatribe.

He tried to dodge into his room, and in an alarming, fluid movement she rose from the kitchen table and flew towards him. 'You know,' she shrieked, 'I've got Siri coming over tomorrow. You know I've been stressed. And this is what you—'

'Hey, hey.' He flapped his hands in the air, trying to fend her off or shut her up. 'No need tae talk tae me like a haufwit. Ah'm sorry, awright? Ah'll no get cuntit again.' He saw her wince, so said it again: 'Nae mair gaun oot getting cunted fer yirs truly. Ah do solemnly swear.'

Space felt like it was scrolling away from him in a four-dimensional way not known to science, and Angus very much wanted to draw a line under this conversation so he could retreat to his futon and lie still until the sensation went away, but for some reason Lynne was unwilling to accept his apology with good grace. 'The least you could have done was phone me to let me know where you were. You have to start taking responsibility—'

'Oh-ho,' he interrupted her again, 'ah see whut this is now. Sub – sub—' He coughed, got it out on the third go. 'Sublimation!'

'What are you talking about?' she screamed.

'Sublimated . . . anxiety, aye. It's no actually me ye're angry wi at all, is it, doll? What ye're worrying aboot is thingy, Siri, comin round the morra.'

He could tell from her anger that he was right. A devil took possession of his vocal cords then, and made him say, his teeth wolf-sharp: 'Ye know whit's guid fer tension?' He took two lumbering steps towards her, unsheathing a leer like a knife. He didn't have a plan, was improvising based on the situation. ' 'Mon, doll, genuine offer, nae strings. No promisin it'd be the greatest night ay either oor lives – ah'm no even certain ah'd be capable – but if ye'd like tae, Lynne, if ye think it might help . . .'

She backed away, face creased, white, but colouring. 'You're disgusting.'

'Disgustin! How's that? Ah wis offerin a solution. Throwin ye a bone. Ach, forget it. Ye dinnae know *what* ye want.'

She made a strange gesture with her hands, brushing herself down, casting off invisible cobwebs. 'Go to bed, Angus,' she said heavily – as if he'd been trying to do anything else! 'We'll just try and forget about this, all right?'

'Urnae foolin me, sweet cheeks,' Angus called after her as she went to her room. Chortling, he flung himself on the futon, shoving aside the veils and cushions and whatnot. He could hear her stamping about in the next room, and when she slammed her door, the whole flat shuddered. 'Lynne, Lynne, Lynne,' he croaked, shaking his head in amusement. Now that he'd forced her to stop tiptoeing round him and reveal her truer, meaner side, he felt something for her close to tenderness.

EIGHT

He woke late, rancid with hangover. A familiar confluence of sensations: queasiness, the apprehension that this was some aftermath, but not much notion to *what* – a general feeling that all the piano keys had been hammered down at once – plus a rapidly mounting horniness. Supine in his pit, Angus let his eyes wander the pink room, searching for anything to help him get himself off. You'd barely know this was a grown woman's place. Inconsiderate Lynne hadn't left him so much as a laptop to flick through, a laundry basket stuffed with used smalls to plunge his head into—

Raised voices, plural, from another room. Gradually he deduced – dredging to mind a conversation that seemed to have taken place years ago – that today must be Saturday, and therefore the second voice he was hearing must belong to this girl Siri. Under the covers he had a stauner raging. It'd been, what, six months since he'd last had a lumber? He tugged at himself, trying to bring to mind Siri's photograph, and whether she was fit.

When he'd finished, he smeared the thin stuff on his bedsheet – that was going to need washing soon if it wasn't to walk out the house all by itself – then got up, slung on a dressing gown, and dragged his carcass to the bathroom. He stood under the shower, nauseated, feeling like somebody'd been at his brain stem with a machete, until the water ran cold.

It only occurred to him after he'd dried off and primped

himself to a more or less acceptable standard and was standing outside the kitchen door, engaged in some gentle eavesdropping, that the shower noises would have alerted Siri that someone else was in the flat. Plan A surely must have been for him to stay undetected, Lynne's secret. She must be having a fit in there.

'So when,' the voice he took to be Siri's was asking, 'are you coming over? So I can stay out your way.'

'Thursday. Thursday night. But please, I don't want Raymond thinking we've been talking behind his back.'

'It'd be weirder if we hadn't. You know, I'm pretty surprised he made the first move on this. He must really want to work it out with you.' As Angus, to whom Lynne hadn't so much as hinted at wanting to be reconciled with this guy, listened in fascination, she made some sort of mouth noise. 'No offence to you, Lynne, but Ray's a stubborn old bugger. You'll say something, and he'll just sit there silent, waiting, until you . . . compromise yourself. Like, I'd ask him permission to stay at a friend's house on a Friday night and he wouldn't say yes or no, just sit there, completely blank, and before you know it I was admitting that this guy we'd only met online was driving me and my pals down to Ayrshire for an all-night rave.'

'You never came to *me* for permission—'

'My point is,' Siri got in hastily, 'you mustn't let him overrule you, or manipulate you into giving ground you don't really want to. You're a good person, and I'm not saying Dad isn't, just . . .'

'You're saying a lion doesn't change its spots,' Lynne hazarded. In the surprised silence that followed, Angus, boggling, shifted his weight and made the hall floorboards creak, after which he had no option but to stride purposefully into the kitchen as if this had been part of his planned grand entrance. 'Hi!' He sped past the table where both were sitting and went straight to the kettle. Of Siri he had only a brief impression: a skelf of a girl, pale, with white-blonde hair.

Lynne was straight in there with the guilt trip, asking, 'How's the head?' with the infuriating superior tone of a person who never, ever overdid it – who'd probably felt she was going off the rails ordering a white-wine spritzer to see in the millennium.

'Ah've hud better, let's say.' On the table, breakfast dishes with gluey slithers of muesli drying to the sides, food scraps that made Angus feel he might still boak.

'Better *heads*?' asked the girl.

You couldn't play fast and loose with a literalist, so he settled for just going 'Aye.'

She wasn't so much thin as wiry, with firm biceps, in a grey T-shirt and trousers that were all pockets, combat chic Angus remembered from first time round and still found faintly distasteful. Her hair was brush-cut and peroxided, her expression one of great distrust.

'Siri, this is Angus, who I was telling you about. He's staying in the flat for a while, till he gets himself settled again. He had a late night last night, didn't you?' – this last in a tone that could've flaked plaster from the ceiling.

Oh, so she was going to go on tearing strips off him, was she, for a perfectly innocent – well, several perfectly innocent errors of judgement? He chose to ignore her, sweeping round on Siri instead. 'Delighted tae meet ye.'

'Hi,' Siri said, inspecting him with curiosity. 'What is it you need to get settled, exactly?'

Lynne floundered. 'Oh, well—'

'Ah wis homeless,' he interrupted. An intake of breath from Lynne; he bugged his eyes out at her in reply. Evidently she'd got as far as deciding that the truth was too much for Siri, but not as far as devising a cover story. 'Ah wis out on the streets, and yir . . . eh, Lynne here, she saw me and invited me to steiy awhile. Just till I find a place ay ma ain, ye understaun. A temporary measure. Wisnae fer her, ah'd be wan more ay they jakies ye see shufflin up and doon Byres Road, waitin' – he faltered – 'for the pubs tae open.'

'Angus used to be a teacher, at the Glasgow School of Art – used to be my teacher, in fact, many years ago.'

'You? Went to art school?'

'Paintin and printmakin', aye.' Angus knew this only because she'd reminded him. He rubbed under his nose, worrying, even though he'd washed, that they'd smell spunk on him. 'Second year.'

Siri was watching them with greater anthropological interest than the young usually took in their elders. And why not? This guy turns up out of nowhere and spins this yarn. And it was a yarn. He felt a cold worry that Lynne might have implied something going on between them. 'Lynne,' she said, 'you know what? You're full of surprises. I never knew you had an art degree.'

'Oh, no – not a degree, no. I only went for two years.'

'Hold up. Ye mean ye quit?'

Lynne sniffed, puzzled. 'You knew that.'

'Ah nivver did. Ye walked, after two year jist? Och, but Lynne, that isnae even a qualification.' To cover his dismay, he turned to chastising her. 'What that is is a waste ay time – yours *and* mines.'

Lynne fankled with the dirty plates. 'I wasn't suited to art school,' she complained. 'Or it wasn't suited to me, I don't know. That was all. It was easier to make a mistake like that in those days. Mine was the last year you didn't pay fees. It was all a lark.'

Siri shook her head. 'You as an art student. Did you dye your hair green and join a band? Do you have tattoos I don't know about?' To Angus: 'I find it hard to picture.'

Angus, smiling to wrinkle up his eyes, abruptly felt much better. 'Her as a student, or masel as a teacher?'

'Kind of both.'

Lynne cleared her throat. 'He'll show you. Won't you? Go on.'

It was unclear to Angus why the burden of proof should be on him, but he played along. 'What, a lesson? Now?' Lynne giving him a plaintive look. 'Aye, awright, if ye like. Fetch us through some paper an at, will ye? Fae ma room' – just the slightest stress on there, giving permission this time.

99

'Oh, *I* can't draw,' Siri said dismissively. 'Even when I doodle it comes out crap.'

He laughed. 'No at art schuil yirsel, ur ye?'

'Hardly. I'm studying earth science.'

'You're at uni? Ye're awfy young.'

She smiled sweetly. 'Maybe I'm just awfully smart?'

Lynne returned with the cartridge paper and the box of pencils he'd accepted from Dean in the Kelvingrove, setting them down on the table, evidently happy to play the technical assistant. 'Cheers, Lynne doll.'

'You're wasting your time,' Siri warned. 'I've no hand-to-eye co-ordination. I can't even catch a ball.'

'Have ah asked ye to catch a ball?' He essayed what he hoped was a winning smile, or at least parted his lips to show his teeth. He'd slept through the worst of the hangover and its late-lifting phase was making him obstreperous. He had the strong sense of himself as charming, borderline eccentric, a favourite uncle, but both Siri and Lynne were observing his antics with expressions of censure remarkably similar for two genetically unrelated individuals. Noticing this made him want to act out even more, being someone who derived more satisfaction from winning the approval of people who seemed not to like him than maintaining friendships with those who did.

'Okay, fine. I give in. What do you want me to draw?'

He came round to see what was in her eyeline. 'Oot the windae, while it's stopped rainin. They trees, they flats opposite. See the stairwell windaes across the way there, how the lines ay the banisters kind ay cut diagonal through them? Try that. Mibbe ye want tae start wi— Well, okay, that the side ay the block, is that? Ah'd huv . . .' His hand reached involuntarily for her pencil and she snatched it away, irked. 'No, you're fine, dinnae mind me, carry oan. That's jist a straight line, see, ye can manage that.'

'Don't speak too soon. Aren't you drawing anything?'

'Jokin me, state ah'm in? Ah amnae fit tae feed a cat.'

Siri, head bent to the page, working with the amateur's close attention, made a noise in the back of her throat that nearly qualified as a laugh. From Lynne's direction he felt a shiver of warmth fall upon him, as when the sun peeps out from behind cloud on a baltic day. He had to hand it to himself: he could be seriously smooth when it suited him.

'Now that's a guid start,' he said, 'but try tae lay down the lines wi mair forcefulness. The way ye've got them, it's like they're apologizin.' Oh, you never forgot it, this knife edge between taunting the student and encouraging her. 'Try and *grip* the pencil. It willnae bite ye.'

Siri exhaled sharply, frustrated, and set down the pencil. 'Are you doing that thing? Assuming I must be an idiot because I'm young?'

'Of course he is,' Lynne chipped in. 'He's a teacher.'

'*Was* a teacher,' he corrected her. A dim recollection of lecturing the folk in McCalls on this point made him shudder. Sad, though: the sheer unalloyed enjoyment he'd felt as he downed his first pint, and how that had been buried in all the rest of the night's shit and silt. 'Anyweiy, it's no an uncommon problem. Lynne here started out nervous too, but she quickly overcame it. Her lines got confident. She hud promise,' he added, as if Lynne was not actually present, ears flapping, 'but often as not it's the wans've actually shown promise who jack it in early.'

'I had my reasons. I had,' Lynne said acidly, 'to get on in the real world.'

'What ah resent,' he said to Siri, 'is this implication that ma career, such as it wis, involved living in some *un*real world. It's not as rare a criticism to hear as ye might hope. It was art college, no the magical land ay Narnia. All ah'm meaning, Lynne, is it's a shame ye gave it up. Ye werenae bad, ye know? No need to get all uppity.'

'Fine for you to say. You made it, you had exhibitions at the CCA – books devoted to your work.'

'A catalogue,' he corrected her, as Siri looked up, interested.

'Singular. The thing is, it isnae a ladder ye climb in one direction only. It's certainly no like ye get to the top and stay there indefinitely – no sayin ah did either, mind. What it is, ye spend years castin aboot for validation – findin a gallerist tae show yir work, a dealer tae sell it, no tae convince other people of yir worth so much as persuading yirsel you're mair than jist a dilettante. Up ye climb, painstaking. And then, nae matter how long or arduous yir ascent has been, ye discover that wi wan wee signature, wan application tae a teachin post, even the maist prestigious ay institutions, ye can renounce all rights tae be taken seriously as an artist. All they rungs ye've built for yirsel tae climb jist fall away.'

He'd addressed this confession to Siri's developing drawing – her tentative pencil marks, dabbing at the paper as though petting a dangerous dog – while the two women listened in silence. Then Siri, who maybe hadn't been listening at all, said in alarm, 'Hold up, is that three o'clock? Oh my God, I've got to get going.'

'I thought you were staying for tea,' Lynne protested. 'And look, it's raining again. Do stay.'

'I'm sorry, I promised Rose I'd meet her this afternoon.'

'Ah,' Lynne said, rather less tenderly. 'And how is Rose? Still working at the coffee place, is she?'

'She's good,' Siri mumbled. 'And yes, she's still at the Ristretto.'

'Making coffee.' The timbre of Lynne's voice had changed, grown deceptively bell-like, brittle. 'Well, it's useful to earn a little extra.'

'Extra, no, that is her job, Lynne – you know that. She's a trained barista. It's what she *does*.'

Lynne turned to Angus. 'I just think this is extraordinary, that Siri's friend can make a living by knowing how to brew coffee. Don't you? That something we'd think of as so simple could be someone's career. I don't think that could've happened in our day.'

Angus found himself too distracted by what Siri had drawn

102

to comment, though his reply would have been along the lines of telling her not to be so snobby.

'No one ever said it was a career – oh, Lynne, I can't have this same argument again, all right? I'm already late, I've got to go.' Perfunctorily kissing her cheek: 'I'll see you soon, okay? Good luck for Thursday. Call me if you want.' With her eyebrow raised, making him feel his avuncular act had been wasted on her: 'And Angus, I hope you get back on that ladder soon.'

Angus, squinting at her picture: 'Aye, you too. I mean, tae meet ye.' Wavering lines, representing the tenement block opposite, crossed and intercut one another, forming a loose hypercube that flip-flopped between concave and convex, between stage set and the bars of a cage. For an instant, between these lines, there appeared something she had not put there: as if a striped animal, camouflaged in long grass, had betrayed its position by the tiniest parallax movement. A moment later it had stilled itself, vanished again. Siri made to take her drawing and he slapped his hand down hard, trapping the paper. 'Wait one wee minute, doll?' He tried closing his left eye, then his right, wanting to see how the trick was done.

'Oh, just keep it, I've no use for it. Thanks for the lesson, though. I really am sorry, you know.'

'For whit?'

She indicated the drawing. 'Proving you wrong about the straight-line thing.'

Something had put Lynne in the huff. Round and round the kitchen she blundered, making more noise tidying up than seemed strictly necessary: a percussion section of clattering plates, slammed cupboards, cutlery hurled like spears into the dishwasher. She herself remained stewingly silent, her mouth a compressed white line. It was, Angus thought, the most transparent play for attention he'd ever seen, and he let her get on with it whilst he turned Siri's picture this way and that, trying to bring into focus again what he had glimpsed before. If Lynne was expecting an apology for last night, that was a shame for her, because Angus had a credo: never apologize, never complain. He wasn't entirely sure he'd always cleaved to the second part, but his record on the first was unimpeachable.

What Siri had made of the view from the kitchen window was a scene so poorly reasoned – lacking the barest grasp of proportion or perspective – that it almost qualified as outsider art. And yet there was some unintended trick to the drawing, maybe visible solely to Angus – something she had described that bore no relation to what she had actually drawn. It sure as hell wasn't anything she'd seen through the window.

Angus massaged his temples, sighed, groped at the back of his neck where the hangover still nagged – and as if his touch had completed some ethereal circuit, he had it: no, didn't have it, not yet, but could sense it. A field of colour – orange? Sienna, maybe? A scalded, burned-out colour. Old rust. And more – a pale maggoty lavender that trembled over the orange. What he'd seen wasn't in her childish drawing, but in him. Swelling up inside him was the idea that there could be nothing in this world more beautiful, more vital, more *right*, than this particular combination. He stood over the table in stupefaction, tracing his fingers round the sketch pad's edges. In that pairing of colours, as well as in Siri's amateurish line, a possibility was offering itself for his consideration. He tried not to look – did not want to scare off the thing that had crept forward from wherever it had lain skulking all this time.

'The silent treatment, is it?' Lynne bellowed. He leapt, broken from his dwam. 'All right, fine, if you're not going to say it, I will. I don't know why she comes round if she's going to behave like that.'

Angus shook his head, but the feeling of *rightness* was already gone. 'Whit ye oan aboot?'

'She's grown so snide lately. So combative.'

'Seemed fine tae me. Young, ah mean, but no much ye can dae aboot that—'

'If she just withdrew, fine. I'd understand that. Her first loyalty has to be to her father. But I don't know why she feels the need to test me like this – punish me—'

'Punish ye!'

'Didn't you see how she got all nervous when I mentioned Rose? She must know that I know what's going on. Does she think Raymond and I never talked to one another?'

Angus, who had spent considerable time this last fortnight watching game shows on daytime telly, was starting to feel he had accidentally passed through the TV screen and was appearing on one himself – a show where questions could be answered only by questions until you could figure out what subject was under contention. 'Help us out here, Lynne. This isnae aboot the coffee hing?'

'You think I'd be this upset about coffee?'

They glared in mutual incredulity. 'Honestly?'

Lynne opened and shut the ventilation shelf over the cooker several times. 'This girl Rose. The archaeology graduate who went to London for a postdoc then came back home to stand behind a counter all day making coffee. With the holiday home in Portugal and the frequent-flyer miles so Siri can come and visit for free, any time she likes. Not that I've heard this first hand, you understand, but apparently she's all Siri ever talks about – Rose this, Rose that. But always to Raymond, only Raymond. All he says is he's concerned about her sexuality, but to me it sounds like she's already made her decision. But then he told me that this girl Rose is in her twenties – woman, I should say. It's ridiculous. It's sinister. Nearer my age than Siri's, but she's hanging around with a, with a kid, basically. Dazzling her. Doesn't that seem odd to you?'

'Ah, stop. Lynne.' Angus's head was throbbing. He poured his tea away – left unattended it had, like so much in life, gone bitter – and made himself a fresh mug. 'So she's got hirsel a girlfriend. So what? Really, what business is it ay yirs?'

'But when I even mention her name – you saw how she

clammed up just now. She's refusing to confide in me. Punishing me,' she repeated, her face pinched.

'Mibbe she was feart ye might, ah dunno, overreact a tiny bit?' But Lynne's face, angst-swollen, didn't move. He noticed her gold cross necklace deliberately laid over the top of her sweater. She'd talked about Siri spiralling away from her, but all it seemed like to Angus was the girl growing up, exceeding Lynne's conception of her identity. Coming out, he'd told more than one student in his time, was a radical act. They'd always seemed pleased. He had his own reasons for flattering them: now I've legitimized your existence, will you please give it a rest with your frenzied nudes, your phallic clays? 'So Siri's young. Ye think she isnae old enough to know her own mind. But when d'ye think she is gonnae be? The day she turns eighteen? Twenty-wan? Or is sumdy jist gonnae randomly wave a chequered flag one mornin?'

'Don't be facetious.' Sullen Lynne nodded, piped down, did not necessarily concede that he was right, though he undoubtedly was.

Slyly, he added: 'Ah'm sure ye can discuss all aboot it wi yir man – when was it? Thursday night.'

'And you're taking that tone because . . . ?'

'Look, ah know ye'll no want tae hear this, but see him summoning ye tae him without even a hint ay an apology? Ur ye sure it's wise?' He'd pieced this together listening outside the door earlier, and rushed on before she could accuse him of snooping: 'Ah'm lookin out for you is all.'

'Oh, yes. My great defender, always with my best interests at heart. Like yesterday – I was *so glad* you rode to my rescue when I was in danger of a night's unbroken sleep. Your support – my God, Angus, I can't begin to put it into words.'

'Hie, Lynne. Ye want a fight?' He gestured at the window, against which rain, wind-flung, dabbling with sleet, was crashing now in great sheets – seemed to be hitting the glass from *below* somehow. 'Away doon intae the street and fight wi yir

106

shadow. Ach, forget it.' His warmed-over blood had started flowing more fiercely: in the last few minutes his hangover had resurged like a bastard. 'Know whut, hen? Ah'm headin back tae ma scratcher. This has all been a bit much for me today.'

'So we're not going to talk about what happened last night at all, are we?'

By Christ, she did want a fight, the cheeky besom. Left to his own devices Angus might eventually have told her the whole story; instead he gussied up a simper and the usual bundle of half-truths. 'Look, Lynne, ah'm sorry, okay? Ah bumped intae sumdy ah used tae know—'

'Somebody from . . . the street?'

'No. Christ, no. They guys werenae exactly the socializing type, Lynne, ye know? No, jist a pal fae . . . before. We got chatting, went for a couple bevvies, before you know it it'd gone midnight and ah'd hud wan too many for ma ain guid.' Her eyes went haywire, darting all over his face in search of signs he was lying. 'Like ah said. Willnae happen again.'

Had he really – the memory drawing up from last night's murk – threatened Rab with a dart to the puss if he didn't spring for a last pint at McCalls? No wonder the poor bastard hadn't been in evidence later on.

'I wouldn't have minded,' Lynne wheedled, 'only, I'd appreciate it if you could tell me in future if you're going to stay out late.' Her anger had dissipated – her whole demeanour altered. It was quite a transformation from the fight-seeker back to her normal pliable, concerned persona. Angus thought he preferred the feistier Lynne. 'Just so I have an idea where you'll be. I was worried. The things you've told me. How people hurt you before.'

'Doll. This isnae me renouncing one ay ma life's great pleasures for yir sake. It's that ah don't fancy spendin any more ay ma time wi that lot. In pubs and that. Ah amnae that person ony mair,' he assured her, knowing that this sounded conciliatory enough to prevent her clocking, for a while at least, that it wasn't an apology at all.

Lynne's expression cleared. Boy, even hung over to fuck he could still play a blinder. Now the kill: he went in for the hug, held her long enough to reassure her, not so long as to revivify her hopes. Honestly, he could teach a masterclass. But this safe haven of hers was a bloody minefield.

He was done coddling her anyway – no energy to squander on Lynne, not when he had those pigments to think on: the orange and the dry-bone colour. The thing to do was not try too soon to pursue them; it was enough just to think around them, letting them hang in the mind's middle distance, protean, choosing their own form. He took himself back to bed, and as he lay there on the low futon he could feel, shining in his arms, the memory of muscle cramps brought on by the nights-on-end painting sessions of old. In his rush of anticipatory elation, Angus felt that this ache was echoing back from a point in the near future, from work he could barely imagine, yet which he must, any day now, be about to begin.

NINE

Driving home from Raymond's four nights later, sad and enraged, Lynne thought she might keep on driving – drive south, disappear. Let Angus have the flat, let Siri go about her life however she wanted. But she ended up on Glendower Street as inevitably as if every street in the city had been designed to draw her home.

Leaving the bin bag he'd given her slumped on the landing, Lynne let herself into the flat. It was cold, and as she went round adjusting radiators and drawing curtains, setting things right, she started to see, highlighted, as thermal imaging shows up where a house leaks wasted energy, all the things Angus got wrong. Glaring from the kitchen shelves, the tumblers he consistently replaced upside down; neon outlined the windows left unlocked; in the washing machine he failed every time to empty, damp clothes, all melded together, seemed to phosphoresce. She shook, angrier with Angus now than with Raymond. Glendower Street was her sanctuary, and with every bit of thoughtlessness, the invader was wrecking it. Yet she could no more have told Angus how his mistakes infuriated her than she could have listed the numerous small gestures she made that favoured him: ironing his socks, making sure she always served him first at supper. In Lynne's mind lurked the idea – juvenile but somehow persisting – that these subliminal acts would have a cumulative effect in eventually winning him over. She laughed meanly at herself; already hurting, she

109

sought to hurt herself further. You wouldn't even know what to do if he did fall into your arms.

It was tempting to leave the bag out there in the close, but eventually she retrieved it, humping it into the flat, then tore open the plastic knot and, disconsolate, began removing the junk it contained. It was as if Raymond had kept a list for the past five years, noting down everything she'd ever left at his house. Certainly, what he'd returned to her seemed extraordinarily comprehensive, including items even she wouldn't have remembered – she who sometimes prided, sometimes excoriated herself for remembering everything. Here was her little plastic vial of sweetener, a nail file she'd left in his bathroom years ago. Their time together itemized in objects that now seemed at once imbued with significance beyond themselves, yet to be lacking, too: vapid reminders of nothing very much.

He'd sounded conciliatory on the phone before, and she'd driven over to the High Street smugly confident. She would be aloof, she would be superb: he'd end up begging her to take him back and she'd say so nicely, so sweetly, 'I'm sorry, but there's someone else in my life at the moment.' Then it'd be his turn to go to pieces. If she left it at that, it wouldn't even be a lie.

How green could a person be? In fact, she had been lured into a trap. She understood it, that was the worst thing: when she thought about the times she'd cursed Angus for smoking in the house, or sluiced from the bathroom sink the toothpaste spit he'd slathered it with, she understood why Raymond would want to expunge every trace of her from his home.

She hung the old clothes in her wardrobe, then filed the books. As well as hurt and indignant, she felt an odd disquiet she only identified when she went to return to the living-room mantelpiece a travel alarm clock she'd taken to Raymond's years ago, and found she didn't need to clear any space for it. There was a gap there between ornaments, a gap that had waited patiently for the clock's inevitable return. In all this time the house hadn't changed – no, worse: Lynne had never allowed it to change.

110

Never fixed the toilet flush, the work of minutes. When she heard Angus's key rackling for the lock, rage swelled up in her, a howl stoppered in her throat. Soon, far too soon, barely eight o'clock. Was she not entitled to one single uninterrupted evening to herself? At that moment, offered a lit match, she might gladly have burned Glendower Street to the ground.

But being who she was, she tried to compose herself and met Angus, when he came panting and huffing into the flat, with feigned warmth. 'You're back early.'

He grunted and shoved past her. 'Spot the genius.' She blinked. From his room, he called, 'Been in here again, huv ye, Lynne?'

She took her time inhaling and exhaling. 'I was simply putting something back on my mantelpiece. How was class?'

Again he walked straight past her, into the kitchen this time, where he deposited his bag on the table and went to fill the kettle. 'Oh aye. It wis jist dandy.'

'Really. Because you don't seem—'

'Naw, Lynne,' he interrupted, pityingly, 'no really.' He didn't seem to have registered her sarcasm, as though believing her incapable of it. '*Really*, ah'd say it was a waste ay fuckin time.'

'Angus, why don't you try and be civil, and tell me what happened?'

'Let's jist say,' he at last condescended to reply, 'you urnae the only wan hus it tough.'

Lynne felt tears gathering. She must not let him overrule her – let whatever had happened to him swamp her own upset. Wallowing, she jagged herself, tried to make herself feel worse, with the thought that he hadn't even remembered this was the night she was seeing Raymond. 'After all I've done for you,' she could have said, squeezing her eyes shut, forcing the tears to flow. But, able neither to speak nor leave Angus be, she stood ramrod straight at the kitchen counter, watching him drink his tea. Her hands behind her back found an edge where the finish on the counter had started to come away, and she began to pick at it like a scab.

111

'Giein me the third degree,' he muttered when she didn't say any more. He had trimmed his beard, she noticed, razored the sharp stubble from his cheeks, run a comb through his hair. Even before this, she'd been aware he was walking taller, his confidence growing. He had been getting better, and Lynne had been happy enough – conceited enough – to give herself credit for helping him heal. Like any scientific theory, though, a single contradictory reading could trash the hypothesis. She had been quite consistent in her behaviour towards him, and yet tonight he was sniping and raging at her. How on earth had she not seen it before? Nothing she'd done, the explicit charity and the secret, was making any difference to him.

Angus finished his tea and went to retrieve the kitbag from the table – a bag that did not, it struck her, seem any fuller since she'd given him all that money for materials – then just stood there, awkward. 'Right then. Ah'm away tae bed. Ah'll see you in the mornin.'

'Planning to get up at a decent time for once, are you?'

Angus paused, squinted at her. 'You all right, Lynne?'

Oh, now he notices. But perverse Lynne, her own nemesis, just shook her head. She wanted him to know what had happened to her, but she didn't want to have to *tell* him. He was the immature one, forever taking, taking: why shouldn't she be infantile for once – hold something back to spite him? In a tone that belied the words: 'I'm fine.'

'If ye're sure.' His expression was doubtful, and she felt a small heat in the base of her spine, a shameful pleasure at the pointless deception she'd undertaken. 'Night, then.'

He went into the bathroom, and through the thin dividing wall she heard him gargle, spit, swallow water the wrong way and commence hacking and coughing – the same disgusting routine every night. It wasn't fair to expect him to be something he wasn't – though wasn't that why it was called a crush? Years ago, in the wake of their kiss, Angus had become, in her imagination, an effigy of a man she'd barely known, and

112

all she had been doing since his re-emergence on Sauchiehall Street was trying to cram all his real person's contradictions and excesses into the not-even-two-dimensional avatar she'd conjured. It was no more logical or dignified to feel aggrieved at his failure to conform to behaviour patterns she'd invented for him than it was to feel she was showing largesse by forgiving him for it.

Let the silence grow between them. Let it sour. It's good to be angry, she counselled herself: if you're angry at him maybe it means you're starting to get over him. But there remained a nub of chill in her heart, and a mocking internal voice that said: Don't lie to yourself.

Raymond had been wearing a V-necked navy sweater and tan pressed chinos, clothes she seemed to remember choosing for him. She'd been too distracted to comment, anyway, galled as she was to recognize that, dressed like this, he closely resembled Angus. His excuses and self-justifications, his accusations – you're too keen, too pliable, I need an equal, an opponent – had gone mostly over her head as she laboured with an ontological paradox. Evidently she had, unconsciously, been buying Angus clothes like Raymond's, but it seemed that she'd used to dress her lover in a way that reminded her of her old teacher. Had she been harder on Angus than she ought because he reminded her of Raymond? Or forgiven Raymond so much because he recalled Angus? Round and round it went, the sheer improbability of these two unsuitable men's inter-resemblance a Möbius strip that had neither beginning nor end, but had generated a waste by-product, Lynne herself. Who'd come first, who was modelled on whom? No matter. Everyone had a type: Lynne's just happened to be the type who disdained her.

'I need to spend more time with Siri, too,' Raymond had said, and had her attention. 'She needs a stable home environment.'

'But the three of us,' she gasped. 'That was a nuclear family. How much more stable could it have been?'

'I just need some space,' he'd said, brow wrinkling at her

intransigence. 'You understand? A little time.' So, what, she possessed no dimension of her own? 'Maybe then we might—'

'You must think I'm stupid,' she'd blurted. 'A real fool.'

'Of course not, Lynnie!'

'I get it. You *know* I am.' He'd looked startled, even frightened. She would never have taken this tone with him in the old days, the pre-Angus era.

Tears prinked at the corners of her eyes as she tried to think of other hurtful things she might have said to Raymond. How dare he try and reason with her, con her into accepting the blame for his throwing her out of his life?

The living-room door flew open and Angus, shirt untucked from his jeans, came barrelling out. 'Lynne. Listen—'

She screamed and screamed and screamed at him to go away, until, in his shock, he softly closed his door. The flat lay still once more.

114

TEN

Winter gripped the city, winter wouldn't let go. Work had long since stopped on the school; the diggers lay inert in the frozen furrows they'd excavated, mechanical arms folded to their sides, resembling nothing so much as the people you saw rushing home at street level, muffled up, hands tucked beneath their armpits for warmth.

On Saturday afternoon, with both of them trapped in Glendower Street and the central heating set to tropical, Angus at last ended their two-day deadlock.

'Lynne,' she heard him softly calling. 'Oh, Lynne? C'mere, doll.' She padded into the kitchen, where she found him sitting at the table, surrounded by the equipment she'd funded him to buy: sketch pads, a huge box of pastels, a jam jar crammed with pencils, their sharpened tips uppermost like arrows in a quiver. He was, to her surprise and faint discomfort, smiling broadly. His lunch dishes, she saw, were stacked unwashed by the sink.

'What ye think, eh? We're no gaun oot anywhere, so how's about a bit ay drawin? You dae me, ah dae you drawin me. Back tae basics.'

Lynne hesitated. She couldn't bear the atmosphere in the house when they weren't talking, and this seemed as close to détente as they were likely to come. And that offhand remark to Siri as he'd been concentrating so intensely on the girl's drawing – 'Lynne hud promise' – had stayed dimly aglow in her mind for days, a talisman.

'Okay, then. If you like.'

She'd been trying to maintain her animosity towards him, feeling this would serve her better than apologizing, and here, at the merest hint that he valued her even just as the only available model, she was brimming again with what she thought of as love. It was useless: she thrilled at the notion that she could be model, muse, student, whatever he liked. If he wanted to draw her, Lynne reasoned as she chose a few pencils from the jar, he must find something about her interesting, though she knew his work well enough not to expect it to be anything flattering. Most likely he had noticed a corned-beef texture in her skin that he intended to depict unflinchingly – slab flesh marbled blue and green. Just her luck he'd chosen to draw her under electric light.

She put on an appropriate CD, a cello concerto sere as winter branches, but within seconds Angus came sweeping over to turn it off. 'Nup. Nae music. Nae distractions.'

'Serious stuff,' she joked. 'And you're sure you don't want me to do anything about my face? Put on make-up?'

Angus faltered for a moment, appalled, then smiled hugely. 'Lynne Meacher, you bluddy dare.'

They took opposite ends of the table. Angus stilled, watching her – she held her expression fixed – then tossed a pastel crayon in his hand like a majorette's baton and fell to work, making swift, decisive marks on the page. Lynne, unable at this stage even to choose between pencils and watercolours, did nothing.

Drawing had never been her strength. She liked geometries, abstractions, colours arranged in matrixial hives. She liked detail. While her peers assembled, as Angus was doing now, a large-scale sketch of the entire subject as the first step in a new composition, Lynne had persisted, throughout her two years at Glasgow, and despite her teachers' best efforts, in starting with a detail and working her way outwards. No matter how often she pointed to Klee or Albers – the delicate, precise little grids and nests of colours she admired and wanted to emulate – her teachers told her the technique was childish. That only gave her

116

the ammunition to reject the criticism, persist with her method. It worked for her, or didn't, depending, but what was the point in doing the same as everyone else?

She settled on starting with the delta between Angus's eyebrows, which frowning had permanently corrugated, and went to work.

'I've been meaning to say thank you. What you did with Siri at the weekend, that teaching stuff?'

'Ah thought she'd be better no gettin the wrang idea about you and me, eh. Though ah guess that must've occurred to you an aw, specially if ye thought she might report back tae the auld man after.'

Why did he have to invoke Raymond? 'Whatever the reason, it was really nice of you.'

He blinked. 'Aye, well, ah am nice.'

It was better they be friends. Intellectually she knew it. So why couldn't she take it to heart? She wanted to test their new truce, and asked, 'Will you be going back to your classes next week?'

He ruminated on this awhile. 'Mibbe. Mibbe no. Depends, ah suppose.'

'What on?'

'Various factors. Stuff.' He cleared his throat. 'People politics, ye might say.'

She envisaged Angus usurping the teacher, going around critiquing the others' work, upsetting a whole roomful at a time – secretly enjoying the ruckus that ensued and swearing blind he'd only wanted to help.

'Ah wantit,' he began, then halted, thought about it, resumed. 'See sometimes, wi a piece ye're planning, it seems within yir grasp – ye've worked it all out, put all the plans in place, you can practically *see* the thing hovering there in front ay ye. But ye've still forgot sumhin, or there's a factor still outwith yir control, so when ye come tae put pencil tae paper, so tae speak, poof, it jist, ah dunno, evaporates.'

117

'That's why you left early on Thursday? You couldn't get a picture to work?'

She wondered what she'd said to amuse him. 'Sumhin along they lines.'

'Well, could it be you're just overthinking it?' Lynne felt that her own propensity for so doing qualified her to identify and correct the trait in others. 'Maybe it's not as unworkable as you imagine?'

'Very possibly. Trouble is, sumdy like me, imagination's all ah've got gaun fer me a lot ay the time.'

Lynne managed next to get the strange sharp line of Angus's nose down quite well, and, rewarding herself, announced: 'Well, while you were out having a mediocre time at class, I was down at the Saltmarket having an even bloodier time of things.'

'With what's-his-name, aye?'

'With Raymond, yes.' She hadn't been expecting Angus to throw his pastels to the floor in jealous rage, but was disappointed nonetheless that he just kept on sketching placidly. 'A nice cosy night in with the ex.' She marvelled at herself. This was the tone to take: wry, putting inverted commas around everything heartfelt or true. 'He'd done that thing people say on television: "We need to talk." And I'm just so deluded that I went along imagining he might actually mean it.' She paused: nothing. She had to stop making these self-deprecating remarks if Angus wasn't going to bother repudiating them. 'I didn't think you knew I was going to see him.'

'Lynne, darlin! No, look – Thursday night this wis? Jeezo, whut you must think ay me. Ah may be a bit ay a loser, but ah can retain basic information. Ah jist didnae want tae trample all over ye wi ma big size tens wis aw.' In a jolly, moronic voice, bopping his head from side to side: ' "Aw, aw, what happened to you, Lynne? Why so doon in the mooth?" A blind man could see ye werenae in the mood tae talk. So, you'd gone down there thinkin he wis gonnae ask ye back?'

'You needn't sound so surprised. I'm not that awful, am I?'

118

'Ye've never gave me tae believe that was sumhin ye wantit is all.' He at last set down his pastels. He seemed poised to issue a statement of great profundity. 'Beats me,' he said slowly, 'why ye'd even want tae see that dobber again, after he treated ye like such shite.' He sniffed. 'If ye don't mind me bein candid.'

She was, absurdly, about to defend Raymond, but decided to let Angus's remark go because of the implicit compliment that she did not actually deserve to be treated like – what he'd said.

Her portrait had gone wrong somewhere, made him troll-like. She rolled a few pencils over her sketch pad to hide it. Here was the problem with her detailed method – the unnoticed early flaw that corrupted the whole image, further distorting it the more you elaborated. On this evidence, any talent she had once possessed had withered to nothing, or else Angus had been exaggerating to flatter her. She didn't want to accept that, however, and without waiting to be told, she turned to a new page and began afresh.

'Even if ah hudnae remembered, ah kin put two and two together. Ah huv ma ain special method ay gatherin information, nivver fails.'

'Which is?'

'Ah keep ma eyes open.' Unruffleable, he wrapped kitchen roll around his index finger and blotted at his picture. 'And ma big trap shut. Seems tae me there's a load more stuff around here since Thursday, ye know whut ah mean? All what he gave ye back, am I right? Look, ah'm sorry if ye thought ah wis bein insensitive. It's the exact opposite ah meant. Pussyfootin, ah wis. Ah barely know how tae speak tae people at the best ay times.' He frowned. 'Why ye smilin like that?'

'I was just thinking you were right. Raymond is . . . he did treat me like that. He behaved' – she drew her shoulders back, gathering herself – 'like a prick.'

Angus guffawed. 'Awright Lynne! Tell it like it is!' He seized a fresh pastel and scrubbed it flat-sided over the paper, laying in a reddish-black background to her emerging portrait. 'Go on, then. Ye arrived there wi a girlish feeling high up under yir ribcage, couldn't make it stop even though ye werenae even sure whut ye were hopin fer. Despite that, all hope jist vanished soon's he opened the door.'

'It was the lights,' Lynne said, uneasy remembering it. 'All on full blast, every light in the place, in case I, what, mistook one bulb on a dimmer for romantic lighting.'

The blaze, and Raymond at its centre. 'Thank you for coming,' he'd said straight away. 'I was worried after I'd spoken to you that I might have given you the wrong impression.' She'd buckled, gripping the door frame for support, but he'd been too caught up in his own self-important speech to notice.

Now Lynne was glad that Angus had been surly on Thursday night – had denied her the opportunity to rush into badmouthing Raymond. 'It ended in a great rush, you know. Even if he wasn't going to take me back, I wanted to be fair, to give him the chance to explain.' And then reject any overtures he made about being friends again, she didn't say. Angus's eyebrows crept ironically upwards. 'Okay, so the truth is, I wanted to stick my fingers in the plug socket and give myself an almighty shock. And that's just what I got.'

'But ye did love him – before, ah mean. Wi all yir heart.'

Lynne hesitated, sighed, gazed from corner to corner of the ceiling. 'With all my heart I don't know about.' Over the boiler, a long woolly strand of cobweb drifted in the upward air. How had she missed that when she was cleaning? 'With the eighty per cent that was on offer, maybe – available for the purpose. I'm trying to be honest,' she told him. 'I know my limitations.'

She squinted at Angus's drawing. 'Ho, love's young dream! Nae peepin.' But in the instant before his hand swept down to cover his work, she'd glimpsed what he had made of her: a solitary figure in a darkened room, like the widow or spinster of a Hammershøi.

'It's not easy being a woman.'

Angus shifted in his seat. 'That right?'

'I know so many women – colleagues, old school friends . . . and I am talking about women, my age, not girls – who choose to go out with men they know are unsuitable, even ones they've already broken up with once before, just because it's so difficult to meet anyone new.'

He nodded, absorbing this, then said: 'Well, then, they wimmin're lunatics.'

She drew. She worked down the edge of his beard, twitching the pencil to describe the unkempt line of it, then the side of his neck, the broad tendon disappearing into his collar. 'There's this real fear' – she made herself phrase it impersonally – 'of being alone. And anyway, "dating".' She dangled the word at arm's length. 'Surely only teenagers *date*.'

'Did you?'

'Hardly.' Teenaged Lynne had spent her time trying to figure out sex – worse, love – from questionnaires in magazines, acquiring from these a patchy and unreliable knowledge base. To actually try to put what she'd learned into practice had been unthinkable: the sense that everyone around her was already *doing it*, that she was permanently disadvantaged, made it easier to absent herself. When she thought back to those days, she remembered picturing herself as a small candle guttering in a vast cold sepulchre – she had wallowed in the notion that choosing to be alone was in some way noble – and her palm itched with the wish to slap sense into that girl.

'Well, then. Nae shame gaun oan dates. Ye know – websites and that.' As she'd pronounced *dating*, so he enunciated *websites*, cautiously, apparently by no means sure that such things existed.

'But it's humiliating,' she protested, dismayed to hear the whine that had entered her voice.

Angus set down his pastel crayon and pressed his smudged blackened fingers together under his chin. 'Awright, well – talk me through it. Lynne Meacher headin out on a date. Tell me how it goes.'

121

'Oh, no, Angus—'

'Naw, ah'm interestit. Whut's the worst you think's gonnae happen?'

This conversation was uncomfortable, yet she didn't want it to end; it was not unpleasant – not unproductive – to play this game of discussing your feelings with someone to whom you couldn't fully admit them. You had to talk in allusions, name no names. Not that it mattered: she knew Angus would treat everything she said as confession regardless.

She had created a passable likeness of his face's lower right quadrant, but when she tried to draw his mouth, it all went wrong again. Everything pulled downwards and to the right, as though stroke-afflicted. She scrapped it. Started over.

'I guess the worst thing . . . and I'll admit' – she was lying – 'this is based a little bit on personal experience . . . is to go through that process of dressing up, polishing all your best stories, slapping on the make-up, the veneer of confidence and optimism, then hauling your carcass down to whatever busy, well-lit, non-threatening environment you've selected, only to find—'

'Wasted effort?' Angus nodded. 'The guy's wearing a fleece smells like he's no washed it since the year dot. He husnae bothered tae shave. He's boring. If he notices he husn't impressed ye by his total gash effort at gallantry by buying ye wan drink, he takes the sulk, blames you.'

'God, were you there at the next table?'

'Jist the ither side ay the experience, darlin',' he said sadly.

'Maybe that isn't even the worst part. That's when you realize, maybe during the date, maybe once you've refused a second drink and safely extricated yourself—'

'Refused the second, that's harsh, Lynne – surely ye should at least get in one round each?'

'You've never heard of cutting your losses? Why waste your money on someone you've already written off?' She'd never in her life walked out on a date in the way she described: she

122

was extemporizing, but enjoying seeing Angus intrigued by the novel, unforgiving Lynne she was inventing. 'I'm hardly *obligated*.'

'Well anyway, ye're off, with or without yir second drink. And as ye're on yir way back hame, you're turnin it over in yir mind, dissectin whut went wrang. And that's when it sinks in. Mibbe they boring things he said *were* his best stories. Maybe that fleece genuinely was his best claithing . . .' He trailed off, possibly remembering that Lynne herself favoured a fleece as outerwear.

'It's the way it reflects so badly on you. If this is the calibre of person you're attracting – well, then, what does that say about you? Meanwhile, he's gone off home in a stink too. "That frigid bitch." '

'Hardly. And surely it wisnae like that every time. No wi what's-his-chops, ah presume.' She had noticed Angus going out of his way not to use Raymond's name, a code of practice he'd set himself; she was grateful for it.

'There were . . . exceptions.' Two exceptions. She saw them in opposing corners, like boxers: Raymond, who each morning laid his comb against the line of his nose then ran it up over his forehead to determine where his centre parting should start; who believed that wearing trainers if you weren't playing a sport at the time was tantamount to criminal. And Angus, who was – Angus. Uncapturable Angus: wrong likenesses littered her sketchbook, each failed in its own distinct way. 'The problem is that after you've done that even twice or three times, your stories are smoothed to routines. Putting on your best outfit feels like dressing a doll, and trying to be all confident and optimistic is just another costume you're putting on. So you go and meet this next person, thinking maybe this time, maybe this one'll be' – shaking her head at herself – 'a catch, but you're pumped full of bad faith, you don't give them a proper chance. Totally cynical.'

'Lynne,' he said, in all seriousness, 'if there's a word ah'd use tae describe ye, it isnae cynical.'

123

Smiling, she rolled her eyes. 'It makes me so tired to think I might have to start that again. All that getting-to-know-you stuff, the time you might waste on a person who doesn't deserve it.'

'Be a lot easier,' Angus mused, 'if ye could jist skip forward, whit, three month? Six? To when yis're already comfortable with one another. Take all the hassle out. But since ye cannae dae that, ye persevere, like ye tried to with that feller ay yirs the ither night. Mibbe ye can improve him along the way.' His eyes flicked to her necklace. 'Besides, yous lot're meant tae turn the other cheek, urn't ye no?'

'Please don't tell me' – betrayed again, she fought to keep her tone level – 'how I am or am not meant to behave. You do not have that right. I get it, Angus, it's just a joke to you.' He lifted his chin: he was smiling. '*What?*'

'See that passion? That strength ay feeling? That's what ye should be putting intae yir pictures. Dinnae bottle it up. *Get* cross. *Be* wild. That passion – try and utilize it.'

'Passion,' she exploded. Incensed, she considered grabbing the black pastel and effacing her likeness on his page. 'What makes you think you have the faintest idea what I'm passionate about?' Then, afraid that he might respond frankly: 'Half the time, I barely know myself.'

'You've got your faith,' he said, eyes sealing in mock piety, 'and ah've got mine.'

Dig, dig, dig – goading and goading her – was this what he was like when he drank? When other people had tried to help him? Or did he save it just for her? She stayed silent and he went on at last: 'Ah've felt the hand ay God maself, ye see, doll.'

'In your art, you mean?'

His eyes sprang open. 'No, Lynne, ah do not mean in ma art. Jesus.'

'Angus, please—'

'Lynne, naw, wheesht, listen. Believe me, ah huv. Wan time, ah nearly orphaned masel.'

She sat impassive, resolved to do nothing to encourage him, but it did no good. He told the story anyway.

'Each summer, ma da'd take a week aff and we'd huv a holiday thegither, just the two ay us. This wis after,' he explained briskly, 'ma mither'd left us. We'd go tae Elie, St Andrews, they sorts ay places, places he minded gaun when he was wee an aw. He hud quite the gift for choosin the week in August it'd bucket doon rain. Anyway, this wan summer – nine or ten ah might've bin – we went tae Kirkcudbright. And it didnae rain! A miracle.'

Angus paused, recalling not the visit itself, too long ago, but elements: the guest house's yellow window frames; a wolfhound, tall as his shoulder, that had rushed into the garden, sniffed him, made him howl with fright, and rushed off again. And the story he'd rehearsed but never told.

'The place we were steiyin in sat right on the watter, and there was this sortay wooden pier oot front, sumdy's dinghy moored tae it. The first mornin ah got up and went oot, and ah saw ma da staunin oot the end this thing, gazin out tae sea – takin a fotie mibbe, evidence sunshine did really exist. Ah saw him there, and ah thought it'd be jist . . . so funny . . .' – here it came, the isotopic chill that suffused him, even so many years later, any time he remembered what he'd done, the clench of horror heightened not just by the memory, but by Lynne's look of total incomprehension – 'tae run up behind him and shove him in.'

'How deep . . . ?'

'No deep at aw, naw. And all jist rocks. He'd've died if ah'd did it. Struck his heid and died, ah know it.'

'Not necessarily. No. Anyway, it's academic. You didn't do it. Did you?'

Angus shook his head. 'Ah took a big long run-up at it, but. Ah hud real velocity. But see, as I came harin up behind the auld man, jist at the last instant before ah commit patricide, what happens? Ma toe catches in a gap between two gangplanks. No time to throw oot ma hauns – down ah go, face first, sprawlin ma length, chin hittin the wood. Doosh. And ma da turns round and he's like, "Whit ye daein doon there?" ' Nausea came up in him: he'd thought telling it might have earthed the horror. 'And ah start bawlin, partly cos ah've dunted ma chin or whatever, but maistly because the enormity ay whut ah wis aboot tae dae's just hit me, and he husnae a scooby.'

'And that's . . . that was a religious experience for you?'

Was she stupid? 'Being sent flying tae the deck seconds before pitchin ma ain faither tae his death? Aye, Lynne, ah'd say that wis divine intervention right enough.' In mounting desperation he held up his thumb and forefinger – 'This close ah came!' – but all Lynne did was make a face: sympathetic, not empathetic. A confession he'd never again be able to make for the first time, his excuse for an apology, and she hadn't got it: why wasn't she letting him feel absolved? His stories were starting to lose their power over her. Cynically motivated, this one: he no more believed in divine intervention than in the tooth fairy. He wished he'd said nothing.

She wasn't even paying proper attention. Instead her gaze kept slipping past him, towards the kitchen window: at what, a bird on a branch? He turned, frustrated, and saw what had distracted her: snow, coming down fast on the dark – no fannying about with flurrying, no delicate flakes gambolling in the moonlight, just purposeful, urgent fall. He looked back in astonishment at Lynne, her enchanted expression.

Neither of them suggested going out in it; yet in silence, like mummers, they abandoned their drawings, drew scarves round their necks, did up their matchy-matchy windcheaters. Lynne dropped a camera into her pocket, rolled her bobble hat down as far as her eyebrows, then helped tighten Angus's scarf around his neck, reviving in him a long-dormant and, he hoped, irrational fear of death by strangulation. She raised her chin. Ready? He gave a single nod: Aye.

It wasn't cold outside, not at first anyway, and they made their way quickly through the wet woolly snow swiftly falling to collect on their shoulders, every so often a stray blotch drawn in by breath to land on Angus's tongue, shine briefly, then dissolve. Irresistible, the pure wonder of the stuff – the privilege of being first to walk in the fresh, undisturbed settling, feel its stiff scrunching beneath your boots. The merest few early flakes pullulating under street lights triggered an atavistic feeling in the hindbrain, the same primitive awe that must've gripped the first folk on Earth ever to see this stuff drop from the sky.

After the fiasco of Thursday night, his impromptu art class tonight had been his attempt to recapture the brief glimpse he'd had in Siri's drawing of the work he wanted to make. If he patched things up with Lynne in the process, well and good. He'd carefully used the burnt orange and the off-white, hoping that even in an unrelated image, his captor's portrait, they'd function as a tuning fork, resonating against his sense of the painting to which he sensed they'd be crucial, and by doing so, help reveal it. No spark, no nothing. All he'd produced was a picture of Lynne, a shade haughtier than in life but passable nonetheless. He was just going to have to let that sense of colours, that faintest notion of a structure, simmer away by itself in the subconscious, develop quietly, hoping it would present itself to him as and when.

Lynne wanted to see the university, and Angus took it as a sign that the route there involved going right past McCalls. A test. No worries: as they passed, he'd keep his head down, watching his step. Likely it'd take hours before the barflies registered what was going on outside anyway. He smiled to himself, imagining bleary heads lifting as events penetrated booze-deadened consciousnesses. Shoving each other in the ribs. 'See that? In the windae? Is that . . . *snow*?' Armageddon might come and go unremarked.

On Queen Margaret Drive, nutjobs were charging from pubs and houses and engaging one another in snowball fights – violence stored up for the one occasion it was socially acceptable to chuck a missile at a total stranger. The place was hoatching:

127

running battles between instant gangs, cold-packed fusillades that arced from the Botanics to the roundabout in the middle of the road, from there to the BBC building where Angus'd seen the fox that time. Cars crept along the road as though trying to escape the missile-hurlers' attention. The night sky was a bright, terrible green.

With McCalls successfully bypassed – and the odd thing was that for once he didn't feel the slightest urge to be in there with the other barflies, screened from the world – Angus followed Lynne along the terraced row that led towards the university's main entrance. With considerable restraint, he stopped himself rushing through the scrim of untouched snow on the quad lawns; when he caught up with Lynne, he had to exercise almost as much self-control not to point out her stupidity in taking photos of the sodium-lit central spire from its foot. Had she no sense for perspective? Did she want her pictures diabolically foreshortened? Instead, he squinted out at the horizon, his eye travelling over the distant river's glimmer, the static Finnieston crane; Partick, vanishing beneath snow haze; the fortress gallery in the park; the denuded trees useless for shelter.

The snow grew colder, attained more solidity, came down on their faces stingingly as darts. 'Getting a bit bluddy cauld,' he called to Lynne, swiping in affront at the air.

'Cold as charity.' Lynne studied the camera's tiny illuminated screen before adjusting the controls with an amateur's tentativeness. 'We'll go soon. I just want a good shot, but the flakes keep getting in the way.'

'That thing new?' he asked, and she nodded and – it was visible even in the strange luminous yellow dark – blushed fiercely. Angus did not enquire further, assuming that Lynne, like everyone else, had come to see the potential in owning a device to take photos there was no risk strangers in film labs would see. For all her inhibitions, for all her guff earlier about fast-forwarding through her relationships to avoid, so he assumed, the terrifying business of sex, there must nonetheless be some sleazy side to her after all. For her own sake he hoped so: sex oozing around in there, way down low, strenuously repressed.

Sweet, despite everything, to see her capering about unguarded under the falling snow. He felt sudden solidarity – wondered what she'd been like as a child. Solemn, he imagined. When she saw him watching, she came up beside him and slipped an arm round his waist, and he did not push her away. Flakes in their lashes, they looked up together into the rushing sky. He could afford to be magnanimous, having brokered this reconciliation – not just for their own sakes, trying to patch up their fractured, unsustainable situation that bit longer, but on behalf of whatever was gestating within him. Assembling itself in secret. It made him happy to imagine her reaction when she got to see what he'd painted: so eloquent, so irrefutable, that they would finally understand one another. You couldn't wait for things to rectify themselves, you had to take command. Not through words, cack-handed diplomacy, but through what you did. Your work. And here she thought he was helpless till fucking divine inspiration struck. Earth to Lynne! The hand of God is a phantom limb.

ELEVEN

He hadn't expected to see China again. When she hadn't shown up to last week's class, he had assumed that her attending his first one had been the aberration, rather than the norm. Yet here he was, still hoping, making his cautious way to class once more, along pavements treacherous with ice. The weekend's snow had frozen and refrozen; along the kerbsides it lay shovelled aside in clods and clumps mottled black with exhaust fumes. He went like a novice skater from lamp post to dustbin to road sign to letter box, arms out stiffly for balance every time he skited, worried that if he lost his footing he'd clutch in reflex at an unwitting passer-by and bring them both down.

This week, Dean was taking the group – Angus had muttered something unkind upon seeing it on the list last time – to the Transport Museum. Another childhood post-hospital distraction, one that Angus's father, no doubt sick to the back teeth of dinosaurs, had suggested for variety's sake and one that, after that initial visit, Angus had fiercely resisted repeating. You could, he remembered complaining, see buses and the like any time you wanted just by looking out the window, which you could not say about prehistoric monsters. Quite the advanced argument for a kid. His tired old da acceded, making Angus immediately feel wretched – also pretty advanced empathy for a bairn – but once you'd made such a song and dance it was difficult to climb down, even when you knew that doing so would make the other party feel better. As any Lynne could tell you.

Something was making him so jittery he could barely put one foot in front of the other, and it wasn't just the black ice. It was the feeling of having stalled. Just as you'd prepare for any impending guest, Angus had got his house in order, bought a canvas to soak and stretch on a frame. And then – nothing. Potential had welled up in him then subsided; colours that had sung synaesthetically in his mind's eye, possessed something verging on life, now lay inert. What was burnt orange, anyway? What was bone white? Pigments, nothing more. The canvas lay, prepped and obeisant, face down on the desk in Lynne's womb-pink living room, and he could do fuck all with it.

Unlike the Kelvingrove, the Transport Museum was not as he remembered from his youth. Though its exterior was the same big corrugated byre, the display inside had entered the space age: it was all about buttons for the kids to press, animations, holographic thingmies that followed you around the place reciting their curators' scripts. Everything shone, right enough, but there were only so many ways you could display a parade's worth of jet planes, or chart the car's evolution from go-kart to gas-guzzler to electric buggy, and Angus, fundamentally, couldn't give a toss.

What did interest him, not to say astound him, was that China actually turned up – late, albeit, as seemed her prerogative. Black coat, black boots, clunky silver chain around her neck. She inspected the group, and her gaze did not seem to linger on Angus more than on anyone else. Antsy as any schoolboy, he drummed his heels impatiently through the remaining minutes of Dean's lesson on the basics of perspective.

He didn't need to look hard afterwards to find her: the museum was one vast open-plan barn, and he could see her from miles off, up on a gantry, sitting on a small fold-out stool facing the car engine she'd picked as her subject. He made his way briskly over to her, businesslike, and said her name. Before recognition had time to seep into her blank look, he saw smoky colour around her eyes that he mistook – it felt like receiving a blow just below the heart – for bruising. She held a pencil clamped longways between her teeth, and when she removed it to greet him, he saw with relief that it was just jadedness in her face, she was worn down was all.

'Missed ye last week.'

'Last week . . . Oh, you mean this? I forgot, I guess.'

'Ye shouldnae,' he said, embarrassed for them both. 'You shouldnae jist – forget tae come.'

'I had stuff to do,' she changed. She didn't seem offended, much less repentant. 'Sometimes you have to prioritize things. What did I miss, the Hunterian?'

'Aye.'

'Nice. That must have given this lot a fright. Dead things in jars. Pickled foetuses. What did you draw?'

Angus, not letting on that he hadn't stuck around long enough to draw anything: 'Oh, eh, aye, grisly stuff right enough. Ah dunno, this sortay . . . medical cadaver thing. Sumhin deid,' he laughed awkwardly, 'in a jar. What did ye huv oan mair important?'

She didn't acknowledge his question, just kept on at her drawing. Angus didn't pursue it. Instead, he cast around among the displays for something to draw – settling at length on one of the half-sized military aircraft hanging from the ceiling. A fighter jet, battleship grey, fangs painted in white enamel on its snout. He had the idea that its position, above and ahead of him, might make the perspective interestingly difficult, at least. An old challenge: you chose a problem and, through drawing, worked to solve it.

The jet did not hold his attention long, though, and he was soon sneaking looks sideways at China's work. She was working in charcoal on heavily textured Ingres paper; her progress was laborious, but what was emerging on the page was a proper response to the way the BMW engine was displayed, set like a votive on a lavender-coloured columnar plinth. She was refiguring its precise machine-tooled lines as organic forms, softening

132

the pistons to resemble plump arteries, the valves to knurls of bone. Angus, who had over the last week or so abstained from his daily wank in the hope that redirecting his energies might aid in making his painting, was discomfited to detect in China's impressionistic drawing something erotic – machinery that had warmed, swelled, grown muscular, sweaty, grubby as a Howson. He couldn't help comparing its roughness, its sense of an arrested transformation, with what he'd finally goaded Lynne into drawing on Saturday. Both good, both more than competent, but China's was the snapped shot of something living streaking by, Lynne's the painstaking portrait of a subject safely etherized and pinned for study: himself. But not bad, was the point: like China, Lynne was not ungifted, maybe a little heavy-handed, maybe too unwilling to investigate different approaches to working – and yet Angus couldn't imagine, even with these caveats, praising her to her face.

Momentary guilt regarding Lynne – the person, the curtailed career at art school – made him turn on China. 'Dean willnae like that,' he said, indicating her picture.

'How not?' He detected a trace of Scots accent then, previously buried, one that had travelled.

'Well, he's all about the literal, isn't he, Dean? Strict figuration, nae deviation. Nae imagination.'

China shrugged. 'It's a beginners' drawing class. I'm sure he's seen worse.'

'Well, awright,' he hedged, 'he might no dislike it, but he willnae get it.'

She inspected him, one eyebrow raised. 'Whereas you, I suppose.'

'Well – ah understaund what ye're daein at least.'

She didn't take the bait. 'Dean's okay. Why're you so down on him?'

It came to him that he wouldn't have minded China's eyes being bruised, for her to be in trouble – nothing serious, of course; would have liked most of all to be able to help her.

'Naw, naw, he's . . . harmless. He's jist daein his joab after aw – but that's all it is tae him, don't ye think? A joab. Now, see when ah wis teachin at the Art School' – a second's pause for her reaction, which did not come in any visible form – 'it wis ma *life*. Ah breathed, ate, slept ma work – if ah slept at aw. And suffered the consequences. Ye imagine Dean daein any ay that? Nah, he's strictly hands-off. No even a proper teacher, strictly speakin, if ye discount the ditty at the start.'

'Yet you've come back, what, three times now, and still haven't figured out how to turn up late and miss all that preamble.'

'Cunnin,' he said.

'Yeah, well. You adapt, don't you. He only has about five stock lectures anyway, they just run on repeat. Drive you mad to hear them over and over. What was it last week? Proportion? Yeah, I've heard that enough times.' In the next breath: 'So it's not true what they say, then? Those who can't, teach?'

'That's actually a misquote,' he retorted hotly, having been insulted in this underhand way before. 'It isnae *teach*, it's *criticize*. As any teacher'd tell ye.' He was growing frustrated by his drawing, which was turning out more diagram than piece of art. 'Aw – this is baws, this place. Don't ye think? We urnae engineerin students. We shouldnae be drawin bluddy . . . sprockets all night.'

China, with a mild expression, studied the car engine. 'I actually don't mind it. It's different. Like you said at the Kelvingrove that time? You have to be able to see the way things function, even if it's mechanical stuff like this. There'll be people loving these sprockets. Sprockets'll be what they signed up hoping to draw.'

He was so delighted she'd remembered a remark designed to flatter her in the first place that, in deference to China and her drawing, he shut his yap and sat quietly sketching the plane. He plotted dimly: Drink later? You and me, jist, how's about it? Aye, very good. Very – what's the word. Debonair. Going by how little money was left in the kitty, it'd more likely be a case of Hie, China, fancy joinin yours truly after fer a bottle ay ginger and hauf a Greggs bridie?

Unwilled, an apparition of Lynne doing her bloodhound impersonation bobbed up in his mind like something unflushable. Go away, he told it, and take your skelped-erse hard-done-by yearning with you. The way she'd waited for him to ask about Raymond rather than just tell him how she was feeling? That drove him up the wall. Biting her tongue, thinking that any silent suffering whatsoever ennobled her. They'd cleared the air – a screaming match often did that – but he had his doubts she'd react with sanguinity if she strolled in now and saw Angus trying, failing admittedly, to fire into China. Even if he denied it, she'd say she was disappointed, but actually she'd be furious, and for all she was unable to hide the fact, neither did she respect him enough, weirdly, to admit it.

Well, who was he to criticize? He who'd never admit he'd felt a tremor of misgiving on hearing she was visiting the ex. At the time, he'd gone into a protracted, worrying daydream: they reconcile, they decide to move in together, and that's curtains for old Angus. Later, despite his selfish relief on learning that their reunion had been a disaster, he'd reasoned that if Lynne was allowed to do that, he himself was permitted – even obliged – to try and take China out on this date or whatever.

Beside him, China gave a short irritated expostulation, tore the sheet from her notebook and folded her drawing roughly. 'Whoa, whoa,' Angus exclaimed, flapping. 'Whit ye daein?'

'Giving in.'

'Tae whit?'

'To you! To this constant tutting and sighing you're doing.' Angus opened his mouth to deny doing any such thing. 'Puffing like a grampus. You want to bunk off, let's bunk off.'

He shut his mouth. 'Serious?'

'Deadly,' she intoned – not the unequivocal enthusiasm he'd hoped for. She stuffed the folded sheet into her leather satchel, followed by the charcoal sticks she'd been using, bundled together with an elastic band round them: he could have told her they'd crumble and smudge black everything she was carrying. 'Let's do it.'

Who said persistence didn't pay off? Angus got clumsily to his feet, his legs aching in novel ways from his cautious negotiation of the icy streets. Had he been doing all that stuff she'd said, sighing and that? So transparent. He was concerned, though – and wasn't this just like the thing, to achieve moderate success then immediately start interrogating it – about what kind of person gave in so easily to such tactics.

A wincingly bright clear moon on a blue-black sky, cloudless, frounced with stars. The air sharp with winter; the smell of woodsmoke and frost. He fumbled with his cigarettes, glad that gloves had been among Lynne's gifts, and, 'Can I borrow one?' China asked.

'Borrow!' He slid a cigarette from the pack.

'Ta. And a light?'

'Where's it ye steiy?'

'Not far from here.' She didn't elaborate, nor laugh at the implied, adolescent offer to walk her home, and so Angus, keeping silent, simply continued along Dumbarton Road, his own route home, figuring China would soon enough let him know if they were going out her way.

As they turned on to Kelvin Way an ambulance went birling past them, all lights and sirens, on its way to the Western – URGENT BLOOD. China clapped her left hand to her right shoulder and murmured a superstitious invocation: '. . . hope it doesn't come for me.' She might have been right to worry, Angus having inadvertently selected probably the least passable street in Glasgow for a short cut: gnarled roots had deformed the pavement, had at points irrupted right through it, and there was ice, too, bedded deep in fissures in the warped tarmac, the whole street aglitter, a dicey proposition. He proceeded cautiously, while China went on ahead, nimble as a gazelle, in boots up to here.

Angus tossed his spent cigarette into the park grounds on their left, drew a smarting breath of unfiltered night air, wondered what she thought his plan was, wondered himself.

When they reached the main road – treeless, safer – China indicated the newsagent on the corner. Angus, who did not want to risk her seeing his eye drawn inexorably to the magazines on the top shelf, waited outside. He sparked up a second cigarette and kept an eye out, just in case, for Lynne's green windcheater. No people, however, on Bank Street, and precious few places for them to go anyway: a defunct laundromat, a shuttered shop front that had once been a bookshop. He let his mouth hang open so smoke spilled slowly into the frozen air. What businesses might replace these, as gentrification hit Bank Street? A champagne bar? A shop dealing exclusively in pens made from the quills of ecologically farmed porcupines?

A commotion behind him: he turned and saw, through the newsagent's glass door, that China had barged into the shelves and was scrabbling to prevent magazines plummeting like shot birds to the floor. He was contemplating heading in to help when a voice piped up from his side. 'Eh, pal? Pal. Penny for the guy?'

A boy, aged maybe nine or ten, was standing beside him. At his side, nearly as tall as he was, stood the upended cardboard box from a DVD player; a sky-blue felt jacket, its nap worn bald, was draped over the box's uppermost corners. 'Jesus Christ, whaur'd you spring fae?'

'Gonnae gies a pound fir the guy?'

'Hie, it wis a penny a second ago.'

'C'moan, gies sumhin.' The lad, with ivory hair and dun-coloured eyes, looked scarcely more robust than his creation. 'Be a pal.'

Angus shook his head, expelled a column of smoke. 'Wee man, no meanin tae be funny, but that is the single worst effort at a Guy Fawkes dummy ah've seen in all ma puff. It's shockin.' As China exited the newsagent, Angus dropped his finished cigarette to the ground, scrubbed the dowt underfoot. 'Couldn't ye've tied a balloon tae it or sumhin? Thing disnae even huv a heid.'

'Aw, don't,' China chided – chuckling, though, enjoying herself, so what was he going to do but pursue what made her laugh?

'A paper plate wi a face drawn oan even?' The boy's chin still jutted out at an aggressive angle, but his eyes had gone round with affront. Angus chapped his fingers against the sad offering. 'This is constructive criticism, wee man. Take it fae wan who knows, this is no way tae make money oot ay folk.'

The boy's shoulders straightened. 'Fuck you, pal.' He scooped up the guy and went staggering off along Bank Street, leaning backwards to hold the box to his chest, its sorry jacket hanging halfway off, dragging along the dirty ground.

'Charmin,' Angus called after him. 'Kids, eh?' he marvelled to China. 'Ivver see the like?'

'Too right.' She wiped her nose on her forefinger. 'You'd have thought I'd raised him better than that.' Angus stared at her, until she prompted him, not the barest smile on her face: 'Joking?'

'Oh, aye, right. Funny. Well done.'

They turned left and started up the hill towards the university, and soon found themselves going against the tide of students tottering homewards after an evening's cramming. Rucksacks, clumsy rollies, iPads, backpacks weighed down with textbooks; Angus didn't miss being among their sort every day. China ripped the cellophane from her Lucky Strikes and let the wrapper drop. 'Here, take one.'

'Christ, you were serious.' One cigarette was extended from the middle of the packet – slightly confrontational, Angus felt. 'It was a gift, ye ken? A gift?'

'I just don't like being beholden to anyone. Is that okay?'

He snorted. 'Beholden. Fine, whatever makes ye happy.' On the evidence thus far, China seemed no likelier to exhibit happiness than an Easter Island statue might. He took the proffered smoke and tucked it behind his lug. 'Ah don't huv tae be watchin the number ay sentences we say tae one another, do ah?'

Up the hill, along a high-walled alley that skirted the library and overlooked Ashton Lane's festive lights and alcopop two-for-ones, then led back down towards the fine hostelries of Byres Road. China must have seen his expression because, mis-interpreting it totally, she asked: 'So, do you want to, like, take me for a drink?'

'Oh God, no. Ah mean, aye, obviously ah do, but that wisnae the only reason ah wantit ye tae come wi me . . .'

'Okay, that's . . . Yeah. That's cleared that right up.'

'Dinnae get me wrang, it's jist it might be better if we dinnae huv a drink – better fer me, that is.' China didn't react. Angus faltered – usually folk didn't need it spelled out. 'But you, ah mean, you can huv anyhin ye like.'

A change occurred in China's expression – understanding dawning with tectonic slowness – and then, casual as anything, even considerate, she said: 'Well, shall we go to the Ristretto instead?'

Angus had long eyed with scorn those who spurned McCa-lls in favour of the try-hard café on the facing corner – whose signage peed you off before you even entered by declaring it not a café but a coffee shop, a distinction he found the height of pretension. Well, here he was giving in, joining the enemy. Though now, warily scanning McCalls, he spotted the words SALOON BAR graven on the pub's frosted windows, which was pretty pretentious too when you thought about it; misleading as well, implying something significantly more salubrious than the reality.

The Ristretto was stuck in a post-war time warp, faithfully recreating a mod era that to Angus's mind wasn't Glasgow at all. Northern soul on the PA, vintage poster prints on the walls. In the front window, a vintage Vespa was parked, as if having stopped in on its way to the Transport Museum. To Angus, the groups and couples jawing over their teas and coffees gave off an unmistakably smug air: *we* don't drink beer, not like those hoi polloi across the way.

139

He let China go ahead in the queue. When it was his turn to order, he didn't know what to ask for – what was he, one of those no-experience-necessary folk he'd once laughed at the idea of? – so simply parroted what China had ordered, something called a bowl latte. He murmured the order, had to repeat himself when his request coincided with a great screeching release of super-heated steam from the coffee machine, in whose chrome sheen he could see his worried face distortedly reflected. 'Full milk or half 'n' half?' the girl asked, and Angus, experiencing a brief vision of a maid milking Damien Hirst's heifer sawn in two, made a muttered request for full.

'Be a devil,' China twitted him.

They took seats by the window. Angus scraped at the tab-letop with his thumbnail, unable to tell whether the circular marks patterning it were rings left by coffee cups immemorial, or a print designed to seem that way. 'So,' he said, then couldn't come up with anything to add. He wondered how China and he must look to strangers: the world's oddest first date. A pro-independence sticker had been gummed to the table edge and he started digging at it with his nail. 'Is this somewhere ye like tae . . . hing oot . . . often?'

'I guess. I'm slightly obsessed with the retro thing. No one in the fifties knew they were going to be retro one day, did they?' He had a worrying feeling she might not be asking rhetorically.

Their drinks came in a vessel more cauldron than cup. The first sip wasn't bad, though the stuff bore scant resemblance to coffee as Angus knew it, which was black, brutally strong, and customarily administered as an emetic to individuals who'd overdone it, in an attempt to sober them the fuck up before wives, parents or offspring could see them. With his second mouthful he set about parsing the mouthfeel: warm rather than hot, sweetish but strangely salt too, and viscous – like blood! he thought wildly: he was sooking on a bowlful of blood.

China must have seen his expression. 'Don't you like it?'

'Very . . . substantial,' he said weakly, setting down the bowl.

'I was just thinking, no offence, but doesn't you being a teacher make you overqualified for these classes? Don't you find them a bit primitive?'

This was not a direction Angus was keen for the conversation to take. 'Ah could say the same fer you, eh. Show's yir picture again?' She made a face, but retrieved her sketch from her satchel anyway. 'Aye, ye've somethin gaun on there right enough – compared to the auld coffin-dodgers jist takin the class tae steiy oot the cauld.'

'You almost had it there. That was almost a compliment.' She contemplated her picture, the brawn she'd given the engine, its pugilist lines. 'Well, I'm definitely better at this than some other things I've tried to draw – for the time being, anyway. I swear there's a connection not wired properly in my brain. One week I'll be getting the hang of whatever technique I've been shown, but next time I'll have completely lost it. Same pattern for years now, week in, week out.' She swept her hair off her forehead, an oddly vain movement that undermined her plangent words.

'Years? Ah thought ye said ye'd only been goin jist a month or so.'

'Oh, that was just to Dean's classes. I took a break over the summer and then I came back again.'

'But how? Ah mean, why keep comin to these same classes that long? Ye think ye're gonnae learn anyhin new now?'

'Imagine what Dean'd do if I left now,' she drawled, not answering the question. 'His face when I came back after summer? I reckon he'd top himself if I abandoned him' – then fell about laughing, or as near as she was able, a cold, staccato ha-ha-ha. 'Adored by Dean, resented by the fogies – I'd say it just about balances out, wouldn't you?' Angus, feeling unexpected empathy for the tutor, object of so much disdain, did not respond. 'I signed up for life drawing first of all. And I was good, if I do say so myself, when I started at least – but by the end I was noticeably less competent, that's what they said, at producing a likeness of a living person, and there's only so many times you can blame the model for being ugly.' Rattling this out, proud of her failings. Over-caffeinated or nerve-ridden? Angus couldn't tell. 'So I swapped. Painted landscapes instead. They gave me an easel and a little plastic tray of watercolours, and off I went with them to "places of outstanding natural beauty". And the same thing happened again. By the end I was drawing trees that were more like bodies stretched on racks. When I tried to paint Culzean Castle it was like you could see it being ransacked and falling to ruin right there on the canvas as I went.'

'Disnae sound so bad.' Angus pictured beautiful devastations. 'Who'd want tae be on the production line, anyweiy, turnin oot stuff identical tae evrydy else's? See some of them? They're jist copyin actual existin paintings each week. Ah mean, why even bother?'

'I tried to do a beautiful sunset on Loch Lomond and it came out like a chemical spill had caught light on the water.' She set about tugging each finger on her left hand until the knuckles popped. '*I* wouldn't be a teacher,' she remarked, with the young person's aggravating assumption that every avenue in life would remain open to her indefinitely. The young were tiring, they'd never be told. 'Having to try and dream up kind things to tell no-hopers like me. Not in a fit.'

'Neither'd ah. No any mair. This class, but. Ah've seen yir pictures and they're guid. *You*'re guid. There ye go, there's yir compliment, honestly offered.' As China set to work on her right hand: 'Ye know ye'll gie yirsel arthritis ye keep daein that.'

'Early days,' she said, ignoring the medical advice. 'Come back to me in a few weeks, I guarantee I'll have reached my usual nadir. My taxidermy animals'll look stillborn. This' – she tapped her fingernail on her drawing – 'will have rusted on the page. I don't mind. In a way, now that I know it's going to happen, it's become the point. I destroy all the pictures after-wards anyway.'

He was, despite his earlier keenness, starting to lose patience with her. 'Quite the wee Metzgerite, urn't ye, China?'

'No, because I'm not designing the work to decompose, or to unmake itself. It just happens.' She gave no sign she was pleased to catch him out in his name-dropping. 'It's a young person's project, I suppose. Ecological thinking taken to extremes.'

Despite her quips, her goth-with-means clothing, she was older than she pretended – too old for this nihilist schtick. Angus didn't mind a pessimist but couldn't be fashed with anyone behaving more smugly negative. He would lay bets that on her bedside table sat at least one volume of Nietzsche, at least one of Bret Easton Ellis. Much more bettable: odds against Angus's ever being in a position to verify this first hand.

'So why keep oan, then? If you feel yir efforts're doomed?'

She took her phone out and began flicking through it, her thin shoulders curved inwards as if in anticipation of a blow. Her fingertips tapped, twitched, slithered on the device's screen. 'I wanted to ask you something.'

'Oh aye?'

'My father was an artist, you see. Amateur. Still is, for all I know. We didn't know him, growing up.' Apprehension came off her in heat lines.

'No even his name?'

'My mother doesn't like to talk about him. All I've got of him is a painting from a catalogue, which she'd cut the margin off – so no, I didn't have his name. But I . . . Well. I know it's stupid,' she said, miserably, 'but it's just something I've thought about, ever since I found out I could draw too. That it might mean something.'

'So you go tae these classes in case yir auld man turns up one night? Haud oan – did you think *ah* wis . . . ?'

'I didn't think it was *you*. I mean, I didn't know. It's like, I feel I'll know at once if I ever do meet him – you know, my hair'll stand on end. I know,' she said again, 'how stupid it sounds. Here.' She turned the phone around to show him, surprising him in an attempt to unobtrusively pick his nose. 'You can . . .' moving her fingers to stretch the image, delve into it, kindly demonstrating how to use a device she probably imagined ancient Angus considered indistinguishable from magic. 'Have you ever seen this before?'

His first response, peering at the screen, was relief. Not his *Losers*, not his *Best Company*. Not even his style: a landscape in watercolour, sunset over an empty beach, hard stones protruding in silhouette through a graduated wash of sky-reflecting sand, an idealized scene in reds and pinks and muted purples. Summer dusk at the end of the earth. 'Nup,' he said. 'No, ah huvnae.' With clumsy fingers he zoomed the picture right out and saw at its corners, photographically preserved, the multiple worn punctures where the original had been tacked and retacked to various walls. But the sad fact was he *had* seen it before, or if not this precise example, then numerous identically meticulous, pedestrian watercolours. You'd step back to admire this landscape the day you hung it on your living-room wall – doesn't the clouds' mauve match that tone in the curtains? – then never once look at it again. Some quality in it slid off the retina; even now he had a hard time focusing on it, though his top lip had pulled away from his teeth in unintended reaction. Say what you like, as an artist he'd never taken the course of least resistance. Whatever he did next, this thing bobbing at the edge of his mind, it wouldn't be *pretty* like this.

He returned her phone, smiling in embarrassment. 'Sorry, doll. That could be anebody's.'

'No worries. It was a million to one chance. I just thought . . . Whatever.' She smiled, an uncanny thing to see, and dropped her phone into her pocket. 'It doesn't matter what I thought. But you seemed like someone stuff had happened to.' He looked down over himself, feeling less hurt for himself than for Lynne: her ministrations, the money she'd spent, but the essential him still showed through. 'And then when you said you'd been a teacher . . .'

Outside, a child in a pushchair hurled a toy into the road, and they watched together as the mother bolted out into the traffic, nearly causing a pile-up, retrieving the stuffed toy just before it was swallowed up. It left Angus wondering what he habitually did seeing kids out after dark: why wasn't that wee girl home in bed by now? Two year auld at most. What sort ay parent—?

China had fallen silent. Glumness had settled down over her. He couldn't have said exactly what he'd been hoping for the evening, but it wasn't to spend time in the company of an attractive girl unanimated, as if calculatedly so, by any magnetism whatsoever, sexual or otherwise. Even if she'd been different, keen, how could he flirt with someone who'd imagined – the ultimate cock-witherer, this – he might be her long-lost father? Here was the antithesis of Lynne, who could mistake a slammed door for a declaration of love; Lynne, with her blandishments too freely offered, her gifts, her sulks, the way she sidled up close beside him, assuming proximity and intimacy were one and the same. This disparity between what you hoped somebody was and how they actually behaved was what she, too, was trying to resolve. He should be kinder to her. The flip side was that China's total disinterest in him made it seem like he might talk to her more openly than he could to Lynne. Here was a girl he had no stake in – no longer wanted to plant his stake in, ha-ha – and that meant he didn't need to care what she thought of him. How frustrated he'd been when Lynne had totally missed the point of his story about the trip to Kirkcudbright – but he'd told it seeking a particular reaction. It seemed unlikely that China here, her shoulders slumped, would admit to being shocked – would react even that strongly to anything he said. He might not just talk, then, but confess.

Remembering how China had responded to his treatment of the boy with the crappy Guy Fawkes doll, he figured that provoking her cruel laughter was one way to get her intrigued. 'Talkin ay destruction,' he said, and when she was paying attention, proceeded to tell her how he'd lost his job.

'Ah alwis imagined ah'd get back intae it eventually – the paintin, ma "career" – and the teaching'd jist be an interregnum.

Only trouble wis, ah felt nothin. Nae dazzle ay inspiration, nuhin. Ah'd sit in the studio night after night waiting for it, like a visitor ye know's on the way but not when they're due. But naebody came. And meanwhile, all these young bucks, ma students, were coming up fast from behind. Ah'd feel their breath hot on ma neck as they moved in tae overtake me. And a few werenae bad, don't get me wrang. That made it harder, in fact.'

She shifted, sat back on the chair with her left leg folded under her. 'So what did you do about it?'

'Ah tripped them up. Ah docked them marks, whenever ah could. Any pretext. Fer bein late tae class. Fer submitting their work late, and since when did an artist ivver stick tae deadlines? Ah fucked them,' he told China, whose eyebrows slowly lifted. 'Ah dinnae mean literally.' Well, in some cases literally, but that was a whole other story. 'Ah devised this elaborate secret system ay demerits, almost an art project in itself. Taking it oot on the students for ma even being in the position ay *havin* students. Ah hud this deranged notion ah wis keepin the field clear for ma glorious return. But ah nivver did make a comeback, still nivver huv. So it was aw pointless. Even then ah wis popular, at least till they sussed what ah wis up tae.'

China cawed laughingly. Absolution the Angus Rennie way: he could divulge his worst behaviours without censure, and even tell himself he was helping her by taking her mind off her hopeless quest – oh, the two destroyers, they were perfect for each other.

'Here, listen tae me rattlin oan. Let me get ye anither coffee.' He had been delighted, going through his trouser pockets earlier, to discover two tenners seemingly left over from his night at McCalls. He strongly suspected he had extorted these from Rab at dart point, and he was keen to spend the evidence. 'Ma treat, nay arguments.' He was buying himself time, sure that he had other stories he could tell against himself, worse ones: 'See when ah hud a comfy bed, a roof over ma heid and a good pal watchin oot fer me? Still ah wanted to crawl underneath St

George's Cross and kip in a bin wi all the other vagrants.' Try and tell Lynne about that, the eyeballs'd pop out her head. As for revealing his sabotage tactics, ye gods, he could see it now: how she'd chew over the confession for days then ask, white with charity, pretending this was not the very first question that had occurred to her: 'Was mine one of the careers you ruined? Did I give everything up, alter my life's whole trajectory, because you were playing some game?' What could he say to that? Which answer would she find more hurtful: the truth or the falsehood?

This time it was a young man in earnest spectacles taking orders. Angus queued up again, trying to decipher what the items printed on lit panels overhead even meant: what in the name of the wee man was a mango icebox? Rockabilly on the sound system, digitally remastered to preserve vinyl's susurrations. He was thinking about the café's painstaking simulation of a time no one here had experienced personally, and how it resembled carefully prepping a corpse for open-casket display, when the colours rushed up on him once more – burnt orange and bone, not the image itself but something like the pools of colour cast by sunlight passing through stained glass; and Angus, as in a dream of paralysis, was unable to turn his head the short distance to see what had generated the amorphous shapes, which were not, properly speaking, even shapes yet.

'Angus,' a voice said. He snarled, flailed, tried to shake off the voice. 'Angus? Are you all right?'

The colours shot away. Still in the coffee shop. He had the sense of having been, for an indeterminate span of time, somewhere else entirely. Someone was still talking at him, and he clocked this person's constituent elements – the gleam of her nose piercing, the dry wedge of snow-coloured hair – before understanding fully that this was Siri McKenzie herself, not an additional hallucination.

'Well, Christ,' he croaked, 'fancy running into you here.' Though in his confused state what he meant was: fancy my conjuring you up! He glanced at the table by the window: there sat

147

China, busy with her phone. So she hadn't metamorphosed into the other girl; they were all here together.

'What happened? I thought you were having a stroke. Your face . . .'

'No. No – ah wis in a dwam, jist.' Impatient customers insinuated themselves between him and the counter; he took a step sideways; Siri did too, a slow *pas de deux*. She was wearing a grey denim jacket, collarless, vaguely military in cut: she was a foot soldier. 'Sorry tae disappoint ye.'

'I thought Lynne said you had some drawing class on a Thursday night?'

'Usually ah do, aye. Only tonight it wis . . . it finished early.'

'And you decided,' she concluded, in the ironizing tone teenagers employed when stating simple fact, 'to come here.'

Angus, who had since their drawing lesson come to imagine them pals, wanted to tell Siri she had inspired him, however unwittingly, to – what, see colours? He stalled, struck with a primitive fear that even to admit the possibility of the new work might chase it away for ever. 'And, eh, whut brings ye here yirsel? You wan ay these . . .' He indicated the overhead light boxes' mysterious legends. 'These coffee folk?'

'I'm meeting Rose, actually. Her shift just finished.'

Oh, thought Angus, of course, why not. This is just Christmas. 'Rose is here?'

'Wasting my time if she wasn't.' She tipped her head backwards: a little behind her stood the girl who'd taken Angus's order earlier, shift finished, a black leather biker's jacket zipped over her barista's uniform. 'Rose, sweets? Don't loiter. Come and meet Angus – remember I told you about him?' As Rose approached, Siri gripped his shoulder, a reminder that she could probably ju-jitsu him into next week. Out the corner of her mouth, and none too sotto bloody voce: 'Be nice, okay?'

'Ah am nice,' he protested. 'How's naebdy ever believe that?' Demonstrating it, chivalry incarnate, he bobbed as he greeted Rose, grabbing her slim hand in his apelike own. 'Delighted tae meet ye. Delighted.' Brunette, cool-eyed, with a point of high colour on each cheek: a knockout, all told. The age difference between the girls didn't seem all that pronounced to Angus, to whom both fitted into the generic category 'young'. The resemblance was in their standard-issue lesbian undercut hair-styles, and their clothes: Rose's leathers similar in cut to Siri's military-effect jacket. For some reason, what looked natural on Rose hung on Siri like dress-up.

Jackets. Why had he been thinking about jackets earlier? Windcheaters. 'Ye're no,' he ventured, 'meetin Lynne too, ur ye?'

'God, no. Could you not tell? Things are a bit weird between us at the moment.'

'Och, that'll pass, doll, doan ye worry, jist . . . gie her time. Try not to be too hard on her,' he ventured. 'Lynne's . . . guid, ye know? She'll come roond.' Addressing Siri, he was monitoring Rose, who looked on, guileless, face dollishly blank: oddly uninvested, he felt, in Siri's problems.

Ignoring his attempt at bridge-building, Siri said dismissively: 'Anyway, we're going to see Ten Dwarves? At the QM Union? Not exactly Lynne's scene.'

'Gaun tae see . . .'

Siri said pityingly, 'It's a band?' – like he was meant to keep up with the trends.

'It's just one guy, really.' Rose, stepping forward, mistook Angus's mystification for a desire to know more. Her description involved conjoining unrelated words – eight-bit, chip-hop – and left Angus as baffled as, no doubt, she would have been had he started prattling on about armatures, contrapposto, egg tempera: terms of art meaningless to the outsider. Then she shrugged in winning self-deprecation. 'It doesn't sound much, but I find his stuff really moving. There's something so appealing about how he never lets you forget the primitive technology he's using. These ancient, clapped-out synthesizers.'

'A sortay sleight ay hand.' Something about Rose – how her eyes opened very wide as she gave this explanation – made

Angus keen to show he was keeping up, even to impress her. 'Misdirectin ye, makin ye look at wan particular hing while really there's a whole load other stuff gaun on simultaneously. Like Bacon's arrows.'

The imaginary graph you might plot to describe his regard for Rose would peak here, in the gap between his stopping talking and the look of pretty bewilderment forming on her face – the instant where he still mistakenly believed he was making a connection, that she understood what he was on about.

Too much to hope, too, that China would have remained meekly sitting at the table, waiting for him to return with their coffees. Nonetheless, he was taken aback when she stropped over, long black coat already on, and said: 'I'm leaving now, just so you know.'

'Oh, naw, don't go, ah wis jist . . . Wait, no, look, this is Siri, ma, eh, ma landlady's sortay stepdaughter, wid ye say?' First the exertion of the evening's walking and now this prolonged standing around had brought hot, slick, pulsing pain to Angus's knee, and he went to clutch a chair-back for support, free hand flattened to his spine. He was grateful for the frosted windows of McCalls: no danger of anyone from over the road seeing him in this Mexican stand-off. 'And Rose there is her—'

'The world's best barista,' Siri supplied, with odd haste. 'And my best friend.' Rose's smile waxed faintly mortified: the look of a minor celebrity accosted in public by a fan.

'And awright, ah admit it, the two ay us're skiving off our class. Gonnae no tell embdy?'

'Yeah,' China said, the one word somehow contradicting him. 'Nice coincidence us all being here at the same time. You two don't mind taking over my shift as his therapist, do you? Tell him about yourselves – really dig deep. Then wait and see – is he going to sympathize? Is he going to ask you how you feel? Hell no, he's going to muscle on in with *his* story instead. Has he told you about his students? Get him to tell you that one, how he fucked them all.'

150

Siri turned on her. '*Excuse* me?' Even Rose looked startled, then abashed.

'Aw, she disnae mean . . . China, pal, a joke's a joke . . .' In his rush to tell his misdemeanours, he hadn't anticipated that what he revealed might make China despise him. To the others, scoffing: 'Dinnae listen, she's no ma therapist or any such hing.'

'Well, no, that's true, I'm the cheap alternative. Take a girl out for a drink and just let it all spew.'

'China!' he shouted. 'Gonnae shut up a minute?'

'Yeah,' she snorted, turning to leave. 'Yeah. That'd be right. Let you get a word in edgewise.'

He had changed his mind: he'd welcome being spotted from McCalls if it meant Big Shelagh might come sprinting in right now with a tray of glasses, hot from the dishwasher, to smash over his head. He held out his hands to Siri and Rose, supplicant. 'Ah'm sorry aboot that stuff. Ignore her, she's . . . Christ, ah better go after her, try and sort this oot.'

'I dunno, Angus.' Was Siri *smirking*, the wee besom? 'That didn't sound like someone wanting you to chase her.'

'Ah'm sorry ye hud tae . . . It was so nice,' he said in panic, stumble-john, 'meetin ye, Rose. Yous two make a cute couple.'

He was surprised to see the faintest, sweetest quizzical crease deepen on Rose's brow. And Siri, smile erasing itself, turned her head with appalling slowness, slowing still, as though to forever defer meeting her friend's eye.

A hoarse bellow from the barista wiping coffee-machine steam from his glasses: 'That's two bowl lattes to stay on the bar!' Angus's coat and bag were still by the table where he and China had been sitting, and on the tabletop, between their empty cups, coins were neatly stacked – payment for the coffee he'd gone to buy her. Owe nothing to no one: it wasn't a bad philosophy. He wondered if it was too late to ask the barista for his money back. He could even make a moderate profit.

Between him and the counter stood Siri and Rose, looking deep into each other's eyes, but not with romance. Oh, but what was unfolding on Siri's face: a story of fear and hope and being caught out, a weighing up of whether to confess or devise a swift, corrective lie. He could have stood for days and watched the look's minutely evolving modulations, a work of art itself. And the slow, rich blush creeping upwards from her collar to her nape, where her cropped-clean hair had begun to shade faintly in once more.

TWELVE

Even his set-to at the Ristretto didn't prevent Angus waking energized the next morning, in the slate-grey near-dawn, laughing at something he'd been dreaming, which hadn't migrated into his waking consciousness. The soles of his feet were prickling; he knew this feeling of old. Something thrilling was drawing near. New work.

He'd chased after China as she tramped down Byres Road with the stilted gait of the person who knows she's being watched. 'Don't follow me,' she'd called over her shoulder. 'Don't you dare.' Okay then: he'd taken her at her word, though she hadn't spoken with conviction. He'd spun on his worn heel and headed for Glendower Street. What had she got so het up about? Hadn't they just been swapping darkest secrets, quite contentedly? Years of experience and he still couldn't fathom the young.

When Lynne came home that night, it was to find him hard at work over the stove. 'Guid evenin! How wis yir day? Ah'm makin supper – dinnae argue, sit, sit.' In her astonishment, Lynne complied without argument. 'Pour yirself wine. Or a beer, there's plenty mair in the fridge. Or both! Ah'm making beef bourguignon – at least ah hope ah am.' In the instant he'd taken his eye off the pot, the stew had agglutinated into one large lumpen mass. He turned the heat off and cast round for an implement to divvy it up, possibly a carving knife.

'What a treat to be cooked for,' she said when he deposited

153

a plateful in front of her. Cautiously she nibbled a lump of the stuff from the tip of her fork. 'Delicious.'

'There wis meant to be soup tae start too, only . . .' Angus indicated the open window, the blackened pan balanced on the sill. 'Ye ought tae get yir smoke alarms tested, ye know, Lynne.'

He upended a fresh can of beer into a glass, tilting both to keep the head level, nice and easy. Noticing her watching with eyebrow raised, he shrugged, still pouring. 'Thought ah might've needed it fir the stew, eh. No sense letting it go tae waste.' Neither this, nor the impossible task of applying fridge-hardened butter to a slice of supermarket pan loaf could stop him grinning like a maddy. It was making Lynne smile too. Domestic bliss.

It was a new era in their relationship, and it lasted about forty-five minutes.

Lynne scunnered it. She didn't mean to, but there it was: dabbing her mouth with a napkin – a napkin! The lengths Angus had gone to – she announced that she couldn't eat any more. 'I'm sorry, it's great, but it's so filling.' There was plenty left over, but she wasn't wrong: the stew was sitting heavy on his stomach. Worried that the sauce had seemed too watery, he'd thickened it mid cook by free-pouring flour into the mix. 'Maybe Siri'll want some. You know she's coming round?'

'Ah did not, no.' Casually, cautiously: 'Ah wis under the impression you two werenae . . .'

'Well, we weren't, I suppose, for a couple of days. But I remembered what you said about how we have to try and move forward in' – she sketched quote marks in the air – 'the "post-Raymond era".' Angus didn't believe he'd ever said any such thing. 'I have to at least try to keep things on an even keel. I invited her over to talk. You don't mind, do you?'

'Naw, naw!' He topped up his drink, effortfully steady-handed. 'Ah'll jist make masel scarce – head oot on wan ay ma walks. Leave yous two tae it.'

'You don't need to do that.'

'Och no. Now the snow's aw gone . . .'

'But you got on so well the other day. It'd be . . . I mean, I'd like you to be here.'

He contemplated worst-case scenarios. Perhaps better he stay here as peacemaker after all. Should Siri take it upon herself to tell Lynne that she'd seen him and China at the Ristretto, he could explain what had happened – paint China as a local simpleton who'd attached herself to him – before Siri could put her own interpretation on the situation. There was also the fact that both times he'd met the girl before had coincided with his getting a sense of his next work. He told himself it was trite superstition. No matter. He couldn't pass up the chance to get more of a fix on the scale, the subject, of what he would do next.

Half eight, and rockets going off outside the living-room window: they shrieked sizzling across the black sky; burst, in petulant silence, into trailing stars; or, the ones Angus had never liked, up they hurtled with a deflating squall then – wait for it, wait for it – exploded lightlessly, firelessly, in a howitzer crack that came from nowhere and everywhere at once, loud enough to rive the night.

In blew Siri, like nuclear winter. She had boosted her height with platform trainers, but seemed unaccustomed to walking on three inches of cushioned sole and staggered like a wet foal to the table. Angus, meek, offered her some dinner. She grunted a refusal. 'How've ye been anyway?' he croaked. Siri turned her baleful gaze on him and didn't speak. He started feeling just the faintest misgiving.

'Answer Angus, then,' Lynne prompted – kind, decent, oblivious Lynne; couldn't she see Siri had a face on like a bulldog chewing a wasp?

'Can't we just get on with it? Get the gloating over with? That's what I've been summoned for, I take it.'

'Hey, now,' Angus protested. 'Dinnae be mad at Lynne. If ye've an issue with anyone, Siri, doll, it's wi me, only me.'

There was still a puzzled smile on Lynne's face. 'What's going on?' Someone else's life flashed before Angus's eyes: a good and generous someone who life was about to seize up and dash against a rock like an unwanted bairn.

'Ask *him*.' Then, without pause, she turned on Angus. 'You fucked it, you stupid drunk dick. You ruined everything.'

Angus waggled his hands in the air, desperate to stop Siri talking. 'Hey, hey, there's no need fer that. Let's get our facts straight a minute, ah wisnae *drunk*. And what precisely did ah ruin?'

'You know what Rose said to me? "I like you, just not like that." This is like the smartest, most articulate person I've ever met, and that's all she could think to say. So, you know, well done.'

'You mean you werenae gaun oot? But Lynne said—'

'Course she did. She put you up to it, I bet. Like that girl said, what, you just happen to be in the Ristretto on a Thursday night? I bet you were back here like a shot last night to tell Lynne the good news, that the plan had worked, you'd managed to humiliate me. In front of your *friend*, too. Or, no, she wasn't your friend, was she? Your therapist, she said. Or was she one of your students too? Another one you fucked?'

'Ya wee clype,' he cried, horrified. 'Ah nivver breathed a word about seein you and Rose, not one bluddy word.'

Lynne's face had fallen in on itself like a failed cake, but her voice kept steady. 'Siri, listen to me. He's telling you the truth. This is the first I've heard of this – any of this. All I told Angus about this girl was what Raymond told me. I didn't mean to drive a wedge.'

'Oh. Oh, well, that's okay, then, if you didn't mean to. I bet you're still pleased you did, though. Never mind this is someone I care about, never mind what I feel.'

'That's a horrible thing to say. Of course I'm not happy.'

Lynne was managing to stay brisk and no-nonsense. Angus, fearful, thought he understood now what she'd said about fights like this making her feel properly maternal towards Siri. 'Are you all right? Please just tell me what happened. Was it—'

'I don't want to talk about it. She's made it perfectly clear she doesn't want me hanging around her. Cramping her style.'

'Then she isn't a real friend,' Lynne suggested.

The sky clapped white. Fireworks popped and popped, feather bursts of soft stars drifting windwards over the rooftops of the tenements opposite. 'What the hell,' said Siri, 'would you know about friendship or anything else?'

'Siri, lovey, listen. You're seventeen. I know – I remember – how intensely you *feel* at that age. How thrilling it is when things are going well, and how devastating when they're not. But Siri, you've your whole life ahead of you. You'll meet someone new – lots of new people. Rose just wasn't the right one.' Siri's face was blotchy and the whites of her eyes had turned ruddy, but she was quiet – seemed to be taking Lynne's words to heart. Angus started to feel less tense, until, with a look of swinish cunning, Lynne added: 'You've experimented, you've tried this thing, and it didn't work out. So now you can get on with the rest of your life.'

Holy shit, Angus thought. He wondered if they'd notice if he dropped down off his chair and crawled under the table – the old duck-and-cover.

'You mean now this phase of mine has come to an end,' Siri suggested pleasantly.

'Well, no, that's not what I said.'

'No, no, I get it. So I take it that since Dad's dumped you, you might start going out with women? I mean, that was a phase too, and now that it's come to an end, I guess you're going to start from scratch again? Because that's basically what you're saying. That's basically your argument.'

'What I'm saying, if you'll listen, is exactly what you said to

157

me when I was going to see your father. About how blind we can be to other people's faults – the things that are obvious to everyone but us. Isn't that what you said to me before? That I might be too stupid not to let your father walk all over me when I next saw him?'

'What are you, Lynne, some sort of . . . misery vampire? You've failed to achieve happiness in your own life, and now you're deriving pleasure from other people's unhappiness as well.'

'Don't compare my life with yours. That's not what this is about.' But Angus thought it was, almost broke cover by thanking Siri for daring to say to Lynne something he'd felt but failed to formulate, or flunked putting into words.

'Go on, then – prove to me you were more committed to Dad than I was to Rose.'

Outrage made Lynne's squawk an octave higher than normal. 'Of course I was committed.'

'No, I said prove it. Just look at this place – all the time you were together, you had your bolt hole to flee back to, in case things didn't work out. How's that for refusing to commit?'

'Glendower Street is *mine*,' she howled. 'I've worked so hard for this place. I've slaved. I can't believe this – don't you remember begging me to let you stay when you and Raymond were fighting? And now you're . . . bollocking me.' Siri had the decency to look abashed. 'It's nothing to do with your father. I couldn't afford to give it up. You don't understand. I'd have lost so much—'

'So it's about money? Gosh, Lynne, that's principled. Wow.'

'Please will you stop turning everything I say on its head? Okay, listen – say I had sold, moved in with Raymond. Where would I be now? We're all on thin ice, Siri, all the time. One bad decision and I could have ended up on the street.' She gestured helplessly at Angus. 'Like *him*!'

I am surrounded, Angus thought, in the sense of besieged, by smart women. As Siri thumped ungainly towards the doorway, he retreated from the table until his back was against the kitchen wall. He had the feeling that, were he to push a little harder, the fragile plasterboard might give way, letting him take refuge in the bathroom.

'That's it, Lynne, I'm going. I hope you're happy to have got all this stuff off your chest. Honestly, though, I doubt it. I doubt you ever will be.'

After Siri had left, Angus and Lynne took their accustomed seats at opposite ends of the kitchen table. Siri had ruined, by one thoughtless mention of China, the ideal Lynne had hugged close for so long – that she alone could heal Angus, regenerate him, have him fall into her arms. In the manner of anyone in a crisis for which he was partly responsible, he found himself regretting, far too late, not having been straight with her from the start.

Lynne fiddled with the salt and pepper shakers at the middle of the table, and he, unable to dream up any panacea to rectify the situation, waited with dread for the tone she'd take. Resentful, cringing, furious; it wasn't going to be good.

'What's her name, this girl?' The fight had hoarsened Lynne's voice, and the words came out strangely staccato – a wooden doll that had just learned to speak.

'China,' he mumbled, feeling an obscure desire to invent a pseudonym for her.

'What an interesting name.'

Angus struck the table edge hard. 'Aw, don't gies it.'

'I don't know what you mean. Or is it a nickname? Fragile, is she?'

'Ye know fine well what ah mean. Play the innocent,' he muttered, shaking his head. 'This is gonnae turn intae yir usual passive-aggressive guff, and ah'm no staunin fer it, okay? Ah went oot wi sumdy fir coffee. And no, she isnae ma therapist either, so ye can forget that angle. Ah've nuhin tae be ashamed of.'

'Of course not.' Lynne drew a breath he fancied he could hear go cold as it entered her mouth. 'I just think it's funny that this is how you repay me.'

'Coffee,' he repeated, with frosty emphasis, 'wi a pal.'

'Contrary to what seems to be everyone's opinion, I do have a brain in my head. Feelings, too, if you hadn't noticed. I gave up a lot for Siri, not that she'd thank me. And now you—'

'Feelins,' he scoffed. 'Ye mean prejudices. Lynnie, one thing ah *have* noticed—'

'Lynne! My name,' she nearly screamed, 'is Lynne.'

'All right, *Lynne*. Sit down, doll,' as, disgusted, she started to get up, 'this may come as a shock to ye. See when ye're confronted wi sumhin disnae suit ye? Sumhin ye dinnae like? Ye never seem tae consider altering yir attitudes, jist bulldoze blindly oan. Achieve yir aims by way ay sheer bloody-minded persistence. Try and make things ye don't like jist – disappear.'

She went silent. You're doing it right now, he wanted to cry out. Then, 'I took you into my home,' she croaked. Oh, that he might live without ever hearing that again!

'Aye, took me in's right.'

'I dressed you, fed you—'

'So an act ay charity,' he leapt in, 'is just a way to make yirsel feel good? A donation tae the karma fund? Lynne, listen, let me reassure ye, you are gonnae be rich, rich, rich in the next life.'

She stood. 'My God!' It burst from her, a real scream. 'I can't do this any more. I was stupid to think I could.'

The wind picked up; rain, startled, slapped against the window. 'Christ, Lynne.' He recalled his resolution at the Ristretto: be kinder to her. With an effort, he moderated his tone. 'You saw what nick ah wis in, that day on Sauchiehall Street. How much longer d'ye think ah'd huv managed unaided? That wis jist *days*'d done that tae me.' Expecting her to break in at any moment that now was their chance to find out, and kick him out. Of course she didn't. 'Ah am . . . profoundly grateful. Every time ah pass by Kelvingrove Park ah nivver fail tae think whaur ah might be without ye, and ah give thanks. Okay, mibbe ah should huv thanked ye directly once in a while. But – and ah do mean this kindly – ah cannae give ye whit ye're after. You know that. You've alwis known that, just willnae admit it.' Her face was morose, cowish – and despite everything, she *still hoped*, Christ's sake, you could see it in her eyes, unwilling to believe that this wasn't just a test of her selflessness. He dropped his voice. 'Admit it tae me now, darlin.'

She drew a deep breath. 'What I'll admit,' she cried, and though her shoulders rose as she tried to rile herself up again, he could hear right away that her heart wasn't in another tantrum, 'is that it's made it damned easy for you. It's given you all kinds of licence, knowing how I feel, knowing I'd never . . . say anything. Try and push things.'

'Ye nivver needed tae *say* anyhin,' he protested. 'Ye think ah huvnae got eyes in ma heid? What you call not pushin things isnae how the rest ay mankind would describe it. Christ, do ye think ye've *nuance*?'

'I can't help it. It's what I feel. It's who I am. I'm not like you, I'm not able to just pretend.'

'Pretend whit? Who's pretendin? Ah nivver led you oan. Let me state categorically. Ah nivver said anyhin ye could misinterpret. This is all you.'

'Yes. No. I know. But you've been careful not to rock the boat, or set me right. Go on, deny it – if it was up to you, I'd never have heard about this girl from your class, I bet.' Her eyes went wide as a thought struck her. 'There *were* classes, weren't there?'

'Of course there were classes. My God, Lynne, listen to yirsel – in fact, no, ye know whit, listen tae me instead. Let me spell this out for ye. *Not – interestit*. There, okay? *Nivver – gonnae – happen.* Ah'm no tryin to fight it, life is not one constant furious struggle tae repress ma base desires, and ah dinnae go tae ma bed nights and crack wan aff thinkin of ye.'

In a tiny voice she said, 'You don't need to be crude.'

'Ye think no? Right, look – here's me literally haudin up ma hauns. Ah'm sorry ye're upset.'

'No, you can't do that – insult me, then pretend it's my fault I'm offended.'

Angus, exasperated: 'Ah love it, aw these rules ye set me, nippin ma heid. "Dinnae say this, dinnae do that, ah'm so innocent and unworldly ye'll make ma hair curl if ye so much as swear. Don't dare go treating this gaff as yir ain, ye're here oan my sufferance and dinnae forget it. Oh, but if ye do happen tae go oot – which ye will, by the way, any time ah demand it – ah'll need full details on whaur ye go, who ye're with, et cetera." *You*, Lynne, cannae dae *that*. Attach conditions tae yir charity, it isnae charity any mair. And sometimes it frightens me, the way ye act.' He stopped, worried that this last statement might, in a weird way, flatter her: you still have power, even if it's only the power to scare.

Her face had gone pale and still. At last she spoke. 'Is there anything you'd like to add?'

He laughed, incredulous. Here was a tactician's trick, allowing him to exhaust his rant, then, when he was spent, challenging him to begin it all over again. He remained unconvinced Lynne was half the innocent she pretended. 'Nup. No, ah think that just aboot covers everyhin.'

'Well, thank you,' she said finally.

'Christ, Lynne – can ye no—'

'No, no, don't say anything more. You've been very thorough.'

She stared out past him, through the scrim of rain streaming down the kitchen window, through the frail screen of bare tree limbs, through the windows of the tenement facing on, into those other kitchens, where other people were living their anonymous, warm-blooded, oblivious lives – going about them so easily. In the tiny twitches of her jaw, mechanically clenching and loosening, he thought one moment he could discern resignation, the next, fresh resolve.

In Angus's experience, a big blowout of a stramash like this was often followed by a period of strained and excessive politeness. The thing was not to let the fight get forgotten, absorbed into the goings-on of their lives, and to that end he gave a great sigh and asked, 'So, whut we gonnae dae now?'

To his surprise, Lynne had an answer ready. 'Did you mean what you said to Siri last week? About your plan being to get a place of your own?'

'Aye. That wis the plan awright.'

'Then we need to think,' she said, and had no difficulty saying it, 'about finding another place else for you to be.'

Call his bluff; fine, he'd call hers right back. 'Ah think that might be for the best.'

She stared at him with those big round appealing dolly eyes, but he was resolute: he wouldn't plead and he wouldn't apologize. As far as he was concerned, they could each go to their graves convinced they were right. This was the trouble: they'd been complacent. From the day they met, their relationship had been so skewed and unhealthy that neither of them had ever imagined the situation getting so fucked it couldn't be salvaged. Still, he wondered exactly how either of them would be able to back down from this ultimatum without starting the whole damn merry-go-round trundling again.

'The waitin lists for cooncil flats, but. Ye any idea? Seven, eight, nine year if ye're no disabled, if ye're ay . . . sound mind,' he concluded, risking a smile.

She wasn't looking anyway. She had reached into the cupboard over the sink and was turning mugs upright, checking inside each one first to ensure it was clean. He had the sense she was already putting things back how they'd been before she'd taken him in – how they would be again once he'd gone. Fresh skin growing over a healing wound. The other day he'd noticed that her old artwork had disappeared from the wall above the telephone, replaced by a framed photograph of some forested Swiss valley which might have been the original she'd once worked from. 'Just leave it with me.'

'Ah could alwis try makin masel a mair suitable candidate

163

so ah could jump the line,' he suggested. 'Hack off a limb or sumhin.'

Lynne turned to him, a mug in each hand, looking ready to smash them together. She didn't laugh. Indeed she seemed, for a while, to be taking the suggestion quite seriously.

THIRTEEN

A big fuck-off unfriendly city, this, in many regards, but at other times it felt like just a small town with ideas above its station. Angus was not, therefore, altogether surprised, as he waited beneath the arches of Central Station for Lynne to park nearby, to spot Cairry-Oot Aidan entering the Arundel office party. A cracking bird on his arm, as well, the sly so-and-so: one of those ladies impressed by the silent type, Angus presumed. The others entering comprised a glum set of Lynne's more or less antipathetic workmates, filing like doomed animals into one of the arches and down a brick staircase towards the unhinted-at catacombs underground.

On the tracks overhead, with a shattering roar, a train accelerated south out of Glasgow, shaking down fat droplets of brackish condensation from the tunnel roof.

What people forgot about the phrase 'the least you could do' was how it tended to lead to doing a lot more than you actually wanted to do. When he'd agreed to accompany Lynne to what she had described as just an office party, Angus had anticipated something low-key at the St Vincent Street offices – 5 p.m. kick-off, couple of boxes of supermarket wine, paper hats, a chance to act on the year's pent-up resentments and crushes. You'd see snogging, you'd see fighting, you'd be home by ten. It was his fault for not asking, but he resented her withholding the information that this was an actual night out.

In his back pocket, his newly reactivated mobile phone

quivered. He assumed this'd be Lynne saying she still couldn't park and he should go on in alone – a suggestion he would disregard – so he was surprised to see Cobbsy's name come up on the screen. Still sending out APBs about likely easy touches to everyone in his address book? When the little electronic envelope opened, all the message said was: 'Hear about Bobby?'

The only Bobby Angus knew was Bobby Imison, the gay kid who Cobbsy'd once introduced him to, who'd come to Glasgow hoping to find a sugar daddy, or whatever they were called. Bit daft, but harmless – he wondered what the boy might have done that called for one of Cobbsy's messages. He texted back: 'Heard what?'

Lynne turned up as he was sending the message. 'Everything all right?'

'Oh, aye, uh-huh. Think so.'

'Shall we go in?'

The party was taking place in a section of disused tunnel deep beneath the railway station, converted into a nightclub for folk who didn't mind a curved roof so low over your head you could touch it without stretching. Poor Arundel folk, going from one lightless underground location to the next. The air smelled of mildew; there was the tang of brick dust too, as though the chamber had been very freshly excavated. For the party, it had been filled with superannuated office furniture – old chairs and desks topped with unwired computer screens. Seamily illuminating one end of the arch, an antediluvian photocopier lay open as an invitation to anyone stotious enough to hop up and scan their underwear, or worse. The sound system was playing what seemed to be music composed for kitchen cutlery, over which a robot-tuned voice gabbled at a pitch no human being had ever reached, and two individuals were reeling about in a strobe light's twickering green cone. Angus checked his phone. Hardly seven o'clock and dancing already: a worrying sign. Noticing him watching them, the pair in the strobe paused and turned to face him. They were suited and booted, but in the flickering he glimpsed inhuman countenances: one wore a clown's sinister gurn, the other had the head of a donkey. Masks, just masks, but for a moment his heart froze in real misgiving, and he wondered what underworld Lynne had brought him to.

'Fuck is aw this?' he asked Lynne.

'This is the reason you're lucky you've never had to work in an office. It was Struan Peters's idea to have all these computers and things.' She indicated, standing by the neon-topped bar, the strawy-haired cunt from Arundel, who was conferring with a short, rotund wifey old enough to be his mother.

'Awright, now ah get it – theme ay the office pairty is "the office pairty". That's . . . postmodern.' Still difficult to say the word, despite two decades' practice, without his lip involuntarily curling.

The guy must have realized they'd been talking about him, because he suddenly turned and bellowed across the space, 'Awright, Lynne! 'Mon over tae the dance flair, show's yir moves.' No chance of his seeing Lynne's minute, forced smile of response at that distance: Angus could hardly make it out, and he was standing right beside her.

She was dressed to the – to the sevens, let's say – in a sleeveless top of gold-tinted fabric seemingly designed by NASA to be worn in space: fancy for her, almost a disguise. She had put in a hairband and worked it forward so that her hair, backcombed, rose over her forehead in a springy coxcomb. Angus, meantime, had allowed himself to be compressed into smart clothes, even a tie. Not his style at all: he felt that at any moment the buttons might start pinging off the shirt, the fabric rupture as the real him, the unwashed animal, the werewolf, long repressed, burst forth.

Lynne was frowning. 'You must have to get permissions to do a place up like this, don't you think? Certificates?'

'Lynne! Wheesht. Gonnae stop bein so practical aw the time. Let folk enjoy their enforced fun.'

The place was filling up around them – he spotted the beardie from the office, then the G-string wearer, who was strutting about, obviously inviting compliments on her new hairdo. Side-swept fringe gelled flat at the front, the back of her head sprayed up in a rigid chrysanthemum: did she and all the other plus-size ladies dedicated to the style not realize it was the exact same worn by neds and teenybopper pooves as well?

'The way ah see it,' Angus said, smacking his palms together, 'there's basically wan way and wan way only we kin make the best ay this situation.'

'And what's that?'

He grinned, daring her to be appalled. 'Get hammered.'

A term Lynne had encountered in one of the science books Siri had pressed on her kept recurring to her: punctuated equilibrium. Some scientists thought that evolution proceeded not smoothly but in hops and starts – that life forms that had gone about their business unchanged for centuries suddenly took an apparently spontaneous evolutionary forward leap, as if, bored or demented by their current way of life, they had decided en masse to try something new. Though Lynne suspected she might be projecting.

In the week since Siri's visit, she and Angus had circled one another like cats. She'd set her alarm a few minutes earlier than usual to ensure she'd leave the flat each morning well before he woke; Angus had contrived either to be out in the evenings, or to shut himself in his room before she got home from work, staying in there all evening, never emerging, making no sound. She tried not to worry what he was doing. Dosing himself with sleeping tablets? Drinking beer all night, urinating in the empty bottles? When they did encounter one another, they conversed civilly. Funny how they could coexist so easily now, maintaining a dual pretence: that she didn't want to evict him any more than he wanted to escape her.

She would have liked not to care. She could easily ask, too, now that they seemed to converse exclusively within quote

168

marks: when you take care to make everything you say sound facetious, you can get away with the most heartfelt questioning. 'Not drinking yourself to death, are you?' 'Nup. And yirsel? No wastin away wi loneliness, ur ye?' 'Goodness, no.' Sweetly smiling all the while.

He'd even learned to tidy up after himself. No more dishes piled by the sink; she felt like joking that they should have got that fight out the way much sooner.

The woman Struan had been speaking to was working the room, interrupting conversations as she went. She was made shorter by stooped posture, and her expression was a little wild. Lynne didn't know her, though she rather coveted her dark-red tank top, and she watched as the woman barged in on one knot of guests, then the next. People seemed nettled at first, then she spoke to them for a while and they broke into smiles, peering at one another in delight. What could she be saying? She had the obnoxious manner, discernible even from afar, that Lynne associated with the charity workers who obstructed her route to work every other morning. She thrilled for a moment to the appalling idea that, to spite her, Angus might have invited China – but surely this creature couldn't be her? Angus, on his way back from the bar, walked past her without a flicker.

He returned with his hands behind his back and a mischievous expression. 'Ah've an important question for ye, doll. Could be a life-changer, so dinnae rush it.' He revealed his hands, each holding an identical bottle. 'Alcopop or alcopop? Red or blue? And before ye ask, that is literally all that's on offer. Free bluddy bar, ah thought ma luck wis in.'

'Red it is.' The liquid – she couldn't quite consider it a drink – glowed in the bottle like a cartoonist's idea of toxic waste. She sipped; it was like swallowing a whole packet of sherbet in one go, sour-sweet, throat-scaldingly sugary. 'Goodness. Goodness me, that's . . .'

Angus drained half his bottle in a single draught, wiped his hand across his mouth. 'No exactly the nectar ay the gods.'

'No, but I know what I can use to top up my car battery if it's gone flat later.'

The strange woman had moved on to talk to Donna from Maintenance and her seldom-seen boyfriend, described by Donna as working in hospitality but who Lynne had, she was sure, seen stacking broken-up wine crates outside an off-licence on Byres Road some mornings. The stranger was one of these unfortunate women prone to adult acne: her jawline lumpy in the greenish lights. She was rudely made up, mascara clumped in her lashes, and much younger than she had first seemed.

'You didn't invite your friend along tonight, did you?' She had to shout to be heard above the music.

'China, ye mean?' Intermittent disco light bloated his face one moment, left it haggard the next. A belch travelled up his throat – she could see it – and he held it in his mouth before letting the breath out slowly. 'Ah did not, no. Christ no. No exactly the hot ticket, is it? No offence. Anyweiy, like ah said, she wis barely even sumdy ah could call a friend. Ah mean, that stuff she said tae Siri . . .' He shook his head.

'I'm sorry,' Lynne screamed, yet again, 'for what she said.' Each time, she meant this to open a conversation in which the apology could be expanded to include herself; but each time, she was too cowardly to manage it, and the same misbegotten blame-shifting crawled out instead, maggot-like, unwanted. But it took two to apologize, and Angus deflected this attempt as he had all her previous efforts:

'Ach, that's awright, doll, ye urnae answerable fer her. She prolly thought she wis watchin out for ye – proof yis raised her well, widn't ye say?' Lynne grew vexed. Was she implicated, then, in Siri's bad behaviour too?

'What about your classes? Will you go back?'

'What'd be the point? Amateur hour at the Glesga galleries, exactly as ah said it wid be. Christ.' Angus gulped another burp, made an apologetic face, raised the empty bottle to inspect. 'It starts gaun down a touch easier after a while, eh? That's deeply worryin.' He took a couple of steps towards the bar, and Lynne followed. 'Get ye anither?'

'Oh, Angus, I don't know if that's—'

'Wise?' he mocked. 'In ma best interest? Och, lighten up.' He was smiling raffishly. 'Check the label. Two per cent proof! Yir tapwatter's mair alcoholic than that.'

'Fine.' She followed him, fretting. Their truce was based not just on mutual deception but on mutual contempt. 'But can we have something different next time? It's making my teeth feel weird.'

'Did ye no hear me, darlin? That's yir lot, red or blue. You urnae gonnae find yir New Zealand chardonnay here, put it that way. Your party organizer must've cocked up – or else he actually likes drinkin this weans' stuff. Me, ah'm startin tae get a taste.' To the bartender: 'Eh, two ay each, please, pal? By the way,' he said to Lynne, wanting, she was sure, to twist the knife, 'talkin' ay ma interests, ah'm makin guid progrees investigatin' where tae go next.'

He handed her a fresh bottle, the remaining three clamped by the necks in a fist held chest-high, inviting comment, she was sure. Surreptitiously, she turned the bottle until she could see the label: four per cent proof. Why would he lie about something so easily verified? She looked at him, his white face, and didn't say anything, just thought about how soon this, he, would be someone else's problem, and wondered how that made her feel.

'Angus, why don't you stay? I mean it. At least until after Christmas. What will I be doing anyway? Sitting in with Radio 3 on, eating turkey sandwiches from the supermarket.' Facetious though she made this sound, it was exactly what she feared she'd be doing. She anticipated the obvious rejoinder: should have thought about that before, shouldn't you?

A slow smile worked into his mouth, and he shook his head. 'Ah cannae steiy at yours ony mair. It isnae even *you*, Lynne. Sumhin's . . . ah dunno. It's haudin me back.'

171

'From what?'

At this point, the strange woman blundered into him, causing him to spill one of his bottles, Lynne mildly surprised not to see it rotting an immediate hole in the concrete floor. When Angus rounded on her, she let out a stream of disjointed not-quite-words, 'Sh . . . ch . . .', through her teeth. She was drunk, or unwell, and Lynne was about to offer to help when the woman's sibilants focused into words. 'A drag,' she was saying, 'a pain.' She pronounced it *pine*, and it dawned on Lynne that this was an attempt at a cockney accent. 'You guys should overthrow me – take me out into that alleyway behind the office, a shot to the head, gangland-style. Put me out of everyone's misery.'

Angus's face was stuck in the same curious rictus as Lynne's own. Taking their silence for encouragement, the bewigged woman – you could see now that the hair wasn't real – continued, in her mangled Estuarine: 'No more of my bullying. No more catty comments. You don't need to force me, I'll go willingly. I don't want to be your boss any more. I hate you all, and you all hate me.' Lynne only got it when the woman put a finger round the crucifix chain on her neck and tugged it upwards like a hangman's noose. They were parodying *her*, the boss from hell: a reflection conjured up by pooled bad will, the grotesque her juniors saw in her brought to shambling, vulgar, self-pitying life.

'I *want*,' her impersonator insisted, looking from Lynne to Angus, 'to die.'

Seeing Lynne incapable of mustering a response, Angus emerged from his trance. He bent at the waist, brought his face close to the impersonator's and said, in a low and dangerous tone: 'Go – *away*.' And the woman, taking no offence, simply pulled a face, shrugged, and limped off, muttering to herself once more, towards the next guests.

Silent for a moment, then both started babbling at once.

'That was—'

'Ah know. But who—'

172

'Why did she say I *want* to die?'

'A joke, darlin, a nasty, nasty . . . Jist try and forget it.'

They drew breath.

'Ye ken who's responsible, don't ye, Lynne? That wee runt—'

'Struan. With the blond hair, and the—'

'The attitude, aye.'

'We can't be sure,' she said, agreeing. 'How can we prove it?'

'By, ah dunno, lookin at him? Wi oor eyes? Lynne, did ah no tell ye ah've incredible powers ay observation?' He swigged from his drink, coughed, wiped his mouth. 'Ye no see them conniving thegither when we came in?'

'It's not enough,' she said miserably. 'I can't haul him up in front of everyone. He'd just deny it. Or say I'd misunderstood, that I was being paranoid – or humourless. People will forgive almost anything except a lack of humour. Somebody who lacks *fun*.' She shook her head. 'What authority would I have left come Monday morning?'

'What authority huv ye now, if this is the kind ay thing folk think's appropriate? You,' he said, 'need a new bluddy job.'

'A new job.' She thought again of those evolving animals hauling themselves in fits and starts through the fossil record. 'A new life.'

'These fuckers dinnae respect ye, Lynne. Ah'm sorry, but they don't. That . . . wummin, whatever she is, got that right, surely. It's not like you actually enjoy workin there, is it? Sorry tae break it to ye, but there isnae a reward for puttin yirsel through things ye hate. Life's too short. Ah mean, ah've hud mortgages and that in ma time, and ah know ye've got tae dae what ye must for money.' Was this – was he giving her a row? 'But huv ye considered findin a joab that isnae sae . . .'

'Evil?'

Angus, thoughtfully, embarking on his last drink: 'Stressful, ah wis gonnae say, but evil'll cover it right enough.'

'Of course I have. It's not as easy as just deciding to leave and going.'

'How no?'

One song failed to merge into the next, indistinguishable one, and in the brief silence, over derisory hoots, Lynne heard bellowed laughter. She turned to see Faraz, hands on his knees, bent double in hysterics while Lynne's impersonator wobbled and curtseyed, grinning cockeyed at him, face halfway between lascivious and demented. 'You know, actually, you're right. Okay, first thing Monday morning I'll start uploading my CV. I can't carry on at Arundel. I should go round them all now, tell them they've won.'

Angus's face had grown oddly rigid. He looked round at the dance floor, where dry ice was skooshing from jets at ground level, dancers moving ghostlike in the haar as the music, the sonic torture, resumed – then thumped the empty bottle down on a desk and yanked his tie knot away from his neck. 'Get in the next roond for us, Lynne, eh? Something ah've got tae go and dae.'

As he lumbered off, Lynne took the smallest sip possible from the saccharine stuff in the bottle – it felt like it was corroding her throat on the way down – and tried to think calmly and realistically about the consequences of handing in her notice. Already it was mid November, and she knew nothing important got done at this time of year. Come January, head office would be busy with all the admin from the previous year-end; it would likely be February before anybody in HR looked with any seriousness at her resignation letter. Even then there'd be the three months' notice still to serve. The resolve that had been swelling up in her reached its apogee and began to subside. The mortgage on Glendower Street was nearly paid off. She had been so careful – so sensible. Why give it all up now?

There was something else. She liked to believe she was someone who didn't quit, quitting being to admit weakness: but she had given up at art school, hadn't she? If only Angus had said at the time that she had talent. The sad thing, though, was that when she imagined what the Lynne who'd persevered with that course might be like by now, years on, all she could bring to mind was an identical copy of herself. What it comes down to, she told herself, is that you don't have the guts to walk out of this job.

It was oddly warming, this self-torture, such a reliable way to make herself miserable – so much so that Lynne only became aware of the altercation unfolding nearby when people started to scream.

This dayglo gloop in the bottles, give it credit: piss-weak, yet Angus, having ingested it in sufficient quantities, could feel it working on him – seething in his blood, blue-glowing. Urgent need to piss. But when he saw Struan jiving away beside the photocopier, next to Lynne's impersonator, he altered course and made straight for the runt. 'Hie, you. Baw-jaws.'

The wide wee bastard pretended not to recognize him. 'What you want?'

'How's about an apology tae Lynne fer starters, fat boy? Aboot tonight, and that stuff ye pinned up on the lavvy door aboot her.' To the impersonator woman: 'Take a hike, sweet cheeks.'

'You.' Struan looked him up and down. 'You were at the office.'

'Ah wis, aye. Ah *saw.*'

'Whit are ye then, Lynne's boyfriend? Her bodyguard? She's got anyhing tae say tae me, she kin say it hersel.'

Angus prodded him hard in the shoulder with a finger. 'Ye go through me, fat boy.' He wasn't even particularly fat, a little plump was all, but Angus didn't feel he could back down on the nickname now. 'Jist go on over there and apologize nicely, and mibbe then ah'll let ye walk away.' Struan didn't move, and Angus, swaying, uncertain how to escalate, could only repeat, 'Ah mean now, pally. You know ye've been makin her life miserable, and that stops right here.'

'Aw, come aff it. Her life's already a misery. Mardy fuckin mare. Thinks jist cos she goat promoted she's better'n the rest ay us. Thinks—'

175

Struan didn't have a chance to say what else Lynne thought, because Angus barrelled into him then, dropping to come in low, as in a rugby tackle, his wrecked leg protesting. His shoulder struck and sank into Struan's pulpy body, and the impact, the surprise at least, threw the short-arse off his feet, Angus grabbing his arm to spin him about and stop him falling. Lynne whirled across his vision: she wasn't even looking. What was the point in defending someone's honour when they didn't pay attention? Then Struan's fist got him beneath the ribs, provoking a childhood blurt of pain, 'Ah-yah!' and a retaliatory jab to the blond's chin, shocking back up to Angus's elbow. A shriek nearby – Lynne now? Angus lucid enough to feel this a bit of an overreaction – and as he and Struan tussled, slapping and grabbing, weirdly silent themselves, a stray elbow or hand struck the copier, which began to document the fight, its light beam rolling over them.

Struan's clenched fist clouted him once, twice on the right ear. He tried to lift the guy off his feet, felt his back spasm, dropped the effort. Pages wheezed into the photocopier's out-tray: a forearm, a murky profile, a hand flattened on the glass like a mollusc. Struan's podgy hand came up, tried to yank at his beard, but Angus lurched away, managing at the same time to crook his arm round Struan's neck. As he was trying to wrest his opponent's face round into the photocopier's scrolling glare to blind him he felt his arms seized, and he was swung by his own momentum around and away from the fight. A voice came in close by his lughole, through the bloodrush: 'Angus. Gonnae cool it, chief?' He was almost delighted to recognize Cairry-Oot Aidan's still-courteous baritone. Who else should intervene but the guy who spent every other night neutralizing rowdy drunks?

Short-breathed, drookit with sweat, Angus let himself be held, exaggerated his grunting and struggling somewhat to disguise the fact that his attempt to batter Struan had been a disaster. Over Aidan's shoulder he again saw Lynne, aghast now. He wanted to set her right: don't go acting so appalled by what ye think ah'm capable of; be appalled by the fact that it seems ah amnae capable ay anyhin.

Into Struan's flushed face wriggled the beginnings of a sneer, a rodenty triumph. Angus relaxed, and when he felt Aidan's grip slacken, he sprang forward and drove his forehead hard into the middle of Struan's face – seeming to hear Lynne's yelp even before the blow connected. A monumental crack and Angus reeled back, dazzled, hands flying to his own face. Conventional wisdom stated that, done right, a headbutt shouldn't hurt the instigator at all, which suggested he hadn't done it entirely correctly. Blood flew like sparks. He was aware of turmoil around him, but it was inaudible through the blazing brass roar in his ears.

And then it came upon him once more: the luminous non-colour standing out on a field dawning from black to infernal red. Why not? Who else's fault but Siri's that he'd been guilted into accompanying Lynne tonight? Struan had fallen, his hands pressed to his face, and people were ignoring Angus in their rush to help him; Angus, standing over his enemy, felt nothing but slow wonder as a bead of blood slipped from his nose and broke on the concrete floor. White light from the still-running copier swept across the archway, its beams and supports, and through his pain and the clearing colour, Angus recognized what he was seeing – his picture, his new work, staring him in his broken face.

FOURTEEN

'I'll sue,' Struan threatened.

'Don't be absurd.' Lynne hesitated. 'On what grounds?'

'Wrongful dismissal.' He folded his arms emphatically, like that was an end to it.

'That's just . . . something you've heard on television.'

It was Friday. Lynne, Struan and Scott Flint, the HR manager who'd driven down specially from head office in Aberdeen, were in the conference room, which had last been used to host a leaving do. A foil banner that read WE'LL MISS YOU was still strung across one wall, flaring gently beneath the air vent; Lynne couldn't for the life of her remember whose party it had been. Flint had shut the Venetian blinds on the internal windows, screening them from the office floor, then dragged a seat into one corner, where he sat making notes on a yellow notepad, leaving Lynne and Struan to face one another across the conference table.

'Yir pal Angus, he's for it an aw.' Struan raised a hand to the great patch of bruise that spread around the bridge of his nose, now buckled and puffy – a domino mask of empurpled skin. 'Ah'm speakin tae the polis. Grievous bodily fuckin—'

'Please don't swear, Struan. We all deeply regret what happened at the weekend, but that isn't anything to do with why we're – I'm – talking to you today.' Oh, lies, lies. Under the desk, she was tearing a worn paper handkerchief into ever smaller fibres.

178

On Sunday, Angus had, after much prevaricating, described to her what he insisted on calling the 'work' in the gents' toilet – first this, he explained, hand to the half-moon bruise on his own forehead, then that horrible impersonator at the party, was the reason for the assault. He'd done it for her sake. Lynne said she wished he'd just spoken to her instead; his taking retribution into his own hands like that had made the situation seem like a private dispute between the two men, from which she, the true wounded party, after all, had been excluded.

'Ye cannae fire sumdy out the blue one Friday eftirnoon,' Struan told her condescendingly, 'jist cos ye dinnae get oan with them. Ye've hud it in fer me since that promotion ay yirs. It's alwis me,' he averred, swivelling in his chair to appeal to Scott Flint, 'she'll call out for no answerin the phone quick enough. Any excuse tae have a go. Who didnae clean up the cups in the kitchen, Christ's sake.'

He wasn't mistaken, that was the worst thing. She'd disliked him on sight – his stupid frosted hair, his cheap shiny suits – and rarely kept it hidden. Worse yet, she'd failed him too: a manager was meant to treat her charges evenly. As the HR man nodded, wrote it all down in his pad, Lynne had a horrid intimation that he might take Struan's side, that this inquiry might all at once turn against her. She might hate working here, but that didn't mean she wanted to be forced to leave. She laid a hand on the buff-coloured folder on the desk before her, a gesture Struan saw and did not misinterpret.

'Be reasonable,' he changed, looking to Scott. 'Ah've alwis met ma targets, which ye must admit's impressive given this company's frankly diabolical way ay dealin wi its clients. And ye cannae hold me responsible for that.' Scott's expression remained mild – almost disinterested. 'Maybe ah'm no the maist eloquent oan the phone, but she'll tell ye ah've nivver wance said a bad hing tae a caller. Ye record all they calls, mind?'

'Yes,' said Lynne, 'I've heard the tapes.' She had not heard the tapes. 'But I'm not talking about how many customers hang

179

up on you – even though you sometimes seem more concerned about winning on that scoreboard in the kitchen than in doing your job properly. It's about your attitude.'

'Look, we all know this joab's gash. None ay us's daein it out ay love. This might come as a surprise tae ye, Lynne, but workin in a call centre disnae represent the pinnacle ay ma ambitions in life, even if it dis yir ain. And so ah try tae have a little fun, so what? *Fun*,' he sneered, 'if that's a concept ye kin grasp? A wee bit banter. Jist trying tae relieve the cripplin boredom ay workin here.'

Here was Lynne's moment. 'All right, then. Let's talk about fun.' Willing her eyes to go colourless, neutral, and her hands not to shake, she opened the folder and withdrew from it the diorama of doctored page-three girls. She unfolded it like a map, looking over it briefly to show she could, before sliding it across the tabletop to Struan. She wanted to see his face change colour until it matched the redness round his eyes, which of course it did not, since that would have meant admitting he felt even the slightest shame. 'Why don't you explain, then,' she asked stiffly, 'how this particular display fits into that category?'

She had intended to come in early on Monday and take the thing down before her colleagues could see her, but in the end, due to an alarm clock she'd failed to set properly – a Freudian slip – and a delay on the Underground, she'd ended up getting into the office well after nine. Plan B: devil-may-care, with everyone watching, she'd rapped twice smartly on the gents' door, waited a beat, then stepped inside. As she'd stood in the warm, fetid gloom, so distinctly different from the ladies', listening to the snigger of a recalcitrant cistern refilling, she had experienced a feeling like satiation. Partly it was the sense of trespass, partly it came from imagining what the others might be saying outside about her – but mostly it was because she knew, even before she saw the pin-ups stuck to the stall door just as Angus had described, that Struan was finished.

But Struan didn't seem to grasp that. Inspecting the images, he stayed silent, toying with the YES SCOTLAND lanyard round his neck, to which she'd turned a blind eye rather than quoting workplace dress regulations. Calculating, maybe? Or maybe he thought that if he remained still and silent long enough, Lynne and the HR man might, like hunters frustrated, simply lose interest and move on.

'Struan,' Flint said, voice soft, 'we're going to let you tell your side. If you've anything to say in your defence, now's the time to talk.'

'You cannae prove ah'd anyhin tae dae wi that . . . whatever it is,' he said at last. 'What about Faraz? Donna? Ah take it ye'll be hauling all thaim in as well? Interrogating thaim an aw?'

Flint's eyelids flickered. 'I already spoke to your co-workers, Struan.' This was his masterstroke: he'd started to describe to Lynne before the meeting how he intended to claim that the others had already pinned responsibility on Struan, so that— She'd cut him short; she knew all about the prisoner's dilemma. But surely Struan would see Flint's eyes shifting, as Lynne did, and realize it was a lie. 'They all said the same thing. That's why you're the only one in here.'

'Is it fuck.' He addressed this complaint solely to Lynne – Scott Flint, a nobody from head office, seemingly undeserving of acknowledgement. 'Yous're stitchin me up here.'

He drew a breath, and Lynne, uninterested in whatever grandstanding he was going to attempt, found herself entranced by the single fibrous black hair that seemed to have sprouted from Struan's left nostril in the time they'd been talking – questingly, like an insect's proboscis, vibrating when he inhaled. When she tuned back in, he was mid spiel: a mixture of appeal and attempt to shift blame on to others, even Lynne herself. The quaver in his voice was as good as an admission of guilt, an invitation to punishment. 'Mebbe if we hud a better workplace environment – if there wisnae jist this unending conveyor belt ay targets and deadlines, the same routine day in, day oot, makin folk plead wi us—'

181

Lynne thought: *enough* of this.

'Struan,' she cut in. 'You may have a point. But the fact remains, you chose to make things harder for other people – for *me* – to work here than it might already be. Before I go any further, we should thank you for the contribution you've made at Arundel over the past two years.' What his contribution had been was to help Lynne realize it wasn't necessary to believe anything you came out with, or even *act* like you did – just deliver the appropriate rote-learned speech at the apposite juncture. She drew herself up, though the urge she felt was the opposite – to slouch down in her chair, cackle, let the inebriated feeling swamp her. She foresaw a future, and it chilled her, in which she had come to relish the speeches. The hollow platitudes. 'We wish you luck in finding employment elsewhere. But your contract here is terminated, with immediate effect.' The death sentences.

Showstoppers of sunsets you got this time of year: tangerine and ice blue, acid greens, a luminous red sun standing cold and near-static in the sky for hours on end. Braw colours, but useless for Angus's purposes. In George Square, street sweepers were collecting up the previous night's detritus, using stiff-bristled brushes to scrape disintegrating paper off the sodden red tarmac, retrieving cans and wrappers from the meltwater-pooled cenotaph and between the paws of the two stone lions that guarded the city chambers. Before it vanished into the maw of a dustcart, Angus glimpsed a mud-besmirched leaflet with the CND symbol printed on it, which made him feel a brief nostalgia, imagining what his da might have asked, bemused, upon seeing it: they still daein that?

Cobbsy had received his *Big Issue* seller's accreditation and a stack of magazines. 'The hoops ye huv tae jump through,' he marvelled, grabbing Angus's hand and making a botched attempt to turn the handshake into something Masonic. He indicated the red gilet he had on. 'Six month I wis tryin tae get

182

one ay these.' Banter ensued – comical remarks that centred mostly on the yellow-blue bruise on Angus's forehead – but it was like trying to hold a conversation with the parent of a new baby: Cobbsy was forever breaking off to step forward, shrink-wrapped magazine brandished before him, to declaim: 'Help this guy find a place for the night, gie it a read, you'll find it's awright – *Thaa Biig Ishhoooo-ahh!*' Angus didn't know, but he speculated the company must vet people for the public-facing positions: 'You're too obviously skaggy. And you look too down in the mouth – folk'll think you're a lost cause. Ah, but you, Cobbsy, big man, you've the kind of face we're looking for – the approachable homeless. Out there and do us proud.' Nevertheless, the passers-by defied him, intent instead on mobile phones, smokes, chewing gum.

'Ye no wantin tae sit doon a while, Cobbsy?'

'One ay the rules ay the joab, eh, no sittin aroond. Looks lazy. Gaun yirsel, but. *Big Issue*, madam? Sir? Naw? God bless yis anyweiy.' Angus couldn't fathom how his pal tholed the rejection.

Angus took a pew on the nearest bench, planting his carrier bag between his feet. Cobbsy eyeballed the bag but said nothing. Angus knew you never asked what the homeless were carrying around; the answer would only upset you. In fact he'd come straight from the art store on Queen Street, a place he'd sworn never to set foot in, and the bag contained a starter set of acrylics, half a dozen hog-hair brushes, a few other odds and sods he'd spanked the remainder of his money on. Dilettante's equipment, as if by pretending to be a novice he might ambush art itself while its back was turned, so to speak.

With a month until Christmas, half the square was cordoned off for the winter carnival. Behind low walls patrolled by over-zealous security guards stood a half-height helter-skelter; a gently undulating thing that failed on the most basic levels to qualify as a roller coaster; a whirligig in the form of a big, sappy-faced purple octopus. Angus watched this last as it gathered speed, lifting and lowering its thick plastic arms, drawing delighted screams from weans in accelerating orbits.

'So ah got yir texts aboot Bobby,' he said, when Cobbsy returned. 'Poor basturt. Is he—'

'Went tae see him yesterday, aye. Intensive care it wis – a room ay his ain, not that he'd know it. Christ, man. Like a fuckin piece ay meat. His chest gaun up and doon's the wan sign ay life, and even that's a respirator daein the work, no him.'

'Whit happened exactly?'

Cobbsy swung his head from side to side. 'Got his heid kicked in, eh.' Funny to put it that way, passive, as if no one but Bobby himself had been responsible.

'Aye, but how?'

'I doan know, dae I?' Cobbsy grew defensive. 'Bobby certainly isnae tellin. For sure he hadnae anyhin on him worth stealin.' He rubbed a finger under his nose, trying to pretend, Angus felt, he wasn't frightened. You looked out for one another on the street, but that didn't bar stuff like this from happening, and when it did, you didn't dwell on all the things you'd done to help folk – only grew skeery it would be you it happened to next. 'Mebbe sumdy jist didnae like the look of him. Followed the wrang guy doon the darkened alley. Or wan ay they what's-it, they motiveless crimes mebbe?'

'Nae luck, poor fucker.'

'It's his folks I've been thinkin about,' Cobbsy confessed. 'How they'll feel when they find oot – if they even do.' Everyone knew the story: it had been the first thing Bobby said about himself, challenging folk to take his parents' side, though he never seemed placated by the universal condemnation: fancy kicking your bairn out the hoose just because he likes it up the jacksy! The boy had held it out like a calling card: in the three weeks Angus had been on the streets, he had heard Bobby's story maybe three, four times. He couldn't move on from his misfortune – he revelled in it.

'Bein fed nutrients through a tube up his you-know-whit.

184

Lookin like a fuckin . . . sea urchin, by the way, aw these tubes comin and gaun in and oot ay him. Felt heart-sorry for the wee bugger, so I did.' Cobbsy shook his head. 'I should hae done sumhin before. I dunno. Bin a bit mair kinder.'

And of course folk tired of hearing the story; of course he'd start getting snide remarks, the disapproval he'd been courting, whether he knew it or not. No street smarts, that was Bobby's problem: hanging out near business hotels, bragging any time he got taken to dinner or given gifts. That this would go badly for him eventually had seemed almost inevitable.

'Ye know ye couldnae have protected him,' Angus ventured. 'Ye're alwis helpin folk oot anyway, yir texts an that. But some-times . . . sometimes—' He faltered, and Cobbsy was straight in interrupting, clearly had not been looking for himself.

'So I'm sitting there wonderin whether I should be talking to Bobby or whit, feeling a bit stupit like, when this nurse come in tae check his charts – and that's a laugh, I'll tell ye. Belter ay a ridheid, six foot zero in her fuckin Crocs, man, in proportion an aw, bendin right doon over him – see the view if he'd opened his eyes that minute?' Cheered by his own story, Cobbsy attempted a gesture to describe the girl's physique, but was hampered by his stack of magazines. 'Wasted oan Bobby, naturally, but see if it'd bin me lying there in a coma, that'd've got me sittin bolt upright quick enough, know what I'm sayin, *that* leanin over me . . .'

'Eh, ye were sayin – his charts?'

'Oh aye. Well, see, one minute she's liftin an eyelid tae shine a torch in, next she's got out these instruments – stickin stuff intae the soles ay his feet an that. Ah wis like, "Whut's that ye're daein?" "We check Mr Imison every day to see if there's been any change in his condition." Ah'm like, "Show's that chart a minute?" And ye ken whit they call it?'

'Dae ah luik like a doctor?'

'Get this – checkin each day tae see how he measures up on the Glasgow Coma Scale.'

Angus shook his head, whistled. 'Who's like us? Christ. Oor ain national measure ay unresponsiveness. And folk wonder if the country'd cope bein made independent.'

'No joke, pal – how comatose are ye, on a scale ay wan tae fifteen? Kin ye feel yir brain, or no? And Bobby's scoring, like, a seven or an eight, at the minute, right bang in the middle, and so what ye wonder is, dis that mean his cup's hauf full or hauf empty? His eyes dinnae open when ye poke him.' He jabbed Angus in the ribs. 'Believe me, I tried. And then – then they test his speech.'

'Guy's in a fuckin coma. What're they expectin, a chorus ay *Jesus Christ Superstar*?' Surprised himself with that one – evidently he had spent too long in the company of Lynne's record collection.

'Naw, naw, there's a whole, like, fuckin list. No just kin he speak or no – which Bobby obviously cannae. But if all he can come out wi's . . . incomprehensible sounds.' They kept their heads – Cobbsy solemn but his eyes darting to Angus, daring him to break – until he added, in a strained squeal, 'Inappropriate words.'

'Like whit?' Angus got out with an effort. Incredulous, his voice like air escaping a balloon. 'Wakin up, call one ay the nurses "cuntybaws"?'

' "Gonnae gies ma morphine, Sister, ya fanny!" '

The guffawing sent pigeons up in flight all round the square.

'Och,' Cobbsy said, recovering, speaking with empty optimism, 'prolly be back on his feet quicker'n ye can say knife. Back oot daein his thing – scuse me a second.' He stepped forward to intercept the next wave of arrivals from Queen Street station as they made their way diagonally through the square towards the Merchant City. Angus was left glumly pondering Bobby's prospects, his *thing*. Unconscious or cracking on to random strangers in the hope of scraping through to another day: neither exactly ideal.

'How ye manage to keep yir spirits up?' he asked, when his

186

pal returned. 'Stoap yirsel chuckin yir magazines in a bin and fuckin off?'

'It's work,' Cobbsy said simply. 'I nivver wanted *not* tae work. Why fuck it up?'

'But when they jist storm past ye like ye dinnae exist . . .'

'Got other things on their minds jist, that's what I tell masel. They're no in the right frame ay mind this time, but mibbe things'll be different next time they go by. A potential customer today,' Cobbsy explained, clearly reciting his employer's script, 'will be a potential customer again the morra. Some people'll always want tae help us, even if they doan know how tae go about it.' He coughed hard. 'Talkin ay which, heard ye'd found a place tae stay.'

Angus bit his lip. No point denying it, but the old cautiousness made him play it down. 'Thinkin ay movin oan soon, but.'

That wasn't entirely true – at least, he wasn't the one thinking it. Two mornings ago, he'd got up to find a stack of brochures on the kitchen table, one of Lynne's signature long-winded notes – a dissertation, a justification – clipped to the uppermost magazine. Angus didn't need to read it; the photo on the cover told him everything. Here were sanctuaries for those unable to cope with the world, with themselves. You had to give Lynne credit for not backing down. Since their showdown at the weekend, he'd honestly been expecting one of the customary reparations – a gift more suited to that other, better Angus she wanted him to be. Climbing boots, maybe, or a cravat. He'd accept the inappropriate gift with good grace, and there would be an end to it. Instead, she'd left him these magazines with their staged photographs of happy people strolling the hypersaturated gardens of former mansions the state had taken over and divvied up into units for, what, the sick, the insane, the unliveable-with.

The kitchen had been looking bonny, all gilded with winter sunshine, but seemed already to be diminished in his eyes, Glendower Street packing itself away, withdrawing from him. But as Lynne was so fond of pointing out, Angus had never asked her to take him in, and like hell, he'd sworn, sweeping the brochures on to the floor, was he going to let her force him out.

Cobbsy was smirking with superior knowledge. 'Six-week rule, was it, aye?'

'Whit?'

'We're no like thaim.' Cobbsy lowered his voice, nodded scowling at the folk mobbing past through the square, heads filled with shopping, Friday-night drinks with the girls, trains to catch, real places to be. 'We've seen through aw the bullshit. We've seen stuff they don't know about, wouldnae believe ye if ye described it to thaim. We know whit goes oan round they dark alleyways, whit's happenin beneath their feet, underpinnin it aw. We see a city their eyes jist skip over, oblivious. Seen that, ye cannae unsee it again, Angus, ye know what I'm saying?'

'Us who've rent the veil,' Angus suggested.

'Every so often sumdy feels they kin help, and by helping, help thirsels. We warp the place, disturb their lives too much. Ye cannae just shove a hawk in wi doves, know what I mean? They can put us up all right but they cannae *accommodate* us. And in ma experience six weeks is about as lang as any ay thaim can stand tae put up wi us.'

Angus laughed curtly, howked a gob of phlegm to the ground to show what he thought of Cobbsy's theory. 'Mibbe ah should go tae see these *Big Issue* folk an aw, see if they'll gie me whatever the fuck you've been smoking.' He mocked, but he was counting on his fingers nonetheless: right enough, it'd be six weeks come Sunday since Lynne'd borne down on him on Sauchiehall Street, all fluster and favour. He glowered at Cobbsy, feeling obscurely as if his friend had gulled him. 'How'd ye hear about me findin a place, anyway?'

'Well I heard it fae Wullie, and he heard it affay sumdy in a pub somewhere, so he says. Oh, wait here a minute . . .'

Who else but Wullie, Angus was thinking as Cobbsy went off again. Says nothing, sees everything; one unshod foot in the barflies' territory, another in the homeless's, a barefoot envoy

188

between worlds. Preternatural sensitivity to all around you: where'd that come on the Glasgow Coma Scale? Like you'd woken from darkness and just carried on, scoring fifteen, sixteen, seventeen, kept on gaining consciousness, insight, couldn't stop waking up.

'Mightn't be the worst idea,' Cobbsy mused when his tour around George Square brought him back close to Angus. He toted the magazines in his hand. 'Speakin tae these guys, ah mean. Earn some readies, get a roof over yir heid – no bad, actually, this time. This big hotel wis meant to open up doon by Central, only the purchase fell through, so noo they've shoved aw us poor basturts in there till they find another buyer. Tryin tae lower the value ay the joint, no doubt.'

'Lots ay it about. Money there tae tear the place doon, no so much for rebuildin it.'

'Ah'm in a suite,' Cobbsy said proudly. 'Nae telly, nae sofa, shower disnae work, bare as all fuck, but a suite. Ye credit it?'

On Glendower Street, the gleaming towers on the hoardings round the old schoolyard seemed more science-fictional than ever. COMING SOON! And when you looked through the railings you saw just a quarry, nothing whatsoever coming soon. He'd spent Thursday evening, this week as last, sitting on the dyke wall, part hidden by one such hoarding, waiting for the light in Lynne's window to go out so he could sneak into the flat and avoid having to lie about going to his classes. Come the witching hour, as he watched the boiler steam cascading down the tenement sides in the gathering cold, he'd heard an unearthly grunting and coughing from the schoolyard ruins – a gang of fox cubs play-fighting, nipping each other's ears, gambolling amid the broken concrete slabs, chasing through thickets of braided steel that had once helped hold together whole buildings.

He watched Cobbsy entreat the crowd: 'Gie it a wee try, ye'll find it's awright . . .' What did he get in return? Talk about incomprehensible sounds: a shamed phoneme, a mumble that might've been 'Sorry'; often nothing at all, not even eye contact;

occasionally a 'No thank you', either po-faced – what could *you* possibly have that *I* might want? – or apologetic; occasionally outlandishly chirpy: No, ta, content to be complicit in denying you the bare minimum standard of life. Maybe one in a dozen said yes, smiled, paid up, had a blether. He was making a go of it – Cobbsy, who Angus, perennially scornful of the good-natured, had thought was basically doomed, his consideration for others likely to get him exploited. The kind who'd become involved in something bad because he was too guileless to say no, who'd end up like wee Bobby, passed out in Intensive Care, his head staved in, unresponsive on a scale of one to fifteen.

When rain started to spit, Cobbsy drew up his hood, then favoured Angus with a brilliant smile. The tiniest luxury. As the rain stung his ears, Angus tried to imagine himself in Cobbsy's place, could not, realized he actively feared the idea.

Undeterred by the rain, another batch of youngsters was wailing as the octopus swinger trundled into life. A safe peril, likely none of these tots worrying, as Angus did watching them, about a connection working loose, a bolt coming away, your helpless body being flung off into the void. Lynne, God love her, must have wondered, each time he blundered in the door, what nick he'd be in this time: drunk, crabbit, fresh from dropping anchor in some bird whose existence he'd then proceed to deny. What role for her this time: confessor, counsellor, victim? Never the one she wanted. It would never stop, he knew that now. Her two conjoined, paradoxical hopes would remain undimmed, no matter how long he stayed in Glendower Street: half of her wishing he would stride in one day, seize her up in his arms and cover her face in kisses; the other half praying she'd be able to cope if it actually happened – that it wouldn't scare her half to death.

Untenable, that was the word. His position was untenable, in the sense that he could no longer be Lynne's tenant – could no longer, unlike the bairns birling round faster and faster on the fair rides, screaming with delight because they knew nothing could go wrong, just keep holding on.

* * *

Scott Flint had worked on in the conference room all afternoon. It had given Lynne the fear. Was she about to be called in? Dismissed too? She carried on working, and at six o'clock, after everyone else had left for the weekend, he emerged and insisted on giving her a lift home. Relief made her overly grateful – all that had been visible through the light wells all afternoon had been brownish rainwater coursing down the hill outside, inches deep, from which you might extrapolate the whole city underwater.

He'd claimed to know Glasgow, but picked an odd route home, and near Garnethill they became enmired in traffic. He put the heating on full blast and turned the radio to a classical station. Rain hammered against the windscreen, too dense for the wipers to clear. It struck the road and bounced back into the headlights' beam.

'You did well back there,' Scott said over the music, as they waited for the traffic to move.

'Oh, no, you helped.' Instantly she corrected herself, afraid that this sounded high-handed. 'You did the hard bits.'

'It was like a good cop, bad cop thing we had going, wasn't it? I hadn't planned it that way, had you?'

There had, to Lynne's surprise and relief, been no scene: Struan had gone out into the office, where an anticipatory silence had fallen, and after retrieving his jacket and backpack, he simply walked out, leaving his computer terminal on, a mug of tea cooling half finished on his desk. On his phone console, three lights blinking: three disenfranchised clients stuck listening to muzak as they awaited an answer that wouldn't come.

'I was always going to be the villain. You could have said anything. I just can't believe he's gone.' She stretched out her legs, turned up her toes and felt her tendons stretch. Hot air in the footwell. 'My heart's still hammering.' The earlier pleasurable feeling stole over her again – the obverse, she now realized, of the dread being at work normally gave her – when she pictured

191

the ground giving way beneath Struan's feet. 'It never occurred to me I could just fire somebody like that.'

Scott smiled, a little uncomfortably. 'Well, yes. Of course. But I'd prefer you didn't make a habit of it.'

'I feel like the door to the cage has been left open and I don't know whether to fly free or not.' She supposed this wasn't the way a colleague should speak to a colleague, but she had such a high-wire feeling that no admission seemed too frank. Or maybe she was sugar-crashing? She'd been trembling so badly after Struan's departure that as Donna was taking orders for the Friday-afternoon sweets run, Lynne had for the first time ever timorously requested a packet of fruit gums, a chocolate bar, anything. From her juniors' astounded looks, you'd have thought she'd demanded the still-warm carcass of a freshly killed gazelle. And now she was ravenous, faintingly hungry again.

Blushing fiercely, Scott Flint said, as if they were competing for the most inappropriate thing to say to one another: 'Of course, if it'd been up to me, I'd have sent him on his way with a kick in the pants.'

She laughed, then worried it might have sounded unkind. But he was so perjinct in his neat blazer, a Remembrance Day poppy still in the buttonhole, and he sounded like a little boy swearing to defend her honour. After a moment he gave a self-effacing chuckle too. 'It's been good to put a face to the voice at last. You won't remember, but I did your telephone interview? When you got the promotion?'

'Oh. No, I remember. Oh,' she said again, starting to smile, 'so it's all your fault?'

What she remembered of that call was a quailing voice, more nervous even than Lynne, it seemed, and how it had made her picture someone more insipid than he'd proved to be. Less physical. In reality he was rather stocky, with a rufous beard and dark hair, also neat, cropped so close it seemed moulded to his head. His face was what you might call pleasantly ugly. Why was it that when you met such a person, even when he was nicer than you'd envisaged, you slightly resented his failure to match the image you'd concocted?

Pleasantly ugly, that was harsh. Normal. Even nice-looking.

Every light on Great Western Road was against them, and at each junction they sat unspeaking, Scott riding the clutch, making the car toil on the spot in seeming frustration. When the lights changed, the car surged forward for a moment before the traffic refroze. Horns sounded. He smiled at her in apology, and a slow worry punctured Lynne's contentment. These friendly questions, these smiles. Had he sought to prolong the journey, deliberately selected the slow route home? Was she undertaking, unawares, a covert follow-up interview?

By way of experiment, she tried a bland, non-work-related question: 'Do you come down to Glasgow often?'

'Not as often as I'd like. My sister stays in Partick, and a few uni friends live here still. So once in a while. Actually,' he added, a little breathlessly, 'I've a friend getting married tomorrow, so I'm down for the whole weekend' – then fell silent, hushed himself.

On the radio, the strings of some chamber piece had worked themselves up to a frantic pitch, and Scott turned the volume right down, clicking his tongue in disapproval. 'Too much,' he said, smiling at her again. She was increasingly certain. A man and a woman, in a car, in the rain: what other reason could there be? Maybe this was what Angus had meant about it being important to keep your eyes open and mouth shut, compiling the various bits and flecks of information that came in – assemble the whole pattern first. Something was condensing in the air. Any minute now, Scott might voice the question he'd been preparing ever since she'd accepted the lift, a prospect that alarmed Lynne – not the question itself, but how she might answer, and what she might be caught up in if she responded, as she might do once more, as events were making her want to, spontaneously, recklessly.

'You know,' she said, as the Botanic Gardens' dim-lit onion domes at last came into view, 'you could drop me here, if you like, and I can walk the rest. If there's been an accident it'll be backed up all the way to Kelv— to Maryhill.'

As she had expected, he demurred. 'It's no trouble – I'll have to go as far as Byres Road anyway to get to my sister's. I'm sure I can get you a little closer . . .'

'No, no.' An additional dismal scenario occurred to her: his car pulling in to Glendower Street, beside the little minimart on the corner, Scott's face grotesque in the lights shining through the shop-window decals of pizza slices and apples beaded with glycerine dew; the question he'd ask – all observed from a second-floor flat by a figure in silhouette, a bearded face pressed to the bay window's cold glass. 'I think the rain's starting to ease off a bit, anyway,' she lied bare facedly. 'Look – you could stop here, by the chip shop.'

'Here? Well, if you're sure?' He brought the car in, sitting in what seemed to Lynne an agitated silence as she slipped her shoes back on and took her handbag from the footwell.

'God, this weather. I hope it clears up for your wedding tomorrow – is it tomorrow?'

'That's right. Though it's not my wedding.' She'd deliberately waylaid him, and felt he must sense it too, but found herself tarrying, feigning a search for her keys, wondering what exactly the offer had been, what she'd have been refusing. She was waiting for a word, a hand on her leg – surely not that? He had the air of someone to whom the idea could never occur.

'Well, enjoy it. Try not to – what was it, kick anyone in the pants?' She opened the door and rain gusted in on her. 'Thank you for the lift and . . . everything else.'

'You too,' he said, nonsensically. 'Stick your head out that birdcage you mentioned, eh? Go for a wee scowp about.'

It was brinkmanship – his prisoner's dilemma again. Leave it too long to say anything, waiting for the other person to compromise himself, and both lose out. But maybe she had misread him, because Lynne was able to get out the car and slam the door with no further word from Scott, without him following her on the dash to the chip shop's awning. She waved at the car, couldn't see if he'd returned the wave.

She'd been so sure he'd wanted to say something. 'Ah, well,' she said aloud to herself, wishing she had thought to put an umbrella in her bag that morning. All she could do was wait out the rain. Meantime, though, her hunger, a weight with sharp corners, had been improbably intensified by the smell of grease and fat and salt she usually found disgusting. What was in the fridge at home? Salmon steaks, pre-mixed stir-fry. She turned, looking through the blue neon waves tracking one another end-lessly across the chippie window, and thought about silken fish flesh in its crust of batter, too hot to eat at first, so you picked instead at the gummy chips slathered in salt and brine, as grease soaked the brown paper translucent. Reckless, she could be reckless. She couldn't recall the last time she'd had a fish supper on a Friday night.

FIFTEEN

Lynne was unfamiliar with the South Side, and when she arrived at Maitlandfield House she was already running late. The day was too warm for February, and she was dressed all wrong, a cardigan over her dress; the walk from the train station had taken twenty minutes, all uphill, and she felt dishevelled and conspired against. She should have brought the car, but had worried that on seeing it, Angus might, like a pet in kennels, think she had come to take him home.

She gave her name at the gatehouse, was allowed entry, and set off up the long red-gravelled driveway towards the house. Spring had come early, but seemed peculiarly advanced here: the trees that lined the drive were brilliant with soft new foliage; beneath them, in the grass verges, daffodils were almost in bloom. The feeling she had – and this must have been the intention of those in charge – was less of entering a new place than of leaving a former one behind.

Maitlandfield, a sandstone mansion with a colonnaded entranceway, had been first a private residence, then a school, before the charity acquired it. As she approached, Lynne noticed an ugly new conservatory huddled to the house's east side, which the photographs in the brochure had been careful to conceal. Within it, residents – was that the word? – sat in wicker chairs, and as she'd feared, it was games of whist, tea from a bottomless samovar, a television turned permanently to talk shows.

The entrance was on the far face of the house. It was a

mid-sized room unostentatiously decorated, somewhere between a hospital reception and a hotel foyer: friendliness designed by committee. On the wall behind the front desk hung a large daubed painting, an autistic landscape, and there was an overpowering floral smell, seemingly from a vase of star-gazer lilies on a table nearby. Elsewhere Lynne saw posters for courses, classes, non-denominational prayer sessions; the same picture of a kitten struggling to grip on to a tree branch as some-one had stuck on a wall at Arundel. Beneath this, a laminated sign cautioned: ABSOLUTELY NO ALCOHOL TO BE ADMITTED. She gave Angus's name, this time, to the rather severe girl behind the desk, and signed the visitors' book. Then, rather than setting off immediately towards the residents' rooms as directed, she hung back. 'I just wondered . . . How is he? Mr Rennie. Is he all right?'

In an instant, the receptionist's frosty efficiency evaporated. 'Oh,' she stammered, clutching up a tidy stack of papers from behind the desk to disarray then set neat again. Poor girl: Angus probably didn't know she even existed. 'Oh, well, it does take some people a while to adjust. He's definitely making progress, though,' she added, too late: Lynne's smile, pitying to start with, had already ebbed to nothing.

She could leave now: no one would blame her. Hardly anyone would even know. But she would, and so she forced herself on down the hallway towards the residents' rooms. Here the smell was that of freshly laid carpet, pleasantly acrid – though, like the pungent scent in reception, it made her wonder what neces-sitated such strenuous indicators of freshness, cleanliness. Through windows on her left she looked on to a walled garden where some residents sat in deckchairs, keeping to the shade, seemingly unnerved by the weather. To her right ran a series of doors, each with a name plate: a polythene file pocket contain-ing a sheet of paper with the resident's name printed in cursive type, most of these signs further personalized with drawings, stickers, photographs.

The sign with Angus's name was otherwise unadorned. His door stood ajar, and Lynne, finding no solace in the thought that she might yet escape without his ever knowing she'd planned to visit, peeped in through the gap. The receptionist's ambivalence about his progress had made Lynne fear what she might find, and it was a relief to see him looking more or less as she remembered him. He lay on the bed, flicking through a small red book. He was wearing stonewashed jeans and a plain white shirt, nothing like she would have picked for him. He had new, thick-rimmed glasses, and his beard, that thicket, was neatly shaped: a novelty. The glitter of grey hair seemed to have been eliminated from it, and although she was probably misremembering, she had the distinct impression that both his hair and skin had grown darker, healthier, since his Glendower Street days.

Hearing someone approaching from the far end of the corridor, cutting off her escape route, Lynne tapped once on the door and pushed it open. 'Hi, Angus.'

'Hi yirsel,' he returned genially, not yet lifting his eyes from his book. When he did, his expression moved swiftly from suspicion to recognition to open surprise. He sprang up, spraddling the book face down on the bed. 'Oh, Lynne! Come in, come in!'

They met in the centre of the room, performing there an inelegant dance, arms opening stiltedly for hugs, then dropping, both of them uncertain, until Angus tutted, 'Och, Lynne, c'mere,' and they embraced. With no resentment she could detect, he said: 'Ah wis startin tae think ye'd nivver come by! How the devil ur ye?'

She broke the hug – though it was good and substantial, and she had missed it – as soon as seemed polite. 'Oh yes, good, I'm good. And you – you look well.'

'I am well,' he agreed, all jaunty.

'New glasses.'

'Are they?' He mugged going cross-eyed, trying to see them for himself. 'Aye – no bad for NHS efforts anyway, eh?'

'Make you younger,' Lynne suggested.

'Oh, ah'm no that, but.'

The walls were painted yellow, and the furnishings were modest: a desk and chair, a self-assembly wardrobe, even a small fridge, which gave off an inordinately loud humming. On a shelf over the fridge, a kettle and two mugs were arranged on a cloth doily presumably provided, like the white goods, by Maitlandfield. The alternative – the notion of Angus going out to purchase such a thing – made Lynne smile, at least until it occurred to her that maybe he wasn't allowed to go out to buy things.

The room was a generous size, yet Angus seemed to occupy more space in it than he ought: wherever she moved, she seemed to be pressed into one corner or another, or to be vying to get into his arms for another hug.

He clicked the kettle on. 'Please, Lynne, grab a seat. There's the chair there, or you can sit on the bed wi me.' He smiled. 'If that's no too forward?'

Choosing the bed, to show she was unfazed, she took off her cardigan, folding it on her lap. Angus opted first to watch the water starting to effervesce through the kettle's transparent side, then to fuss with pushing back his cuticles. Anything rather than have a conversation? Engrossed in these tasks, though, he didn't stop grinning. Hard to believe this was the same man who'd sat on the sofa in Glendower Street on the first of December with his eyes fixed on the TV while she carried his scant belongings down to her car. He'd refused to help with, or even acknowledge, what she was doing – denial personified, as if engaged in non-violent resistance. Between this and the changes in his appearance, Lynne was starting to feel there must have been a mistake: this was just Angus's namesake, his benevolent doppelgänger. Or maybe, she allowed herself to think, she had actually, inadvertently, in sending him here, done the right thing.

'Cannae mind how ye take it,' he apologized, pouring the tea. 'A splash milk, wis it?'

She nodded. 'This is kind of you.'

'Nuh-uh.' He refused the compliment, still smiling. 'Ah'll grant you mibbe ah used tae be older. But nivver kind.'

What was this pantomime? She supposed he was enjoying the role reversal – her being his guest now. Watching him bumble around with the tea, Lynne was keenly aware of the crease he'd once made in her heart, even if it didn't quite fold along that line any more. What she felt was milder than nostalgia – more a fondness for the self that had been so stricken over him, like a middle-aged woman might recall with forbearance her teenage years as some pop band's lovestruck groupie. If questioned, of course, she wouldn't have dared describe what she felt for Angus, now or at any point, as love.

As Angus hooked his foot around the chair leg and dragged it towards the bed to put drinks on, a greying man in a greying sweater slowed past the open door, saluting. 'Andiamo!' Angus called to him. 'Andy Andy Andy! How's it gaun, big man?' In reply, Andy looked from Angus to Lynne and back again, then, grinning, friendly, raised his hands and made throttling motions around empty air. 'Jist you hang in there, big man. Sumdy'll be along tae visit you soon an aw.' When Andy had moved on, Angus set down the tea tray – kittens, naïvely painted – and shook his head. 'Naebdy's comin tae see that sad dobber any time soon.' Lynne noticed the faintest tremor on the surface of the teas, wondered if this trembling, like his odd buoyancy, might be chemically induced.

She shifted along the bed towards the window, and Angus sat beside her, moving the red book he'd been reading. For an astonished moment Lynne had thought it a Gideon Bible, but as he set it down on the table, she realized almost with relief that it was the little book listing football fixtures that was sold at newsagent counters. She turned away, amused – and saw, propped on the carpet, half out of view behind the wardrobe, a canvas, facing the wall.

'Is that – are you painting again these days?' she asked, wondering why the idea almost dismayed her. 'Properly?'

'Properly ah doan know about, but aye. First time in . . . years mibbe.'

She tried to replicate his tone, which was humorous and lacked sincerity. 'Am I allowed to see?'

He considered the point. 'If ye like. Go easy, but, it's at a delicate stage. Me, whit ah'm daein is no lookin at it, fer a month if ah can manage it, till the next sittin. That weiy, when ah do get tae see it again, it'll be fresh.'

'Then I won't either. "Children and fools", isn't that right?'

He laughed. 'Ah, Lynne.' His grin faded at last. 'Ah'm so glad ye came. Ah've been thinkin a lot about ye.'

When she did not immediately respond, Angus hastened on: 'Aye, ehm, about how ye took me in off the streets, bought me all they claithes, aw that. Everyhin ye did. And ah wanted tae say . . .'

He paused, and Lynne, keeping her expression nicely composed, awaited his next pronouncement with trepidation. How would she respond, now that everything was fixed and irrevocable, when he said he missed her? That he'd been wrong and she'd been right all along?

'Ah suppose whut ah wanted tae say wis, ah forgive ye.'

The view from his window was of the front lawn and the long, curving, tree-lined driveway that bisected it. And there was a person out there, too, Lynne saw: a thin young man, a boy, really. He was crossing the driveway, his gait lurching, pained-seeming. When he reached grass again, he half turned and dropped deliberately on to his backside – a real clowning pratfall, a performance, though he seemed to have no audience and he could not have seen, at this distance, anyone watching him from the house. He rolled around on his back for a while, kicking up his legs and snatching at his clothes with his left hand, trying, it seemed, to remove some invisible encumbrance. His other arm seemed trapped inside his T-shirt. A few moments later, he struggled to his feet and lolloped on over the grass for a few yards, before once again flopping to the ground, writhing there like she'd seen dogs do, disporting themselves amid superscents humans couldn't detect. Should she say something? Was this a seizure she was witnessing? A pioneering workout?

'Lynne, doll?' Angus touched her bare arm, and she started: his dark-haired fingers there seemed tarantula-like. 'Ye did whut ye thought wis right. Makin me leave *was* the right thing, even if ye undertook it fer reasons that were . . . Well, ye were angry. Ah wis too, ragin, fer the longest time. But ye cannae steiy angry forivver. Anyway. Here, now, on ma ain two feet, ye ken, ah jist feel . . .' He shrugged. 'Grateful.'

Outside on the grass, the young man straightened up sharply. He swivelled to face the house and, with his right arm extricated from his T-shirt, began to twine and contort the fingers of both hands, flicking them towards the house, flinging some obeah magic in their direction: take that, and that. Lynne almost ducked.

She wanted to point him out to Angus – make sure he could see the boy, that she wasn't imagining him. And ask, too, if this was what counted as normal behaviour at Maitlandfield – were there others like that who spent their days alone, going about their strange rituals? Was this part of the treatment? Instead, fearing what else he might tell her about what went on here, she looked down at her hands cradling her mug, and said:

'So they're treating you all right, then? Feeding you properly?'

'Feedin me? Aye – feedin me swill.' To her astonishment, he leapt up off the bed and went whirling round the room, almost giggling. 'Aw, Lynne, this place, ah cannae begin tae tell ye. It's a disaster area. Ah'm surrounded by bawbags like Andy there, no-hopers who've drank away their money, their hame, their families. Came here tae dry oot? Fuck naw, they've came tae die. Ah'm the healthiest wan here,' he said in delight, 'and still the staff keep oan tryin tae get me tae exercise. "How's about ye go outside, Angus, get some fresh air?" Aye, or how's about you suck ma chug?' There was a broad, stupid smile spreading over his face, all beard and teeth. 'Sorry. But ah mean.'

Frozen, Lynne ran back what he'd said, wondering what in his tone or the words she could have misconstrued so completely.

'Lynne, your face. Here, go on, huv a peep at the canvas. Honestly. Mair bluddy eloquent than ah could ivver be.'

He went over to the window then, giving her and his painting privacy. She did as she was told, but didn't turn the canvas round until she was back on the bed.

It was the head of a young woman – that was all she understood at first. Then the elements began to coalesce, and Lynne's next thought was unworthy of her: she was glad Angus hadn't picked the lovestruck girl from reception as his subject.

He'd made Siri sickly, like all his subjects: her likeness assembled in broad sweeps of brick red and ultramarine, internal colours; her cropped hair in titanium, a furze of hostile brushstrokes. She wore a fearsome expression, befitting the agitation with which it seemed the paint had been slapped down and scoured away: Lynne pictured Angus obsessively making and unmaking the portrait. Behind the head an apocalypse sky, pollution fire rolling down towards the point of view. And there was a structure there too, maybe – a grid or a cage, parallel lines set at an oblique angle to the portrait, disappearing and reappearing amid the blood red, the orange, the white, the concrete grey.

'They tell me when the meals're served and ah dinnae go.' Angus had turned away from the window and was walking a tight circle in the centre of the room. 'They recommend these wee courses at the gym – twenty minutes per day oan a treadmill or a static cycle – and ah nod along: oh aye, sounds guid, guid tae be healthy, and nivver set a foot in the place. Ah've barely even been outside since January. Seems like everydy's got a function here and mine is tae resist, resist, resist.' He paused at the centre of the spiral he'd been pacing, leonine, majestic, until, laughing at himself: 'Contrary auld fucker, so ah am. There ye go, a dash ay self-awareness, there's a breakthrough. Maybe these reviews ay theirs're daein some good after aw – no the weiy *they* think, but encouraging me tae' – he gave a private little half-smile

203

– 'keep sabotagin masel.' He came and sat beside her and, ruining his plan to keep it fresh for himself, took a sidelong look at the canvas. Lynne, hot with guilt, knew this was the nearest to thanks, or apology, she was going to get.

He had built up the paint in thickly textured layers, sponged and chipped and scoured these away, then applied still more paint over the uneven surface. The resulting palimpsest at first seemed like it might reveal something of his working methods, but really it obscured them further, eradicating any indication of what parts he'd painted when. At one stage he had laid down a coat of crimson emulsion over the whole picture, temporarily obliterating it, then flayed that colour away again: something she hadn't seen before in his work. 'Ma way ay keepin things interestin,' he explained, running a finger over one of the red skerricks. 'Ah remembered how ah used tae start out wi all this enthusiasm, aw this sense ay potential, gaun after the image ah held in ma heid. The first mark ye make on a canvas is like . . .' He shook his head, held his hands up in rapture. 'A big moment. Ye make the mark and spring away, almost feart. Go birlin roond the room. But as ye go on, work intae it, ye start tae feel . . . dread.'

'Of finishing?'

'Aye! Well, no, no exactly. At a certain stage, the hing starts tae close in around ye like a trap ye've set yirsel. The end grows mair inevitable wi every mark ye make. Inescapable. Aw that potential's gone, and all that's left is a chore tae complete. Ah alwis found sumhin morbid about that. Ye know the joke: "So, Doctor, now ye've completed the autopsy, can ye tell us the cause ay death?" And the doctor goes, "Aye – bein alive tae start wi." And this' – he gestured again to the crimson marks that littered the image like survey marks on a map – 'wis me tryin tae shake it up a bit, introduce randomness intae the procedure. Pretend ah wis givin up and startin over, mair tae fool masel than anyhin.' He moved towards her, turned his head round to inspect his picture. 'Tryin to haud ma ain attention, if ye like. Keep masel guessin.'

She was glad for two reasons. His new animation, this apparently unfeigned cheer, had arisen from his being able to work again. And she was thankful, too, for the unassailable self-regard which meant he would not ask her opinion of the new work. Once, his tremulous line and constant, compulsive layering and erasure of the paint had married with his subject choice: you looked at that numbing, terrifying portrait of his parents, for instance, and thought, yes, this was the only way he could possibly have conveyed his feelings about them, communicated to the viewer the regret and regard contemplating his subject had provoked in him. In his head of Siri, they were badly misapplied: a vapid revisitation of old techniques, wasted on a subject whose importance to him it was, for once, impossible to judge. Was this a portrait in praise of Siri or an attack on her? It was so inept, and yet he seemed so pleased with it and himself – a disjuncture that was Lynne's doing, her fault.

'Ah'm no pretendin ah understand it, Lynne. All ah know's there's no chance ah'd've been able tae start this, on anyhin, while ah wis at Glendower Street. Certainly not if ah'd kept oan at the hostel. Wan wis too . . . cosy, mibbe? And the ither, well, that wis just a bluddy nuthouse.' He squinted at her. 'Yir place bein the cosy wan.'

'Thank you, yes. Whereas here . . .'

'Oh aye,' he panted, calming down slightly, 'here. The Goldilocks Universe, isn't that the theory? It's a bazillion-tae-wan chance that conditions'll be ripe for life tae occur, yet bam, here we all are. Ye're no followin, ur ye, doll?'

'Siri's been recommending books to you, hasn't she?'

'Naw, but it's a fair comparison. Ye're tryin tae bring a whole bunch ay invisible sights intae alignment, and ye willnae know if ye've got it right till it's too late tae adjust them. Turns out what ah needed tae galvanize me back tae work was a bit mair charity tae kick against, eh.'

It was her own fault for removing the pages that detailed prices before she left the brochures out for him, but that word *charity* struck Lynne dumb. How could he believe – or dare pretend to believe – that a place like Maitlandfield operated as, what, a purely altruistic enterprise? A wealthy philanthropist's death-bed bequest? She could have set him right, told him what his two months here had already cost her, and once he'd recovered his breath she could have talked him through her calculations – shown him that if you really wanted to do this, if you really wanted to help someone, it meant closing certain avenues off to yourself for ever. She could have told him what she'd been will-ing to do to benefit him, the consequences her decision had had, the other people – bystanders – it meant stringing along. But it wasn't right to shame or antagonize him, not when he was so enthused, so effusive.

Besides, different people had different approaches to life. Here was Angus making a show of putting his methods on dis-play, in the accreted and scoured layers of paint; whereas Lynne – well, it had damaged them both when she had kept a secret before, daring to hope but not to voice the hope. Maybe he was right about people's functions in the working universe, and her station in life was to keep secrets – fine: if these new ones helped protect him, she'd happily adopt the role.

'Has Siri come to sit for you often?'

'Three, four times mibbe? Whenever she kin find the time. Startit in December – wan mair sittin should dae it. She's got exams at the minute, then she's gaun oan holiday.' He looked away from the painting. 'That's why ah'm takin a break.'

'She made friends with Rose again, did she tell you?' It struck her, too late, that she might be breaking a rule Maitlandfield visitors were meant to abide by – perhaps you shouldn't mention the outside world, allude even to the existence of such a place. 'It's half-term at the moment. They've gone to Lisbon together.'

'Oh aye, uh-huh.' Angus bounced a little on the bed beside her. 'Ah mean, she said. Disnae seem tae want tae jump Rose's bones quite so much any mair.' He preened, laughing at himself. 'So it all worked oot for the best, ma interference.'

206

'I'm pleased for her.' Angus's mouth tucked in at the corners sceptically. 'She came to see me at Christmas, asked me what she should do. It was a test, or a sort of serving of notice – this is who I am, take it or leave it. And, you know, I'm starting to realize, in my ugly old age, that it's pointless to disapprove of what someone's doing with their life. You'll never convince them to change.' She had mined this statement with several entry points where Angus might interrupt and contradict her, but he let it pass without comment. 'It usually only makes them more determined to do what they were going to do anyway.'

She did not mention that she had not seen Siri since Christmas; she did not say, could not count on it coming out in a humorous tone, that Angus might, by painting her, have stolen her from Lynne somehow.

Angus sniffed. 'Best jist tae let folk get on with it, aye.' She waited, but this seemed to be as much as he was willing to concede. 'Anyway, what cheer wi you? That joab of yirs. Handit in yir notice yet?'

'Actually, no.' Like the student who studies a minimum of the syllabus then twists the examiner's question so she can give the only answer she knows, Lynne launched into a rehearsed statement. 'What happened was, I sat down with a calculator and worked it all out – in the office, actually, I made a spreadsheet, I should have been working. I thought about going public sector, getting a job that wasn't . . . evil, like you said. You know what? It turned out I couldn't afford to.' She shrugged, as if it was all beyond her control. To her, the story sounded blatantly fraudulent, and she both wanted and didn't want him to question her further. To lie by omission, she knew, was hardly lying at all, but she still felt unexpectedly bad about deceiving him. The urge to confess versus the instinct to withhold what didn't concern him. 'Imagine. My outgoings just kept going up and up. You wouldn't believe how much my bills have increased in the last year. What recession? I thought I was doing well, and it turns out I've barely been keeping my head above water all this time. So I guess I'm stuck.'

'That's a real shame, Lynne. A bluddy shame. Ye're worth more than that stupit joab'll ever gie ye credit fer.' He stood up again and held out his hand; after a confused moment, Lynne handed the canvas over for him to replace against the wall. He wandered back to the window and glanced up at the sky. 'Beautiful day the day. Ye should get oot there, get some vitamin D in ye.' He chuckled. 'Hear that? Ah'm as bad as the folk ah'm jist after slaggin aff.'

Realizing she was being dismissed, Lynne stammered: 'Yes, I suppose I should let you get on. Stuff I should be doing too. Ironing my clothes for another wonderful week at Arundel.' She pulled her cardigan on over her shoulders. 'Thanks for the tea.'

'You're very bluddy welcome.'

She was expecting to have to endure another hug, but Angus didn't shift from his position by the window, so she went over and laid a hand on his shoulder instead, half patting, half squeezing. 'It's great to see you doing so well.'

'Oh, ah'm prosperin, aye.' He turned. 'You're lookin well an aw.' Self-conscious, she drew the cardigan round herself. 'Ah'm likin the brooch, by the way. New?' She froze – nodded. 'Silver, is that?' He put a finger beneath one corner of the brooch and lifted it to catch the light, pulling the cardigan's stitching. 'A birdcage, whit's that, some Christian hing?'

'No. At least, I don't think so.'

'Christmas present?'

'That's right.'

'Check us, eh? New jewellery for you, new gegs for me.' A thought struck him. 'It's no fae . . .'

'Raymond? Goodness, no.'

He opened his mouth, closed it again, then said: 'Well, guid. It suits ye. The question is, has the bird flown off, or is the cage door open fer it tae find its way back in?'

208

The question for Lynne, as she moved away, was why she'd elected to wear the brooch today if she had not unconsciously hoped Angus would comment on it – had she not hoped to actively keep the story behind it to herself? Opening the little parcel on Christmas Eve, she'd made a sharp wordless exclamation that mingled delight and dismay – Too much! Too expensive! Too soon! – as though Scott Flint, her shy and ardent pursuer, had been there to hear her.

'Lynne.' Angus's voice had sharpened: no levity in it now. She turned in the doorway and saw that he'd resumed his supine pose on the bed, legs crossed at the ankles, his thumb holding his book open. 'Thanks for droppin by. Ah mean it. Ye're a guid person, ye know that?'

'Mm-hm?' she said, on a rising intonation, pretending that he'd volunteered not praise but some mildly diverting item of trivia. Her hand rose to the birdcage brooch. She sensed a conspiracy – these gifts and praises she could not accept, could not trust or surrender to.

'A terrific, generous person. Ah don't want ye forgettin that, Lynne, ye hear me? Nivver forget it.'

She shook at his temerity. Would people never tire of bestowing these platitudes on her? Generous, sensible: what did words like these even mean? By contrast, after she'd given Siri her advice at Christmas, the girl had squinched up her eyes to inspect Lynne more closely, then declared, in her offhand way, 'Lynne, you know what, you're all right.' That was as much praise as Lynne deserved. You're all right, you're precisely average; you will never attain greatness, nor should you aspire to it.

People said nice, vacuous things all the time, things they didn't mean, and were at pains to avoid expressing what they truly felt, which was usually the opposite. Tell Angus what she'd done for him and he'd crush her in an embrace for maybe ninety seconds then proceed to resent her interference for the rest of his – mysteriously truncated – stay in the place he found

209

so awful, so perfect. For both their sakes, then, she lifted a hand in farewell and, in that way they had now, undermining by their irreverent tone the earnestness of their words, wished him the greatest good luck.

In reception – 'Excuse me? Mrs Meacher?' She didn't bother to correct the girl – there were forms to complete, signatures in triplicate, small print to scan, and Lynne, who imagined other people might find these practical procedures rather harrowing, seeming as they did to entail the literal signing away of someone's life, set about them with relish. She received in return a pink carbon-copied sheet of paper with details of her payment, all she'd have to show for her latest gesture. She folded the paper in four, put it in her handbag, and didn't move.

'Try not to worry, Mrs Meacher. It's only been two months.' The receptionist was spraying room freshener on what Lynne saw now were clearly fake lilies. 'Sometimes it can take six, seven, eight months before residents are ready to move on.' Lynne, doing the mental arithmetic, felt her pulse drop, her eyes grow very wide. Her hand went to the silver brooch. 'But we'll keep reviewing Mr Rennie's progress every week. And of course you can see him yourself any time you like.' She spoke kindly, but a final question hung unasked: why are you still standing around here? 'There's nothing more you need to do.'

In the lime trees, birds sang without cease. The daffodils seemed to have gone from buds to blooms in the hour she'd been indoors. Places like Maitlandfield House existed in a fold in space, an interzone all goodwill and forgiveness and the buzzwords from the posters in reception: growth, development, harmony, tenacity. But she'd introduced into this anodyne controlled environment a rogue element, and because Lynne – contrary to what people kept telling her about herself – was spite personified, a grudge-bearer, a hopeless case, she took pleasure in imagining how, over time, Angus would warp it. She walked

210

back down the driveway, and the ground already seemed a little aslant beneath her feet.

As she was passing the car park, she saw from the corner of her eye a figure burst out from among the trees and speed towards her. She turned, half expecting to see Angus, but it was the boy she'd spotted rolling on the lawn earlier. Reaching her, he slowed to walk at her side, watching his feet to ensure they struck the gravel exactly in time with hers. He was maybe nineteen – too young, surely, for this place – with dark skin and slightly protuberant eyes that, when he glanced at her, seemed to look towards yet not actually at her: something absent, or depleted, in his gaze. She smiled at him, but he didn't speak, and Lynne, who did not want to seem to be fleeing him, though that was her instinct, found herself slowing her pace. His right arm was back inside his T-shirt, the empty sleeve flapping.

After a while, he withdrew his arm from inside the shirt and showed her what he had been holding to his chest: a home-made card on which glitter, the felt-tipped word CONGRATULATIONS and a photograph of two leaping dolphins, clipped from a magazine, were equally prominent. She wasn't sure whether she was being offered the card, though she did not, in any case, want to take it. Instead, she read aloud, in a bold, schoolteacher's voice: 'Congratulations!'

The young man's response was too garbled for her to catch. When she asked him to repeat himself, again all she heard was a random jumble of syllables. 'I'm sorry,' she said, cringing, 'but I don't quite understand.' He didn't seem offended, this time asking instead, perfectly clearly – though she was certain this was not what he had been trying to say before – 'When's *your* birthday?'

'Oh,' she said, so surprised by the question she was momentarily unable to think of the answer. 'Oh, not until September.'

'September,' he repeated, digesting this information.

She didn't know how else to speak to the boy except as to a small child. 'Yes. Not for a long time yet. Months and months.'

The boy made an extraordinary noise, as though shifting coins around inside his mouth, so that Lynne felt that another voice might now emerge from him. 'Mine's next week.'

'That's why you've got the card!'

The boy pointed at one of the cars parked nearby, a red hatchback. 'Is that your car?'

'No, I don't have my car with me today. I walked here.'

'Walked,' he echoed, awed.

'Yes – well, just from the train station. Since it's such a nice spring day.' They were nearing the gates, and she started to feel panic's slow squeeze: envisioning not just that he might try to pretend that he too was merely a visitor, but that the guard – was he a guard? – in the gatehouse would wave them through, lumbering her with him for life. Slowing slightly, though she did not want to prolong the conversation, she pointed again to the boy's card, which he held in his hands as delicately as a butterfly. 'I've got to go back there now. But I hope you have a lovely birthday when it comes.'

'Can I come with you?'

The boy was watching her – not hopefully, not trepidatiously, not with any real expression, she thought, so that it didn't seem possible he could have asked the question, until he made the coin-rattling noise once more and repeated, a bland enquiry as if on someone else's behalf, 'Can I, though?'

'Oh – no. I'm sorry. I don't think that's going to be possible.'

'I'm ready, though. I've made amends, I've said all my apologies.' She faltered in her step. This was the sort of person who properly belonged here – someone who could evidently barely function without Maitlandfield's help. It wasn't right for Angus at all. Yet he had stayed uncomplainingly – happily! – for two months already. Had the possibility of going elsewhere not occurred to him? Or had his resistance drained away once he realized she'd surrendered him, signed him over? Either she'd got things very, very wrong, or this was a joke at her expense and, as she foundered, Angus was watching from his window, doubled up with laughter.

212

'Well, that's good. It's good that you have. But I don't have room in my house, I'm afraid. No space for you to stay.' How much more simply could she put it? 'I'm sorry. I really am sorry.'

'That's all right.' Dazed-seeming but apparently satisfied, he raised the card to her in salute. 'See you, then.'

Still, he accompanied her a little longer, keeping in lockstep with her, unspeaking, an amiable companion. Then, as the man in the gatehouse looked up from his newspaper, and as Lynne noticed that the petals of the daffodils here were already edged as if in lace with the first brown of decay, the sound of the boy's footsteps on the gravel began to diverge from her own. When she glanced over her shoulder, he was heading for the grove of trees where the driveway curved out of view, his head down, their conversation forgotten as he concentrated instead on the long walk back to the house.

Acknowledgements

I would like to thank Alistair and Vida Stewart, Rebecca Fortey, Tim Jarvis, Paul Murray, Paul Ryding, Sarah Castleton and all at Corsair, Natasha Fairweather, Walter Donohue – and Mark C. O'Flaherty.